PRAISE FOR

THE FINE ART OF *Insincerity*

"Only Angela Hunt could write a relationship novel that's a page-turner! As one of three sisters, I can promise you this: Ginger, Penny, and Rose Lawrence ring very true indeed. Their flaws and strengths make them different, yet their shared experiences and tender feelings make them family. From one crisis to the next, the Lawrence sisters are pulled apart, then knit back together, taking me right along with them. I worried about Ginger one moment, then Penny, and always Rose—a sure sign of a good novel, engaging both mind and heart. Come spend the weekend in coastal Georgia with three women who clean house in more ways than one!"

—Liz Curtis Higgs, bestselling author of *Here Burns My Candle*

"*The Fine Art of Insincerity* is the story of three middle-aged sisters that converge on St. Simon's Island to clear away the cobwebs from their deceased grandmother's island home. But the cobwebs hiding the secret pain that each sister harbors threatens to entangle and complicate each woman's deep sense of order and decorum, especially since one of the sisters is hell-bent on a collision course with fate. Angela Hunt's womanly tale of sisterly affection and protective martyrdom is a well-woven story of self-discovery and personal growth that will melt your heart!"

—Patricia Hickman, author of *The Pirate Queen* and *Painted Dresses*

"*The Fine Art of Insincerity* is a stunning masterpiece. I was pulled into the lives of Ginger, Pennyroyal, and Rosemary—sisters touched by tragedy, coping in their own ways. So real, so powerful. Pull out the tissues! This one will make you cry, laugh, and smile. I recommend it highly."

—Traci DePree, author of The Lake Emily series

THE FINE ART OF
Insincerity
· A NOVEL ·

ANGELA HUNT

HOWARD BOOKS
A DIVISION OF SIMON & SCHUSTER, INC.
NEW YORK NASHVILLE LONDON TORONTO SYDNEY

Howard Books
A Division of Simon & Schuster, Inc.
1230 Avenue of the Americas
New York, NY 10020

First Howard Books trade paperback edition May 2011

HOWARD and colophon are trademarks of Simon & Schuster, Inc.

For information about special discounts for bulk purchases, please contact Simon & Schuster Special Sales at 1-866-506-1949 or business@simonandschuster.com.

The Simon & Schuster Speakers Bureau can bring authors to your live event. For more information or to book an event contact the Simon & Schuster Speakers Bureau at 1-866-248-3049 or visit our website at www.simonspeakers.com.

Designed by Jaime Putorti

Manufactured in the United States of America

10 9 8 7 6 5 4 3 2 1

Library of Congress Cataloging-in-Publication Data

Hunt, Angela Elwell, 1957–
    The fine art of insincerity / Angela Hunt.
      p. cm.
    ISBN 978-1-4391-8203-1
    1. Sisters—Fiction.   2. Marriage—Fiction.   3. Inheritance and succession—
Fiction.   4. Grandmothers—Death—Fiction.   5. Saint Simons Island (Ga.)—
Fiction.   6. Domestic fiction.   I. Title.
    PS3558.U46747F56 2011
    813'.54—dc22
            2010028940

ISBN 978-1-4391-8203-1
ISBN 978-1-4391-8206-2 (ebook)

For the women of the Haynes family:
my grandmother Lela,
my mother and my three aunts,
my two sisters,
and a lovely cadre of cousins.
Thank you for a wonderful heritage.

If I speak with human eloquence and angelic ecstasy but don't love, I'm nothing but the creaking of a rusty gate.

If I speak God's Word with power, revealing all his mysteries and making everything plain as day, and if I have faith that says to a mountain, "Jump," and it jumps, but I don't love, I'm nothing.

If I give everything I own to the poor and even go to the stake to be burned as a martyr, but I don't love, I've gotten nowhere.

So, no matter what I say, what I believe, and what I do, I'm bankrupt without love.

—1 Corinthians 13: 1–3, *The Message*

THE FINE ART OF

Insincerity

PROLOGUE

GINGER

"You can't tell your sisters," my grandmother once told me, "what I'm about to tell you."

I listened, eyes big, heart open wide.

"Of all my grandchildren"—her hands spread as if to encompass a crowd infinitely larger than me and my two siblings—"you're my favorite."

Then her arms enfolded me and I breathed in the scents of Shalimar and talcum powder as my face pressed the crepey softness of her cheek.

My grandmother married seven times, but not until I hit age ten or eleven did I realize that her accomplishment wasn't necessarily praiseworthy. When Grandmother's last husband died on her eighty-third birthday, she mentioned the possibility of marrying again, but I put my foot down and told her *no more weddings.* I suspect my edict suited her fine, because Grandmom always liked flirting better than marrying.

Later, one of the nurses at the home mentioned that my grandmother exhibited a charming personality quirk—"perpetual childhood disorder," she called it. PCD, all too common among elderly patients with dementia.

But Grandmother didn't have dementia, and she had exhibited symptoms of PCD all her life. Though I didn't know how to describe it in my younger years, I used to consider it a fine quality.

During the summers when Daddy shipped me and my sisters off to Grandmom's house, she used to wait until Rose and Penny were absorbed in their games, then she would call me into the blue bedroom upstairs. Sometimes she'd let me sort through the glass-beaded "earbobs" in her jewelry box. Sometimes she'd sing to me. Sometimes she'd pull her lace-trimmed hanky from her pocket-book, fold it in half twice, and tell me the story of the well-dressed woman who sat on a bench and fell over backward. Then she'd flip her folded hankie and gleefully lift the woman's skirt and petticoat, exposing two beribboned legs.

No matter what size her audience, the woman knew how to entertain.

I perched on the edge of the big iron bed and listened to her songs and stories, her earbobs clipped to the tender lobes of my ears, enduring the painful pinch because Grandmother said a woman had to suffer before she could be beautiful. Before I pulled off the torturous earbobs and left the room, she would draw me close and swear that out of all the girls in the world, I was the one she loved most.

Not until years later did I learn that she drew my sisters aside in the same way. I suppose she wanted to make sure we motherless girls knew we were treasured. But in those moments, I always felt truly special.

And for far too long, I believed her.

ONE

GINGER

Even without a calendar, I can feel *Monday* settling into my bones.

I miss the postman because he comes early; Martha, my cleaning woman, arrives thirty minutes late; and the newspaper doesn't show up at all. I trudge up the driveway and sort through the mail in my hand—mortgage statement, car loan reminder, bills from Sallie Mae and Stetson University. Four credit card offers. An envelope plastered with the image of that smirking insurance lizard. Michael's copy of *Civil War Times*.

I walk into the house, step over the cat sprawled on the rug, and drop the historical magazine onto the foyer table. I toss the bills onto the desk in the study, then pause to open the envelope from the mortgage company. Our loan has an adjustable rate, and I need to keep an eye on it.

I turn toward the kitchen, but Martha blocks the doorway, a mop in her hand. "Don't even think about it." She glares at me from beneath steel gray brows. "My floor needs at least ten minutes to dry."

I glance past her, wondering if she managed to get up the spilled candle wax near the dining room table. Probably not, because she hasn't had time to mop the floor *and* do spot scrubbing. But Martha, who passed her sixty-fifth birthday ages ago, has been with me fifteen years. This won't be the first time I've discreetly cleaned up areas she missed.

I give her a submissive smile. "I can wait."

I return to the study and look up when Michael steps out of our bedroom, already in his favorite tweed sport coat. He nods in my direction and gestures toward the mail. "Anything for me?"

"Your magazine is on the table." I smile and tilt my cheek for a good-morning kiss that doesn't come. My timing is off, as usual. My husband is doubtless in a rush to get to the coffee shop and his first class. My coffee, he insists, barely merits a passing grade.

Michael moves into the foyer, picks up the magazine, and pauses to skim the headlines on the cover. In the slanting light of early morning, he looks like a *GQ* cover model or a smoldering ad for Ralph Lauren. My own absentminded professor. My handsome husband who around unfamiliar people is still as shy as a boy on his first date.

I smother a sigh as he drops the magazine into his backpack and glances at me. "Gotta run."

I wait, anticipating some word about whether he'll call later, but he's already reaching for the doorknob. "By the way"—he looks directly at me for the first time—"did I mention that we're having after-hours department meetings this month? I probably won't make it home for dinner all week."

"Meetings every night of the week?" I make a face. "What could possibly be so pressing—"

"Writing up a grant." He opens the door. "See ya, sweetie."

And then he is gone, leaving nothing but dancing dust motes and a trace of his cologne in the sun-streaked hallway. I stare at the empty space and speak to the sunbeams angling through the sidelights. "Have a wonderful day, darling." I smile. "Me? Oh, nothing, just the usual. Picking up the house, doing a load of laundry, and working with my children's choirs all afternoon."

I take a deep breath and remind myself that Michael's silence shouldn't upset me. My husband is a brilliant man, but he's not terribly attuned to other people's feelings. When I need something from him—even something as simple as a hug—I usually have to pin him against the wall and spell out the specifics.

Martha appears in the kitchen doorway. "You talking to me?"

I shake my head. "Sorry. Michael left before I could finish."

"He's a man. Off to do important things."

"Right." I sigh and move toward the sidelight as I watch my husband pull out of the drive. He used to linger in the foyer, used to kiss me good-bye and invite me to meet him for lunch. I know he's facing pressure at the university and I know he's heard rumors of cutbacks. We are only one week into the fall term, and the registrar's office recently announced that the usual wave of last-minute applicants didn't materialize this year. The uncertain atmosphere has taken its toll on Michael, leaving him preoccupied and more distant than usual.

But though he's facing difficulties at work, Michael doesn't referee the bouts between a thin checkbook and a thick stack of bills. Every weekend I sit at my desk and struggle to balance our expenses, our investments, and the cost of two sons away at college. To my husband, financial pressure is a vague, shapeless concern; to me it's the ever-expanding and increasingly conspicuous gap between money coming in and money going out.

Still, Michael knows we're in financial straits and he's taken some of the burden from my shoulders by agreeing to serve on a grant-writing committee for the university. I know he wants to provide for his family. He can be old-fashioned in that way. Though he appreciates my income, he has always wanted to be responsible and set an example for our sons.

I drop the mortgage statement into the folder for unpaid bills and leave the study, closing the door behind me.

We'll survive because we've faced tough times before. A couple can't remain happily married without learning how to cope in lean seasons, and in the past twenty-seven years we've weathered feast, famine, and every stage in between. We can survive an uncertain economy too.

ROSEMARY

Will this be the last time I ever open a mailbox?

After sliding several bills into the battered aluminum box, I lift the flag and begin the long walk back to the house. Beyond the rail fence, five retired quarter horses quietly browse the tall grass, the sun dappling their coats. One of them sees me and begins a slow and stately approach, finally dropping his head over the side of the fence.

"Hey there, Magic." I stroke the gelding's nose, then scratch the bristly area between his ears. His lovely almond-shaped eyes blink as he whickers in contentment. "You're a pretty boy, you know that? Then again, why wouldn't you be? I spent an hour brushing you this morning."

The horse shakes his head as my favorite orange hen comes strutting down the drive, a train of chicks behind her. Betsy the Easter Egger is one of the reasons our booth at the farmer's market stays busy on Saturday mornings. The kids adore her pink eggs.

I wait until Betsy and her chicks cross the road, then I give Magic a final pat and continue my walk to the house, inhaling the mingled scents of manure and freshly cut hay. So many farewells to say, so little time. . . .

Two years of waiting have come and gone. For 730 days I've pretended to be content. I've behaved as if our loss didn't matter and the doll-like infant we buried wasn't real.

But she was. And we lost her because of me, so she's another black mark on my record. God must be tired of debiting my account.

In four days, though, I'll be settling my debts forever. I'll leave my husband to carry on my work, my sisters to celebrate what they knew of my life, and my sweet animals to remind others that every living thing deserves a second chance.

Unlike me, who ruined someone's life with every chance I got.

I climb the porch steps and tug on the sagging screen door, then turn to survey the place I'll be leaving behind. Through the screen I see green pastures, a splintering fence, a weathered garage. A colossal live oak shivering in the fall breeze. This peeling house on stilts. Inside, a few pieces of faded furniture and a collection of brightly glazed pottery. All the things I'm willing to surrender as an act of restitution.

Even added together, it's not so much when you're the reason three people are dead.

PENNYROYAL

Even from a distance, the man's height and good looks are enough to make my mouth go as dry as chalk dust. So when he sits at the next table on the outdoor patio, my first instinct is to grab my lemonade and guzzle like a woman with a hollow leg.

Somehow I manage to restrain myself. I nibble at my veggie plate and try hard not to look at the man next door. I succeed, mostly, while he waits, while he orders, and while he waits some more, but when a waiter brings the guy a hamburger, I can't resist sneaking another peek.

I stifle a squeak when I find him looking at me.

"Excuse me—would you mind if I borrowed your salt?"

The handsome and dark-haired man leans toward me, his left arm extended. The ring finger is stark naked, not even a pale strip where a wedding band should be. I drop my left hand to my lap, hiding the narrow band on my fourth finger, then I surrender the saltshaker and toss him a quick grin to show that I am not ending this conversation. "No extra charge for the pepper, if you want it too."

He sprinkles salt over his French fries, then hands the shaker back to me. "You can hold the pepper."

"Already too much spice in your life?"

"Apparently not enough." His gaze skims over my body—good, he's not gay—then he turns and rests his hand on the corner of his chair. "Have I seen you here before?"

I tilt my head, grateful that he's willing to join the game. "Is that an honest question or some kind of line?"

He grins, displaying a row of perfect teeth. "The reason I ask is because I eat at this place all the time. The food's great and the company's usually interesting, but I don't think I've ever seen you here."

No misunderstanding the invitation in that smile. Or the suggestion in his comment.

"So . . . this place is a favorite of yours?"

"It's convenient. I work at the medical center across the street."

I nod at the chair to my right. "If you're not expecting anyone else, there's an empty place at my table."

"So there is . . . and I'm sure these folks need every free table they can get during rush hour."

I clear the napkin and silverware from the empty place as he stands and transfers his glass of iced tea. While he moves his plate, I slip my wedding band from my hand and drop it into my pocket.

He glances around as he settles at my table. "I suppose the waiter will figure out where I went."

I deepen my smile. "I'm sure he will."

Mr. Attractive extends his right hand. "Miller Conrad."

I take his hand with what I hope is a warm, friendly grip. "Penny Jensen."

Still grinning, he douses his burger with ketchup. "Where'd you get that adorable dimple, Penny Jensen?"

"From the dollar store. Where'd you find that overused compliment?"

He laughs. "It's been a while since I've worked up the nerve to barge in on a lady's lunch. I'm not sure what's gotten into me."

I bite my lower lip, unable to deny the tingling in the pit of my stomach. "Whatever it is, I like it."

"You work around here too?"

"At the mall—I'm an associate at Macy's."

The title sounds silly when I say it, but the attractive man next to me nods and picks up his burger. I lift my lemonade and sip it as

I study him. I know practically nothing about this guy, but already I'd swear he is the complete opposite of my husband. He's older, which is definitely a good thing, since Bob has worn me out with his wheedling about a baby. And if Miller Conrad's job involves medicine, he's not likely to be unemployed anytime soon. Financial security . . . would be nice. Being appreciated would be nicer still.

"You work at the medical center?" I lower my glass and smile into his eyes. "You're not wearing a lab coat."

"If a white coat would impress you, I could step into the kitchen and see if the chef has anything available."

My cheeks grow warm. "Some of the doctors who come here wear their lab coats. So I wondered—"

"If I'm also a pretentious twit? I could be, but I spend most of my day peering through a microscope. I'm in research. Most people find my work boring."

I laugh. "I've met boring, and you're definitely not him."

His blue eyes spark as he lowers his hamburger. "Since moving here from Delaware, I've met a lot of Southern women, but you're the first who actually lives up to the reputation."

"Is that so?" I pick up my fork and spear a piece of broccoli. "Funny, but I don't remember calling you *sugar* or *honey pie*."

"It's not what you say, it's the way you say it. In that accent and sort of . . . oozing with charm."

"Well . . . I'm not sure oozing is a good thing, but my grandma always said you should accept a compliment whenever it's offered. So thank you, sir."

Miller is still smiling when the waiter approaches. "I'll take my check whenever you're ready," he tells the young man. "And hers too."

My pulse skitters when he takes my bill. I lower my gaze and dip a carrot stick into a pool of dressing, silencing my conscience with a sharp rebuke: I'm having lunch with a new friend, that's all. Can I help it if he's attractive, attentive, and delighted by my dimple?

GINGER

Where's Martha Stewart when I need her?

Like a mindless zombie I stand at the open freezer and stare at bags of frozen vegetables, an ancient box of Popsicles, and a stack of microwavable diet dinners. Why should I bother to cook something when Michael's not likely to be home until after dinner?

I finally grab a single-portion box of spaghetti and pop it into the microwave. While the oven hums, I fill a glass with ice and reach for the pitcher of sweetened tea. When the spaghetti is done, I pull the dish from the microwave and sit at the kitchen counter, my thoughts drifting toward my husband as I murmur a quick word of thanks.

I don't know how the university administration can guarantee job security for its entire faculty, but even though Michael has tenure I've never seen him look so worn-out. Lately I've noticed new worry lines in his forehead and darker circles beneath his eyes. He may be worried about other teachers in the history department, several of whom are his close friends.

I am twirling my fork in the steaming spaghetti when the phone rings. Instantly, a parade of fears marches through my mind—Ross has broken up with his adorable girlfriend, Ryan has been in a car wreck, Michael has had a heart attack—but the voice on the line is bright, female, and dripping with Southern sweetness. It's Barbara Jones, the Realtor from St. Simons Island, who for nine long months has been trying to sell Grandmother Lillian's beach house.

"Finally!" she crows after a quick hello. "We have a buyer and he'll pay cash. He loves the area, he adores the cottage, and he knows a deal when he sees one. His offer is twenty percent below our asking price, but since y'all weren't able to get up here and clean the place out—"

"We'll take it." The words slip out of my mouth before I can form a more thoughtful answer.

Belatedly, my brain reminds me that I ought to consult with my sisters before I accept a deal. Grandmother left the house to the three of us, but since none of us was able to buy out the others, we decided to sell and split the profits. After all, Michael and I live in Savannah, Penny and Bob live in Gainesville, and Rose lives with Wort in Jacksonville. St. Simons properties usually fetch a good price, but the real estate market has been so depressed that any offer would look good to us.

"I thought this contract would please you." Barbara is almost purring. "There's only one catch—the buyer wants to use the house as his retirement home, and he'll be relocating from New York. He's already sold his property there, so he wants to take possession by the fifteenth."

"Of *September*?"

"Don't panic, sugar." She laughs. "You still have two full weeks to remove any personal property from the house. Can y'all manage it, or should I hire someone to do the cleanout?"

Do the cleanout sounds so final, so . . . funereal. A shiver glissandos up my spine as the phrase conjures up images of faceless strangers hauling away my grandmother's antique piano, pawing through her drawers and jewelry box, unpacking her cluttered closets . . .

"I'll handle everything," I assure the Realtor. "I'll call my sisters and we'll clean the place out together."

"Labor Day is right around the corner," she reminds me. "And the utilities are still on at the property. Maybe y'all could make it a girls' weekend and have a cleaning party."

My stomach tightens at the thought of the job ahead. Only an agent on commission would think of such work as a *party*, but I shouldn't be so cynical. After all, this sale means we will finally get our inheritance. Grandmother's bequest will go a long way toward easing my family's financial burden.

"Don't worry," I tell the Realtor. "I'll make sure the house is empty and spotless by the fifteenth."

"All righty, then." Barbara's voice brims with satisfaction. "I'll drop by with copies of the paperwork this weekend. In the meantime, I'll fax you a copy of the offer. Sign and return it as soon as possible, and we'll be all set."

"Happy to do it," I tell her, meaning every word.

ROSEMARY

"Dad burn it, woman, I'm not about to go prowlin' under the house for no cat."

I bite my lip and stare into Wort's face, allowing him to see the water welling in my eyes. Tears spring up easily these days, on account of all the farewells. . . .

Wort probably thinks I'm being hormonal, but I can't leave knowing that my house is functioning as a trap for stray animals. A black cat has wormed his way into the crawl space, entering through a hole in the broken lattice. I need to get the cat out and the hole repaired.

I sit back on my haunches and focus on Wort, determined to make him understand. "Sweetie, I can't sleep if that cat's still under there tonight. I just can't. So unless you want me up pacing at two A.M., you might as well help me get him out."

"He'll crawl out when he's good and ready. He got in, didn't he? So he can get out."

"Just because he *can* crawl out doesn't mean he *will*. Animals don't always know what's good for them."

Wort snorts. "Listen to you. Good grief, honey, do you know what could be under that house? Snakes. Spiders, the poisonous kind. Maybe even a raccoon or a possum."

"We have spiders and snakes everywhere, yet we manage to survive just fine. Besides, I'm not asking you to live under the house. Just get in there far enough to grab that kitten."

Wort stares at me, frustration and affection warring in his eyes, then he sputters an oath and drops to one knee. With a critical eye he examines the rotting lattice nailed to the side of our rambling frame house.

"Dad blame cat," he mumbles, ripping off the broken section with his bare hands. "Makin' more trouble than he's worth. Now I'll have to replace this whole panel or we'll have who knows *what* living under there."

Grateful to have won his cooperation, I kneel beside him and search for a few soothing words. "Maybe the cat did us a favor. We needed to fix the lattice anyway, right? After all, if a cat could get through, so could a skunk."

"That hole was tiny. It might have stayed tiny for a year or two, but now . . ." He tosses the broken lattice aside and bends to peer into the dark spaces between the brick supports. "Are you sure the cat is still in there? Maybe he slipped out the other side."

"Use this." I hand him the big flashlight I brought from the utility room. "And there are no holes anywhere else. I checked. He's got to be under there."

As if to prove my point, a mournful meow rises from somewhere in the darkness. Wort clicks the flashlight, which doesn't respond until he slams the barrel against his meaty palm. He shines the golden beam into the crawl space, and after a couple of sweeps we spot a pair of glowing green eyes and an arched mound of black fur.

"There he is," I say.

Wort grunts. "And that crawl space is narrower than I thought. I'm not goin' in."

I stare at him, unable to believe he'd give up so easily. This man has ridden a Harley from Las Vegas to Orlando, he's drunk Mexican tequila *and* eaten the worm, and once he dived headfirst into a lake without having the slightest idea if the water was more than a foot deep.

He's not afraid. He simply doesn't want to do this . . . for me or for the cat.

I tilt my head and try gentle persuasion. "You could slide in on your belly."

He straightens and laughs, brushing his hand on his jeans. "Why don't you go in? You're a lot smaller than me."

I catch my breath, but there's no debating that point. Wort is a big man, with a round belly and a full beard to match. If he got stuck under the house I don't know what I'd do. Call 911, probably, unless we borrowed a tactic from Winnie the Pooh and waited for Wort to starve to a more manageable size.

Maybe I *should* crawl under there.

"Okay." I square my shoulders. "I'll go. Hand me the flashlight."

"Rosie." Wort's hand falls on my shoulder. "Don't worry about the dang cat. Leave it alone and it'll come out when it gets hungry. Or set some food out here—something smelly, like tuna. That cat'll come out soon enough."

I crouch on hands and knees, shining the flashlight until it catches the luminous gleam of animal eyes. "What if he's hurt?"

"It's not even your cat." Wort points out. "It may be feral. Wild cats don't appreciate being dragged out of their hiding places. You need to leave it alone before you get hurt."

"But it's been crying all day. If it was gonna come out, surely it would have by now. I'm afraid something's wrong with it."

"So? Not your responsibility."

I toss a reproving look over my shoulder. Wort should know better. If there's anything Gran taught me, it's that every animal on this earth is mankind's responsibility. So any creature, large or small, that wanders onto our property falls under my protection. I'm presently caring for five dogs, three cats, a rabbit, a python, a flock of chickens, and five retired racehorses. Seems like every month I step outside and find some new critter abandoned in our yard . . . which might explain the appearance of this kitten.

I place the flashlight in Wort's hand. "Aim it at the cat." I lower myself to my elbows. "I'm going in."

Wort's jaw drops for an instant, then he grins. "Better hurry. Sundown's comin', and I wouldn't want to be stuck under there after dark."

"Don't remind me." I lower my head and ease into the dark space, crawling beneath the crossbeams that support the floorboards. The ground beneath my palms feels like pure sand, and my path is littered with bits of broken concrete blocks, wood, and the occasional scrap of paper. Fifteen feet ahead of me, the cat wails again, but I can't tell whether his cry is a plea or a warning.

I drop my hand to the ground and yelp when something stings me.

"What happened?" Wort's voice rings with urgency. "You okay?"

"Piece of glass." I wince as I pull the offending shard from the curve of my thumb. "I'm okay."

"Good grief, you're probably gonna get infected. All for the sake of a stupid cat."

"Hush up, will you? I've nearly got him."

I block all thoughts of black widows, brown recluses, and anything else that might lie in the surrounding darkness as I creep closer to the kitten, now backed up against a concrete footer. He crouches and arches his spine as he watches me advance, but he doesn't run.

"Here, kitty kitty," I call, injecting a playful note into my voice. "Are you hungry? Would you like some sardines?"

The cat releases a plaintive meow in response.

I extend my bleeding hand while keeping up a stream of soothing cat-talk. "Pretty kitty. Pretty, pretty kitty. Come here, and I'll get you some sardines and tuna."

My bloody fingers are only inches from the cat's scruff when the cell phone in my pocket shatters the quiet. The shrill blast sends the cat bolting toward the front of the house. When Wort follows it with the flashlight, gloomy darkness swallows me whole.

Unable to sit upright. I drop flat to the ground and fumble for the cell phone. "Hello? Hello?"

"Rose! I have good news—we finally have a buyer for Grandmother's house."

I groan. My oldest sister has a knack for calling at exactly the wrong time. "Great. Can we talk about it later?"

"Well"—Ginger's offended, I can tell from the huff in her voice—"way to thank me for passing on a little good news."

"Sorry, but I'm flat on my belly in the dirt. Can I call you later?"

"What are you—never mind. I called to see if you're available on Labor Day weekend. Now that we have a buyer, we have to clean out Grandmother's place. If you want anything of hers, this is your chance to claim it."

I don't want anything from Grandma's house—after all, it's not like I can take anything with me when I go—but money from the sale might come in handy around here. Wort can have my share of Lillian's estate. I just hope he doesn't blow it on funeral flowers and a headstone.

"This coming weekend, huh?" I close my eyes. Labor Day weekend is only days away, preceded by the Saturday I was planning to write some kind of explanation for Wort and swallow a couple of bottles of aspirin. His motorcycle club has a charity ride and picnic planned for Sunday, but I figured Wort could use the three-day weekend to grieve. If he wanted to, that is. If I were married to me, I'd probably opt for the picnic.

"Come on," Ginger begs. "Time is of the essence, kiddo. The buyer is ready to move and the real estate agent is anxious to get things done. Besides, we might actually have fun."

That doesn't seem likely, but a weekend away might give me a chance to say good-bye to my sisters. We haven't seen one another since Grandma Lillian's funeral, and that encounter was just plain awkward. We ended up talking about how good Gran looked in her casket instead of how much she meant to us. As usual, we focused on unimportant details and locked up our thoughts about things that really mattered.

If I go to the cottage . . . will I be able to open up and tell my sisters what I'm really thinking?

"Okay." I whisper as the flashlight beam bounces in the darkness to my left. "I'll drive up to Gran's house on Saturday morning."

"Good." Ginger's tone reverts to clipped and no-nonsense. "I'll let you go now because I need to call Penny."

"Right. See ya later."

Looks like my plans will have to be put on hold for a day or two.

I disconnect the call and slide the phone into my jeans pocket. My right hand is warm and sticky with blood, and something tells me I should hurry and get a bandage on the wound. "I'm sure about one thing," I yell to Wort, "that kitty isn't hurt. He ran like a bank robber when the phone rang."

"So you come on out," Wort commands, his voice booming from somewhere behind me. "You'll never catch that skittish cat tonight."

"You're probably right." I shimmy backward through the dirt, grateful that I'm wearing an old T-shirt and work jeans. When Wort drops an encouraging hand on my ankle, I turn and crawl through the gaping hole. Sitting upright, I lift my head and brush dirt from my uninjured hand, wishing I could smack the *I told you so* grin off my husband's face.

"I know what to do." I hold my injured hand aloft and stand on shaky legs. "I'm going to the kitchen for sardines. I'll leave them on the lawn tonight, and if the cat comes out, you can repair the hole tomorrow."

"First you're going in the bathroom to clean that cut. I'll set out the sardines and stuff."

"And if he doesn't come out by tomorrow?"

Wort rolls his eyes. "I guess I'll have to install a pet door or something. But if I'd known that stupid cat was gonna cost me a trip to the lumberyard—"

"Don't worry about the money," I tell him, holding my hand and turning toward the house. "That was Ginger on the phone. Apparently we Lawrence girls are finally about to divvy up our inheritance."

PENNYROYAL

Thirty more minutes, I tell myself. I have to keep it together until closing time, then I can go outside and scream.

"Ma'am?"

The question distracts me from the rack of junior separates I've been sorting for the past hour. I turn, expecting to find a teenage girl, but I find two—and both are accompanied by an attractive middle-aged man who wears the patient expression of a tired father reluctantly pressed into shopping service.

I paste on the professional smile of a Macy's employee. "Can I help you young ladies?"

The younger girl holds up a sequined top. "Do y'all have this in an extra small? I couldn't find one on the rack."

"Let me check that for you."

I lead the way to the display of aqua and peach T-shirts, noticing that the girls have avoided the clearance rack and chosen from an overpriced display of separates produced by a young actress-turned-designer. After peering at the tags on a dozen sequined shirts, I sigh and shrug. "I'm sorry, honey, but we seem to be sold out of your size."

"Can you check the back?" The father gives me an apologetic smile. "She has her heart set on this shirt because her friend has one just like it."

"I understand, but all those shirts are out on the floor. You might want to check the clearance rack by the dressing room. I don't think you'll find the exact shirt over there, but y'all might find a couple of similar styles and colors."

"What do you say, honey?" The father looks at his daughter, frank pleading in his eyes. "Maybe you and your friend can look similar instead of exactly alike. Won't that be good enough?"

The girl—who looks to be eleven or twelve at most—pushes her lower lip forward in a pout, but then she looks at her older sister. The older girl glances at her dad, then nods almost imperceptibly. "He's right," she says, her voice ringing with authority. "You don't want to look *exactly* like Zara, do you?"

The younger girl bobs her head. "Yeah, I do."

"But with a different shirt, you might actually look *better* than Zara. Come on, let me help you pick out something nice."

The older sister leads the younger girl away, but not before giving her dad a glance that clearly says, *You owe me one.*

The father acknowledges his debt with a nod, then looks at me. "Thanks," he says, a world of meaning in his weary smile. He swings another shopping bag across his shoulder and trails his daughters across the floor.

And as I watch them go, I wonder why these girls aren't shopping with their mother. Maybe she's home, maybe she's working, maybe she lives in another state. Hard to know; families these days come in all shapes and sizes.

But no matter where Mom is, this dad is certainly attuned to his girls. I watch as he follows them to yet another display of overpriced garments and marvel again that he's out shopping when he could be snoring in his easy chair at home.

I check my watch—ten minutes until closing. Forgetting about the separates that still need sorting, I tiptoe toward the clearance rack where the girls and their father have finally stopped. Hiding behind a pair of mannequins, I pull sweaters from a shelf and refold them, keeping my hands busy while I spy on the little family.

The younger girl holds up a shirt; the father says it matches her eyes. As the girl jogs into the dressing room, the father asks the older girl how she spent her day at school. The girl shrugs and says, "You know—the usual," and Dad nods as if she's just said something terribly profound. When the younger girl comes out of the dressing room in the new shirt, the father whistles appreciatively. A warm glow flows through me when he checks the tag and pretends to be shocked by the price.

My annoyance with my boring job fades as I fold the last sweater and wonder if those girls know how fortunate they are. Not many daughters get that kind of attention from their fathers . . . not many at all.

T W O

G I N G E R

I am in my pajamas and brushing my teeth when I hear the three-noted chime of the alarm system—someone has just entered the house. I freeze, focused on my startled reflection, as I take a quick head count: Ross and Ryan are away at school, and neither is likely to come home on a Monday night, no matter how desperate they are for clean laundry or a free meal. That leaves Michael, who should have been home long before this. . . .

I resume my teeth brushing when I catch my husband's eye in the bathroom mirror. "Sorry to be so late." Michael walks into the room, his hands behind his back. Then he pulls out an armful of long-stemmed red roses wrapped in cellophane. "Didn't think the meeting would run so late, but this grant is complicated."

"Oh, hon—dose are beaugydlfhl." My words come out in a toothpaste-suds garble until I lean over the sink and rinse. "You didn't have to bring me flowers."

"I feel terrible leaving you alone so much." He sets the roses on the edge of the bathtub and smiles at me. "And I hate that you had to eat by yourself."

"I didn't know when to expect you"—I pat my chin with a towel—"so I didn't make anything for dinner. But I could whip up some pasta or something."

"Don't bother; we had food brought in. But I'm getting awfully tired of Caesar salad." He reaches down and scoops up a handful of leftover bath bubbles, then idly blows them in my direction. "We've barely made a dent in the research, though, so we're still meeting tomorrow night. Even worse, Dr. Collins wants me to attend a conference in Atlanta this weekend."

I drop the towel and turn to face him. "Atlanta? I hope the college is covering your hotel expenses."

"I'm sure they will. So you don't have to worry."

"Actually, I'm not that worried. I have good news—Grandmother Lillian's house finally sold. If you don't mind, I'm going to drive down there this weekend, meet my sisters, and help them empty the place. I've had my eye on Grandmother's antique piano, so unless Rose or Penny wants to wrestle me for it, I'll probably rent a trailer and bring it home."

"Why do you want that thing?" Standing, Michael shrugs out of his jacket and unknots his tie. "I can't believe you're talking about renting a trailer."

"Why should that be a problem?"

"Have you ever driven one?"

"How hard can it be?"

"Never mind. Do what you want. All I want to do right now is sleep."

I lean against the bathroom vanity and study his profile, pondering the motives and meanings behind his last statement: either he doesn't want to watch TV, doesn't want to make love, or doesn't want to hear about my weekend plans. But Michael never goes straight to sleep, so . . .

"Are you feeling okay?" I step toward him and press the back of my hand to his forehead. As our gazes meet, I can't help noticing a flicker of unease in the depths of his eyes.

"I'm fine." He catches my wrist and gently pulls my hand away. "All I need is a solid eight hours of rest."

I walk back to my sink and open a tiny jar of ridiculously expensive face cream, trying to remember the last time Michael slept eight hours straight—maybe when he had the flu? He's always functioned well on five or six hours a night, and he *never* drifts off until after the networks have surrendered their programming to infomercials.

Watching in the mirror, I see Michael vanish into the depths of the walk-in closet. I push my bangs from my forehead and lean forward, searching for developing wrinkles. "I thought this day would never end." I raise my voice to be heard at the back of the closet. "The kids in every single choir were wound tighter than clock springs; I think they were excited about school starting next week. Nobody wanted to sing, and nobody even wanted to *think* about the Christmas program."

When Michael doesn't answer, I wonder if he heard me. But then he steps out of the closet, already dressed in his pajamas. "Who wants to sing Christmas carols in August? It's still eighty-five degrees outside."

When did he start undressing in private? I watch my suddenly modest husband move to his sink, where he picks up his toothbrush and peers at his reflection.

"It's almost September," I answer, studying him. "Besides, if this program's going to be better than last year's, I have to plan ahead. I have to find a middle schooler who'll be suitable for the Virgin Mary and won't have braces on her teeth in December."

Michael squirts toothpaste onto his brush. "You'll pull everything together. You always do."

"But next month I've got that fund-raiser for the crisis pregnancy center. My middle school choir is supposed to sing a full program, but my kids barely know three songs. Reverend Howe specifically asked for thirty minutes of music, but most of the new sixth graders are so raw they don't know the difference between melody and harmony."

Michael only grunts in reply.

I cross my arms as he brushes his teeth, a picture of normalcy . . . except for the circles beneath his eyes and the slump in his shoulders. My poor baby has been working too hard . . . or are these signs of weariness due to something else?

I shrug away the idea. Michael is fine, and thinking otherwise means I must be crazy, paranoid, or even more tired than I realized. So what if my husband wants to go to bed early? Who cares if he puts on his pajamas in the closet? That's where I keep the hamper. Maybe he's trying to make things easier for me.

I touch two fingertips to the fragrant face cream and dot the miracle stuff at points around my eyes and jaw. How in the world did I get a wrinkle at my jawline? I'm not surprised to see a few crinkles on this forty-nine-year-old face, but what would cause a line along my jawbone?

I force a smile, and watch as the wrinkle deepens into a verifiable crease. That settles it, then. I simply have to stop smiling so much.

But smiling feels natural when you have a husband who brings you red roses.

PENNYROYAL

Nothing, Grandma always said, breaks up a beautiful romance as completely as marriage. Time after time, I've proven her right.

As the clock chimes ten, I drop the last plate into the dishwasher and rinse my hands, grateful to be done with the kitchen for the day. Bob disappeared right after dinner, but since I can hear the cultured tones of a History Channel narrator, I figure he's watching TV in the family room.

The man who once brought me fresh-picked lilacs in a milk carton, who composed a sonnet in my honor and named a star after me, has turned into a bookworm who would rather discuss the world's hunger problem than tell me I'm beautiful. He'd rather work a crossword puzzle than massage my tired feet, and he'd rather go to a Mensa meeting than take me to a movie.

Clearly, our romance is over . . . and the surprise I felt at learning that a superintelligent man could also be passionate has been replaced by a restlessness I can't wish away. Grandma always said the grass wasn't any greener on the other side of the fence, but she didn't seem to have any problem with leaving a marriage when the lawn dried up and turned brown.

After drying my hands on a dishtowel, I tiptoe toward the bedroom. Unless something distracts me, I should be deep in pretend sleep by the time my husband comes to bed.

When I turn the corner, though, I find him standing in the hallway, his shoulder braced against the door frame of the bedroom we use for an office. In his profile I see a wistful smile, the one he always wears when he thinks about kids . . . and how badly he wants to use that room as a nursery.

Bob must have heard me coming, because his head turns in my direction. "You know"—he smiles into the extra bedroom—"they say primary colors are best for young children. Most people decorate nurseries with pastels, but a bold yellow might be the better choice. Bright colors stimulate the brain."

I nod and sidle past him, heading toward the bathroom. "That's interesting."

"I was thinking we could paint this weekend." He catches my upper arm. "Doesn't that sound like fun?"

"Painting, fun?" I wince in phony distaste. "You're kidding, right?"

"Not at all. I've been watching the calendar, and this weekend should be prime baby-making time. So I figured we could take the three-day weekend to paint the room *and* create its future occupant."

I turn my head, hiding disgust that's now all too genuine. Honestly, what kind of man sweet-talks his wife with phrases like *baby-making* and *future occupant*? Even more to the point, what kind of man keeps track of his wife's monthly cycle?

I struggle to smooth my voice. "Bob, I don't think you can schedule a conception. Especially since I'm not exactly Fertile Myrtle these days."

"Thirty-nine isn't such an advanced age, and you're perfectly healthy. No reason in the world why we can't have a baby."

Oh, yes, there are reasons . . . a couple of them, in fact. But he doesn't need to know my secrets.

I turn, link my hands behind his neck, and breathe in his scent—a mingling of soap, dust, and the cinnamon air freshener that pervades the computer lab where he works. "You're a man— you could father a child when you're as old as Abraham. Women are different."

Pulling me closer, he smiles into my eyes. "The genders aren't that dissimilar. And I want to spend some special time with you this weekend. I figured we could relax, paint the room, go out to eat. You could go to the spa on Sunday afternoon, and I'll make dinner. I'll even set out candles to enhance the mood."

I hug him, glad that he can't see the frustration that has to be displayed on my face. I'm about to ruin all my husband's plans, but he needs to believe I'm reluctant to do it. I'm not about to dump the fish in my basket until I have Miller Conrad firmly on the line.

"That's sweet." I release Bob, then stroke his cheek and give him a sad smile. "As wonderful as your plans sound"—I honey-coat my words—"Ginger called while I was on my break at work. We finally have a buyer for Grandma Lillian's property, so I need to go to St. Simons and help clean out the house. I promised Gingerbread I'd give her a hand."

Bob's face crumples with disappointment. "Couldn't she hire someone to do that?"

"Bless your heart, you're such a *man*. You don't hire a stranger to clean out your grandmother's house, especially if she practically raised you."

"You want some help? I could go along."

"Are you serious?" I toss him a look of pure horror. "How are we supposed to run around without makeup if there's a man in the house?" I peck at his cheek, then give him another smile. "The good news is I might be able to bring home a few trinkets to help us remember Grandma. And it should be a nice time for us girls. We never see each other anymore."

Bob releases me and leans back against the wall. "What about the sale? You're supposed to split the proceeds, right?"

"I'm not sure there'll be much to split. The housing market is awfully depressed."

I step into the bathroom and peer at my reflection in the mirror. My face shimmers back at me, pale and wide-eyed and tired.

Grandma always said that the woman who complains about the

man she married should realize she could have caught a bigger fish
if she'd used better bait. I try to eat right and stay out of the sun,
but avoiding the sun isn't easy when you live in Florida. But if Bob
still believes I'm only thirty-nine, I must be doing okay.

I turn the faucet at the sink. While the water warms, I slip my
hand into my pants pocket and pull out the napkin with a name
and phone number scribbled on it: Miller Conrad, the doctor who
lunches near Macy's.

A successful, handsome man who yearns for success, not children. A man who might be persuaded to drive over to St. Simons
for the holiday weekend.

ROSEMARY

Will I ever be able to be truly honest with my sisters? The question badgers me for two days.

By Wednesday, I decide the question can't be settled with a yes-or-no answer. I can't know how our weekend will work out until I see Penny and Ginger. My sisters are anything but predictable.

I'm arranging important papers in my desk when I hear the click of Justus's nails on the wooden floor. I watch, concerned, as my eighteen-year-old Jack Russell terrier crosses the room and bumps into the wall. I'm by his side in an instant, one hand supporting his body as the other soothes his calloused nose.

"Poor baby. Getting old is hard, isn't it?"

Justus licks my palm, sniffs the bandage over the cut on my hand, and then does his best to scramble up my bent legs to reach my lap. I surrender and sit on the floor, gathering him to me as he covers my chin and cheeks with doggie kisses.

Justus, who has been with me longer than any husband, has never failed to prove himself faithful. My husbands have disappointed me, lied to me, and broken my heart, but the worst thing Justus ever did was chew up a pair of leather sandals.

"Are you gonna be okay?" I lower my head and whisper directly into his ear, because lately I've begun to suspect that he's going deaf as well as blind. "Mama loves you, you know."

Jussy wriggles out of my grasp and stands on the floor, then, with an effort, pushes himself onto his back legs and waves a front paw at me. His eyes are milky now, but his smile is as wide and engaging as ever.

"Good boy!" I pull a piece of dried beef from my pocket and place it under his nose. "Guess I don't have to worry about you forgetting any of your tricks."

Justus takes the square of beef in his jaws and trots over to his pillow, where he settles to crunch his treat. I sigh and return to my desk, then close the gaping drawer. My will and instructions for my funeral are inside, situated beneath a stack of bills. Not so obvious as to be easily noticed, but not impossible to find . . . when the time comes.

I pull my calendar toward me and stare at the discreetly drawn oblong around Friday, September 2. The 730th day after the effective date of my million-dollar life insurance policy. The day of ultimate release is only two days away.

From across the kitchen, Justus whimpers, drawing my attention. His treat is gone, but I don't dare give him another even if he does another trick. He can't keep large amounts of food down, and an inoperable tumor is pressing on his lungs. The vet suggested that the time has come to put Jussy to sleep, but if I can make him comfortable with medication and TLC, I'm gonna keep him with me as long as I can.

I had everything worked out for September third, but Ginger threw a wrench into my plans. Instead of swallowing aspirin on Saturday, I'll be driving to St. Simons. I'll meet Ginger and Penny at Grandma's house. I'll do my share of the work, and I'll pretend to be happy and content. I might even ask for one of Gran's trinkets or a few of the books on her shelves. Later my sisters will remember my requests and assure each other that my death was simply an accident. On a crowded holiday weekend, an accident would be easy to arrange. In a few days Jussy and I can crash into a concrete support together. We'll go out side by side, the way we've lived for so many years.

For my sisters' sake, for Wort's sake, isn't an accident the best way to go? It's a much cleaner exit than an obvious overdose. Losing someone is hard enough, but since Ginger's call I've begun to realize that the loss will be harder to bear if my family knew I could find no joy in living despite their best efforts to love me.

I'm not out to make anyone suffer after I'm gone. I've done enough of that already.

Maybe I *won't* open the door on the past and tell my sisters the truth about our relationship. In three days I'll look them in the eye and smile, though I'm burning to know why they didn't come to my side on that awful August day two years ago. If I somehow found the courage to ask, Ginger would no doubt say that a miscarriage isn't the same as losing an actual child, so what possessed me to think she'd drive all the way to Gainesville to mourn a few cells? Penny would never be so blunt; she'd be more likely to remind me that babies are like men—if you miss out on one, another will come along sooner or later.

I swallow the boulder rising in my throat and reach for a pen. Wort would say I'm being too tough on Ginger and Penny, but he doesn't know them like I do. Maybe I *am* being hard on them. After all, don't most people try to avoid situations that might bring them close to soul-searing loss?

So it's okay. No need for my sisters to know what I'm thinking and what I've always thought.

At least I could be honest with Gran.

I circle a new date, lightly sketching an oval around Monday, September fifth. Labor Day. By late afternoon the highway will be streaming with people hurrying home from picnics, family events, and the beach. After our week-end at Grandma's house, Penny and Ginger will drive home, happily satisfied with whatever treasures they manage to pilfer. Later, they'll assure Wort that I seemed fine during our time together, that I mentioned being content. (This means I have to *say* I'm feeling content. I should throw in *happy* too.) They'll say I had fun, that I looked like a woman who had everything to live for.

Only Justus and I will know the truth. And that truth will set us both free.

PENNYROYAL

"A romantic fire," Grandma liked to say, "is often kindled by a little spark in the park." I'm hoping she was right.

Though Wednesday is my day off, I slip into a pastel sleeveless sheath and spend an hour browsing at the Oaks Mall, making sure to avoid Macy's and the sandwich shop where my supervisor usually eats lunch. A restless energy keeps me moving from store to store, driving me to zip through clothing racks and devour window displays in one glance. I ought to be making plans for the weekend, maybe looking for beachwear, but all I can think about is Dr. Miller Conrad and what life might hold as a physician's wife. A bigger house, definitely. Charity balls. White-tie benefits. Golf tournaments. And an end to my days as an hourly employee.

I end up at Dillard's, where a salesgirl in a chic suit offers me a sample of a new designer perfume. I rub the scent card on my wrist, wait a moment, and inhale—perfect. I spend way too much money on a puny bottle of toilet water, but today I want something to make me feel irresistible. I need to feel attractive again.

By eleven thirty I'm driving to the strip mall across from the medical center. I park in the lot, then enter the restaurant I visited Monday. I ask for a table on the front patio, where I can eat under the shade of an umbrella . . . and be seen if a handsome doctor approaches.

Fortunately, the hostess leads me to a table near the sidewalk. A young waiter brings water, takes my drink order, and leaves me with a menu. Masked by my sunglasses, I sip from my water glass and pretend to read the chef's specials, though I spend most of my time scanning the sidewalk for signs of a certain pedestrian. No sign of Miller Conrad, not yet. Did he get held up at the lab? Or did he make other plans for lunch?

The waiter, a six-foot beanpole whose face is puffy with pimples, comes back and taps his order pad while I attempt to stall by asking if the poultry in the chicken salad is free-range or bred in captivity. The waiter doesn't know and apparently doesn't care. I end up ordering a shrimp salad, and as the waiter walks away, he wisecracks about how grateful he is that the shrimp served at this restaurant get to live free.

I prop my chin on my hand and study the parking lot, occasionally sniffing my wrist to inhale my new perfume. The fragrance is sweeter now and reminds me of funeral flowers. Did I rub on too much? The heat seems to be intensifying the scent, so I hope Miller likes roses and lilies.

My salad arrives. I thank the waiter, unroll my napkin, and drop it into my lap. Nearly noon, and every table on the front patio has filled. The sticky August sun blazes overhead, and if not for the umbrella, I'd be melting like a wax doll.

If Miller doesn't show, I will simply eat my salad and leave. No harm done.

If he shows up with friends or coworkers, I will finish my meal and either slip away or stop by his table for a quick hello. His reaction will speak volumes about the potential of this relationship.

If he shows up alone, I can smile at him from this corner table. I won't invite him to join me—too forward—but if he comes over to greet me, politeness demands that I ask if he's found a seat at another table.

I drizzle dressing over my salad and try to remember exactly what he said when we parted. Was it "Hope to see you again sometime" or

"Hope *I* see you again sometime"? The first is something you might say to anybody, but the latter is practically a direct invitation.

I'm still debating the question when an unexpected voice startles me. I glance over my shoulder and see Miller standing on the sidewalk, his brows lifted.

"Oh, my goodness—you're here." Not the most beguiling thing to say, but at least my blushing confusion is genuine.

He smiles and slips his hands into his pockets. "Fancy seeing you today. Looks like I won't be getting a table outside, though."

"You can join me." I drop my fork, signaling my willingness to wait for him. "I'm in no hurry."

He glances at the others in line to be seated, then grins. "Be right there, Penny."

He remembered my name.

I look away and try to calm my pounding heart as he walks to the hostess's desk, speaks to her, and gestures toward me. This is nothing; this is only lunch. . . .

As Miller pulls out the empty chair next to me, I cross my arms and smile. "I have to confess, I was hoping you'd come."

"I'm only sorry I'm late."

He lifts his hand to catch the waiter's attention. I sip from my glass, pretending a nonchalance I'm far from feeling. "Busy day at the lab?"

He nods, then gives his order to the waiter. "Sorry," he says, meeting my gaze when the young man turns away. "I suppose you've guessed that I eat here almost every afternoon."

"Well . . . I was hoping."

His lips part in a dazzling display of perfect teeth. "More good news. This must be my lucky day."

I prop my chin on my hand and study him. Miller Conrad has been blessed with a beautiful face, marked by touches of humor around the mouth and eyes. He may not be a card-carrying genius like Bob, but he's certainly intelligent. Maybe he's not a millionaire, but he's probably wealthy enough to live in one of the best neighborhoods in town. Best of all, he's my age . . . and he's interested.

Grandma was right—all it took was a spark in the park. Or in our case, a restaurant.

His smile shrinks slightly under the intensity of my gaze. "Listen, I'm not sure what we're doing here"—he tilts his brow—"but I want to be honest right up front. I like you, Penny. I think I'd like to see you sometime—outside this restaurant, that is. And I want you to know I was once married, but I'm single now."

I lift my right hand, where my wedding ring now circles a finger. "I was married too." I press my palm to the tabletop and look at the diamond winking in the sun. "In fact, my divorce isn't final yet—I'm waiting for some financial arrangements to be settled. But I like you too. I don't want to rush into anything, but if you'd like to have dinner or see a ball game some evening, I'd be up for it."

His gaze travels over my face and settles on my eyes. "I'd like that. If you don't have plans this weekend, the Gators are playing—"

"Don't tell me." I cover my eyes as disappointment strikes like a kick to the stomach. I was hoping he'd want to ask me out, but I wasn't sure the situation would progress this quickly. I am ready to leave my marriage and start a new life, but I've made promises to Ginger and Rose, and I have to find a way to tell Bob that it's over.

I am not—I will never be—the sort of woman who has tawdry affairs.

"Did I say something wrong?" Miller asks.

I lower my hand. "I'm so sorry—*truly* sorry—but this weekend my sisters and I are meeting on St. Simons Island to clean out our grandmother's house. The place has been on the market for months, but it finally sold."

A smile twinkles in his eyes. "That's really too bad. We could have had fun together."

I lower my gaze, almost embarrassed by the surge of excitement sparking through my veins. How long has it been since I felt this way? Far too long.

A waiter walks past us with a platter of sizzling fajitas, but I refuse to be distracted. My gaze catches and holds Miller's as my formerly vague idea solidifies. "We could still have fun. Have you ever been to St. Simons? It's really a pretty spot. I'll be busy part of the time, but I think I could get away for a while if you wanted to drive over. I could show you some of the historic sites on the island."

I keep my voice light, not wanting to push, but Miller leans back in his chair and studies me with a calculating expression. I look away and try not to blush. If he comes to the island I'll have to figure out how to keep him away from Ginger and Rose, but I'll cross that bridge when I come to it.

"St. Simons? That's near Jekyll Island, isn't it?"

"Practically next door."

"I've played golf at a resort on Jekyll Island. I wouldn't mind spending a day or two there . . . and if you could find the time to drive over so we could meet up, that'd be better yet."

I break into a wide, open smile. "That sounds perfect. There aren't as many tourists in late summer, so I think you'd enjoy the trip."

"Do you have a personal connection to that area? Apart from your grandmother, I mean."

Despite my desire to remain cool and detached, my voice thickens. "From the time we were small, my sisters and I used to spend our summers at Grandma Lillian's house. The place holds a lot of memories for me—for all of us."

Miller leans forward and drops his hand over mine . . . and the unexpected warmth sends a shiver up my spine. "I can't make any promises," he says, his eyes alive with speculation, "but I'll see what I can do. I've been looking for an excuse to get out of town, and since it's a three-day weekend—"

"You'll find the trip worth the drive," I promise. "If you come up, I know you won't regret it."

THREE

GINGER

"Michael!"

The neighbors won't appreciate me yelling this early on a Saturday morning, but I need to get on the road by seven and Michael is nowhere to be found. I've checked the garage, the kitchen, and the bedroom because I need to talk to him before I leave for St. Simons.

A minute later he strides into the foyer and looks at me, irritation evident on his face. "Can't a man have a minute's peace in his own home?"

"Where were you?"

"Outside, on the phone. I needed to talk to Dr. Thomas, and I couldn't hear myself think with you yelling."

"Sorry." I take a deep breath and force myself to calm down. "I'm really sorry, but I need to be sure these details are covered before I go."

"What's the big deal? It's not like we've never gone out of town before."

"But we usually go together. This splitting up . . . bothers me."

Annoyance struggles with humor on his face as he stares at me. "I don't see why it should."

"Just humor me, okay? I need to run down my list and make sure we've covered everything. Let me know if I've forgotten something important."

Michael drops onto the foyer bench as I consult the scribbled note in my hand. "I've packed a few groceries, a cooler, my alarm clock, and my camera. I filled a crate with scrub brushes and cotton rags. I've charged my phone and put my laptop in the car, though I doubt I'll have time to go to the village to check e-mail."

Michael props his chin on his hand. "Your grandmother didn't have Internet?" His voice drips with sarcasm.

Ignoring his mockery, I press on. "Okay—are you sure you don't want me to pack some snacks or something for your trip?"

"Sweetheart, I know how to work a vending machine."

"But what about when you get home? I could pick up some frozen dinners in case you get home before I do."

"I'll eat out. Please hurry; they're not going to hold the plane for me."

I glance at my list again. "Mrs. Henefin promised to come over and feed Millicent, and I've already given her the spare key. Make sure you take your house key, because the spare is no longer under the mat."

"Check," Michael mumbles around his hand.

"I'm planning to bring the piano home, and I know I'll need help unloading it. But if you think you'll be home Monday night"—I hesitate—"by the way, when *will* you be home? You've booked a return flight, right?"

"Wrong. I left the ticket open-ended in case we finish up early."

"Oh. Okay. Well, if you're home when I pull in, we could roll the piano into the garage until I can get a technician out here to look at it."

"Are you *sure* you want that old thing?" Disapproval edges Michael's voice.

"W-why," I stutter, unnerved by the revulsion in his expression. "Don't you want it?"

"I wouldn't mind a good piano, but that relic is bound to be in terrible shape. So we'd have to fix it and maintain it, and you'd probably never find the time to play it."

THE FINE ART OF INSINCERITY   41

"I would. Even if I didn't, it's a valuable collectible."

Michael chuffs softly. "Right."

"It's an antique Steinway square piano." I lift my chin. "Anyway, it's the only thing from Grandmother's house that appeals to me. I'll let Penny and Rose squabble over the quilts and dishes; all I care about is that instrument."

"You don't know how to drive with a trailer," Michael points out. "You'll probably flip the thing on the drive back. And unless you pad it properly, the piano will be smashed by the time you get it home."

I stare at him, dazed and exasperated. "Good grief, what's gotten into you? You're acting as though I don't know how to do anything."

Michael crosses his arms and looks at the door, his mouth set in annoyance. "I'm running late," he says at last. "Would you please hurry with your final orders so I can be on my way?"

"I'm done." I swallow the lump of hurt that has risen beneath my breastbone and step aside as he stands. "Have a good weekend."

"Thanks." His voice is chilly, but he does stop and bend to kiss my cheek. At the touch of his lips, I close my eyes and tell myself we're both being foolish. He's upset about his job, and he probably resents the fact that he has to attend a conference over a holiday weekend. I'm worried about my trip, about leaving the house, about being with my sisters and finding a mess in Grandmother's cottage.

No wonder we're being short with each other.

"Michael." I catch his sleeve as he opens the door. When he turns, I slide my arms around his neck and rise up on tiptoe to give him a proper good-bye. His mouth does not soften when our lips meet, but when I bury my face in his neck and breathe a kiss there, he wraps his arms around me. "I'm sorry I'm such a pain," I whisper, inhaling the masculine scent of his cologne. "I know I drive you crazy with my lists and reminders. I don't mean to sound like a drill sergeant."

"It's okay, hon. I love you, orders and all." He brushes a kiss across my forehead and releases me, then bends to pick up the roll-aboard bag by the door. "I'll see you when I see you." His mouth curls in a one-sided smile. "Drive carefully, okay?"

"I will. You have a safe flight. And call me from Atlanta."

"Sure."

I follow him out the door and wave good-bye from the porch. This is not the romantic farewell I would have liked, but I understand why he's preoccupied. I have a lot on my mind too.

I make one more trip through the house, checking the lock on the back door, making sure the washer is empty, and double-checking to be sure I haven't left the coffeemaker or microwave plugged in. I change the water in the vase of red roses; with any luck, they'll still look lovely when I return home. I end in the study, where I wake the sleeping computer monitor and do one last check of e-mail.

I sit at the desk and skim the list of senders, glad that I don't see either of my sisters' names, but I blink when I see an "NSF notice" from my bank. I'm not even sure what an NSF notice is, but the bank wants me to log on to my account for a message.

I log on, then click on the message. My pulse quickens when I read that the check to our mortgage company has been returned for insufficient funds. What? We should have at least nine hundred dollars in our account.

I click on the account history and skim the entries. Everything looks familiar except one check, number 9374, for two thousand dollars. The list doesn't indicate who the payee was, or who cashed the check.

I open the desk drawer and pull out our checkbook, then flip through the pages. Sure enough, the carbon for check 9374 is in the book, signed by Michael and written for two thousand dollars. But the payee is blank.

Why would Michael pay someone two thousand dollars and not tell me about it? He's been absentminded in the past, often not telling me about checks until I can't balance the checkbook, but he's never forgotten to tell me about such a large payment.

I reach for the phone, then stop. Michael won't appreciate me harassing him about the family budget when he's trying to catch a flight. I can call him later, maybe tonight. Or, since it's a holiday weekend and the banks won't open until Tuesday, maybe I can let the matter slide until we both get home. I don't know what he bought or why he bought it, but I do know that he hates talking to me about money.

I force myself to close my eyes and breathe deeply. I shouldn't worry. Michael's car might have needed some repair, or one of the boys might have asked for a security deposit to lease an apartment. Ross has been thinking about moving off campus; maybe he and Michael worked something out without telling me.

Anyway, our days of financial stress are numbered. If all goes well this weekend, my sisters and I will empty Grandmother's house, sign the final papers, and receive a healthy check for our efforts. That money will go a long way toward easing the strain Michael and I are under, and when the financial pressure is gone, we'll relax with each other. We'll no longer have to worry about the balky air conditioner or the worn-out roof. And since Michael always worries about retirement, we will certainly need to deposit a chunk of the proceeds into our investment funds.

We may be able to take a vacation, maybe an exotic second honeymoon to the Caribbean or some other tropical spot . . . anyplace where we can be alone and rediscover the pleasure we used to find in simply being together.

Clinging to that hope for our future, I take a last look around the house, then step outside and lock the front door.

ROSEMARY

Tall structure, hard water, speeding traffic: a death trap, for sure.

As the intimidating Sidney Lanier Bridge rises before me, I grip my steering wheel and resist what feels like an oncoming panic attack. Bridges and I have never been on friendly terms, but I've never had to drive across any structure as tall and arched as this one. The previous bridge across this part of the South Brunswick River didn't feel like a roller coaster determined to fling a driver from the track. But there is no track beneath my car, only asphalt, and nothing keeps me on the road but gravity and my sweat-slicked hands, which are trembling on the steering wheel.

Nausea churns my stomach as I breathe in the odors of coffee and sausage from the remnants of my drive-through breakfast.

Why is my pulse pounding? This is *not* my final day. I have to get through this weekend, then I'll say good-bye on my own terms. I am not surrendering to pitiful panic, no matter how terrifying the bridge.

I glance in my rearview and side-view mirrors, put on my blinker, and slant to the left, lowering my foot on the accelerator as I pass a slower vehicle. I feel safer next to the center divider, but eighty miles an hour doesn't seem fast enough. The quicker I cross this asphalt arc, the sooner my heartbeat can settle back to its normal rate.

I startle when a brown and white blur moves in my peripheral vision— Justus has lifted his head in the passenger seat. I snatch a breath and glance at him.

THE FINE ART OF INSINCERITY   45

"I am not going to panic," I tell him. "I'm a rational woman and I can handle this with no problem. It's like taking a curve on the back of Wort's Harley. I just have to close my eyes, relax, and lean into it."

But I can't close my eyes while I'm driving, and I can't relax on this bridge. Another driver is breathing exhaust on my rear bumper, and all I see through my windshield is my hood ornament juxtaposed against a bright blue sky.

This is where I should jerk my wheel in a stiff turn to the right. A quick crash; a long, silent fall; a crumpling upon impact. A fatal accident that won't endanger any other drivers.

The unexpected thought commands my attention and leaves me breathless. Why drive home searching for an accessible pillar or a vulnerable overpass? Why risk involving other travelers? Driving off this bridge would look like an accident to all but the most cynical observer, and few people would be brazen enough to suggest suicide to my family and friends.

The concept of suicide-by-bridge twirls in my head and settles into my psyche. So be it. Let the girl born in Valdosta Hospital die beneath the Sydney Lanier Bridge.

Now that I've settled the most crucial question of the weekend, my panic begins to recede. The pavement levels and I can see a downward slope beyond the hood of my car. Miles of emerald green marshland appear to the east and west, intersected by the snaking gray highway that splits into a fork just ahead, one road leading to Brunswick and the other to St. Simons Island.

What an incredible place to say good-bye.

I exhale through my teeth as the bridge gently lowers us back to earth. I sneak a glance at the next seat, where Justus has stretched out on his tattered pillow. "How are ya, Jus?" I ask, knowing he won't be alarmed by the residual quaver in my voice. "We're almost there. Almost home."

I shift into the right lane and let the impatient driver behind me blow on by. Easing onto the F. J. Torras Causeway, I smile as the vibrant marshes sparkle against the blue ribbon of water. St. Simons is a beautiful spot, and I've missed it. I haven't spent a summer at Grandma's beach house since high school. Her retirement home was in Brunswick, so once she left St. Simons, I had no reason to go back.

But now I have good reasons to visit my part-time childhood home. I have to say my farewells, and I have to pretend to be happy. And while I'm enacting this final stage play, I might look around to see if Gran left any clues about how to endure the unendurable. She persevered through more than her fair share of grief and loss, but she never told me how she managed to survive all those heartbreaks.

If she did, I wasn't listening.

FOUR

GINGER

Being the firstborn apparently means I am destined to a lifetime of being first on the scene. As I pull up to Grandmother's house, I experience a frisson of sheer panic—what if my sisters have conspired together and don't plan on showing up? No cars sit in front of the fenced yard; no signs of life stir at the window. The FOR SALE sign leans aslant on the front lawn, and someone needs to clear out the kudzu suffocating the oak trees along the property line. The trinkets and dusty treasures of a lifetime wait inside the house, and someone has to sift through it all.

Though I'm used to taking charge, there's no way I can handle this job alone.

I get out of the car and feel years slip away as I cross the graveled lane and walk through the small picket gate. How many summers did my sisters and I spend here? At least fifteen. I didn't stop coming until the year I graduated from college. By that time Lillian had married Walter, the sweet old man we all grew to love. He and Grandmother remained in the cottage until he died in 1998. That's when I convinced Penny and Rose that our grandmother would be better off living in a retirement home . . . and that's the last time I visited this house.

Standing on the sidewalk, I tilt my head and examine the cottage with the appraising eye of a cautious buyer. I gave the real estate agent permission to do whatever she thought necessary to spruce up the building, so several months ago Barbara hired a painter and a professional cleaning service. The paint job is holding up well, and the tabby trim on the chimney looks as though it's been pressure-washed. The front porch is still solid and the stairs unbowed, but that has to be a new swing at the far end of the porch. The dangling chains are shiny and silver, though I remember sitting in that swing and coming away with rust stains on the palms of my hands.

Grandmother spent more time maintaining her face than her house.

I climb the painted steps and run my hand along the railing, now smooth and well sanded, though covered with a patina of dirt. A gray heron on the lawn cocks his head and stops picking his way through the long grass, as if surprised by my arrival. I glance at the sprawling live oak at the front corner of the lot, but the bird feeder Penny and Rose painted and hung from a lower branch is gone.

Why am I surprised? The birdhouse probably fell apart years ago. I walk to the entrance and pull a cardboard door hanger from the knob—some pizza delivery service has made the rounds—and punch the Realtor's code into a lockbox, revealing the front-door key.

After I unlock it, the door swings open in welcome. A tidal wave of sunlight pours in from the tall windows, streaming over the wooden floor and splashing the faded furnishings. I step into the overheated space, feeling a bit like Gulliver in Lilliput. Though the bright room before me is uncluttered and airy, the walls seem closer together and the furnishings seem to have shrunk. Grandmother's sofa seems shorter than I remember, and the overstuffed chair has assumed conventional proportions. The pine dining table that Grandmother, the three of us, and most of the ladies from the church choir used to crowd around now has room for only six chairs. But the piano—the Steinway square piano that captured my fancy in childhood—seems every bit as grand in actuality as it does in my memory. It stands against the far wall, bench tucked beneath the keyboard.

Choking on the acrid atmosphere, I drop the house key and my purse onto the table and move to the thermostat near the staircase. Grandmother had central air installed about the time we stopped spending our summers here, though I suspect she rarely used it. As a child of the Depression, Lillian liked to squeeze a nickel until it squealed. "Make do," she used to tell us when we complained that we'd run out of whatever we needed for a craft or art project. "Exercise your imagination, not my wallet."

Standing in the center of the house, I take shallow breaths until the air handler kicks on and the air begins to circulate. Trusting that the room will soon be comfortable, I move toward the dusty piano and run my fingers over the yellowed keys. I play a slow arpeggio, beginning at middle C, and wince as the keys produce progressively off-pitch sounds. But that's okay. Pianos are like marriages—they can be retuned, and the music can be restored.

I open the top of the cabinet and peer at the strings. Many of them are rusted, so Michael was right; the instrument will need a complete overhaul. But this piano is what led me to fall in love with music, so I'll find the money even if I have to take it from my soon-coming inheritance.

After closing the lid, I move to the bar that divides the kitchen from the dining room and serves as an informal breakfast area with two stools. The Realtor has left a stack of information on the Formica countertop, brochures that describe the house and provide information about the neighborhood. Several visitors have scattered business cards on the blue counter, and someone has left a copy of the St. Simons yellow pages by the wall-mounted phone. A cookie sheet rests upside down in the dish drainer; an empty juice glass squats in the sink.

Against the wall, near the push-button phone, I glimpse the spiral spine of an old address book. I slide the book toward me and lift the stiff cover, then smile at the spidery handwriting inside— Grandmother's handwriting. I can't believe this book is still here. I run my thumbnail down the tabbed pages until I reach the Bs, then flip to see my own name, Ginger Bishop, above an address and phone number we haven't used in twenty years.

Overcome by the feeling that I've stepped back in time, I search for other familiar names and find a letter tucked between the pages. The yellowed envelope is unsealed, and it's addressed to *Ginger, Penny, or Rose.*

Curious, I pull out the enclosed page and unfold it. In June 1998, Grandmother Lillian wrote us a letter.

> *Dear Girls:*
>
> *I've left the house furnished in case y'all ever want to use it. You'll find clean towels in the hall closet and fresh linens too. I left a few canned goods in the pantry, but you'll want to swing by the grocery store for milk and produce.*
>
> *Do be sweethearts and clean the place for your sisters if they want to visit, okay? I don't think I'm going to be coming back here, but I want y'all to think of the place as yours.*
>
> *We had some good times in this cottage, didn't we?*
>
> > *Lots of love,*
> > *Grandma Lil*

I smile as understanding dawns. I've always wondered why Grandmother didn't sell the house after she settled in the retirement home—she could have used the money to pay for a better place, maybe one of those condolike assisted-living facilities. I'm not sure why she believed we'd want to revisit this place. The cottage is comfortable enough, but I associate it with hot summers away from my friends, my books, and my dad.

On the other hand . . . the house does hold memories I've pushed aside through the years.

I drop the letter onto the counter and approach the staircase, ignoring the long hallway that leads to a bathroom and Grandmother's bedroom. I climb the steps, breathing in stale air that smells of dust, mildew, and old memories. The scents fill my head with ancient whispers—"Shh! You'll wake Grandma!"—and the sound of girlish giggling. I turn at the top of the stairs and walk to the farthest bedroom, the one overlooking the front lawn. Two twin beds still hug the walls, their sun-bleached coverlets a pallid pink. This was my room when we stayed here . . . and the smudges on the wall beside the bed came from my younger hand.

The sound of an approaching vehicle jerks me out of my reverie. I hurry down the stairs and stride to the front door, then step onto the porch as a dark blue SUV parks next to my car. A moment later Rose steps out, her face wreathed in a smile. "Hey there," she calls, her voice brassy and bright. "I can't believe you beat me!"

I grin back at her. "Only because I didn't have to feed a dozen animals before leaving the house."

I step to the porch railing as she dives back into the car, but after a minute or two she appears again. This time, however, she focuses her attention on the ground, so my intuition sits up and takes notice. I don't know what Rose has brought with her, but whatever it is *can't* be a good idea. I hear Rose murmuring above a coughing sound, then a tattered-looking dog shuffles in front of the car and follows Rose toward the house. He walks—if *walks* is the right word—slowly, rocking from side to side as if his joints have been fused. I double-check my memory to be sure—I *know* this dog. The poor wheezing creature has to be older than Moses.

Alarm bells clang in my brain. "Rosemary Dodson, I can't believe you still have that animal."

Rose flaps a hand at me. "He's okay. Surely you remember Justus."

"Sure I do, but what's he doing *here*?" She shouldn't have brought the dog without first checking with me. Even housebroken dogs smell, carry fleas, and scratch doors and furniture. I don't care if this animal comes with a gold-plated halo, I don't want him in the house we'll be trying to clean.

"I don't think having him in the house is such a good idea—" I begin, but Rose cuts me off.

"I know you don't like dogs in the house, but Justus isn't doing very well." She opens the gate for the dog, then latches it firmly behind him. "I couldn't leave him at home, especially since Wort is going on a charity ride this weekend. His HOGs are raising money for abused women and children."

I have no idea what she's talking about, but before I can ask if HOGs have anything to do with bacon, she runs up the porch steps and wraps me in a hug. Rose smells warm and faintly doggy, but her cheeks are pink and her eyes bright. She looks so determined—and so different from the last time I saw her—that I can't complain about her canine sidekick.

"It's so good to see you," she says, pulling away. "This get-together was a great idea, you know."

I shrug. "It was practical. We need to empty the house while we still own it."

"This might even be fun. How long has it been since we were together? Just the three of us, I mean."

Though I search my memory, I can't remember the last time I did anything with only my sisters. Penny and I both visited Rose after she got out of the hospital a couple of years ago, but Wort hovered over her, and Penny and I had our husbands with us. That weekend felt more like a social necessity than a genuine visit.

"I can't remember. Seems like lately we've always had our husbands along."

Rose hops onto the swing and drops her quilted purse at her side. "That's really too bad."

I wait until I catch her rhythm before I drop onto the moving seat.

She grins. "Like hopping into double Dutch jump rope, isn't it?"

"Haven't done that since I was a kid." We rock in near silence, accompanied only by the rhythmic *clink-clank* of the dangling chains. Truth is, I don't know what to say to my baby sister. We haven't had a heart-to-heart in years, and we never had much in common. I like music, she likes animals; I've got a husband and two sons, Rose has had three husbands and cares for a menagerie.

Finally I find myself uttering the words women always say to one another: "You look good. Is that a new haircut?"

Rose blows a hank of hair out of her eyes. "It's drip-dry hair. Nothing special."

"Must be a new outfit, then."

"Sorry to disappoint. These shorts are older than my dog."

"Still"—I bite back my rising irritation—"you look nice."

She shakes her head. "Thanks, but I'll never be as put together as you are, Ginger, so I don't even try. But the house looks great. Better than I thought it would."

I sigh and abandon my attempt to give the girl a compliment. "I gave the Realtor permission to fix it up. It'd been empty so long, I knew it would need some cosmetic work. I figured we'd recover the cleanup costs in a higher sales price."

She tips her head back and studies the bead-board ceiling. "I appreciate you handling everything. But if you'd asked, I'd have been happy to help."

"It wasn't a problem."

We continue rocking, the swing groaning in accompaniment to the chains, until Rose murmurs something about the dog. She leaps from the swing and skips down the steps. I gape in surprise when she returns with her decrepit dog in her arms.

"Jussy can't manage the stairs these days." She sets the dog on the floor and slides her hands into her jeans pockets. "He's gotten old and stiff . . . but you probably noticed that."

I give the dog a brief, distracted glance and attempt to smile. "Remind me—what kind of dog is he?"

"A Jack Russell. A whole lot of dog in a little bitty body."

"Oh." I smile, pretending her description makes sense. "Besides the dog, how's everything else at your house?"

Rose dips her head in an abrupt nod. "I'm happy and Wort's fine. We have five quarter horses now, and leads on a couple of others that are set to be sold at auction. My assistant's pretty sure she can get the owners to surrender them to us."

"'Us'?"

"I run a foundation now. A racehorse rescue program. I have sponsors and everything."

"I'm impressed." My reply is automatic, but I really *am* impressed. I've never known Rose to take much interest in anything beyond her own property line. "Why would you take animals from auctions? Aren't auctions a good place for people to buy horses?"

She looks at me as though I've just declared my intention to commit first-degree murder. "Sometimes, but older horses bought at auction can end up being transported to Mexico, where it's not illegal to slaughter them for meat. Those animals have worked hard; they deserve a peaceful retirement."

I retreat from the topic of horse meat, not wanting to jab at one of my sister's hot buttons. "And how is Wort these days? Does he still . . . you know, look like something that blew in with the Hells Angels?"

She rolls her eyes. "He looks like he did the last time you saw him."

"Okay." The first time I met Wort Dodson, I thought Rose had managed to marry a balding grizzly bear. "And how long have you two been married now?"

"It'll be eleven years come June. We're not exactly newlyweds anymore."

I force a smile, not wanting to offend again. If Rose wants to hang out on the back of a Harley and kiss a man with a shrub on his chin, that's her business.

And while I'd never admit this to Rose, I'm privately relieved that they haven't managed to reproduce. I can't imagine Rose chasing a bunch of little Worts around on that palmetto- and snake-infested property she calls a ranch.

The arthritic terrier sniffs the floor until he bumps into my sneakers; then he sits and regards me with the cloudiest eyes I've ever seen in a living face.

"Jussy's blind, of course." Rose's voice dissolves into a broken whisper, and for an instant I'm afraid she's going to burst into tears. "I just couldn't leave him at home. He won't live much longer."

I eye the dog with wary curiosity. "How can you tell? Don't old dogs always look pitiful?"

"Age has nothing to do with it. He's just done, that's all." She reaches for the swing, but she doesn't hop aboard. This time, she stops the rocking motion and lowers herself onto the seat. While I wait, she glances at the dog again. "When he's ready to go, I'll know it."

She utters these last words in a hoarse rasp, as though they are too awful to speak in a normal voice. But Rose has always had a flair for melodrama, especially when it comes to her animals.

"Listen, about his *going*—are you sure he'll be okay in the house? I don't want the house to smell like an incontinent dog when we hand it over."

"I'll look after him. You don't have to worry about a thing."

"I'm holding you to that, Rose."

"Of course you are." Her smile flattens as she bends to scratch the dog's ears. "What about your family? How's Michael? And what are Ross and Ryan up to these days?"

Obviously, she wants to change the subject—okay by me. "Michael's fine, just fine. The boys are focused on school, mostly, but Ross has a girlfriend he's crazy about. We don't hear much from either of the boys unless they're broke, but they seem to be doing okay. Ross made the dean's list last semester."

"Has he decided on a major?"

"He's thinking about business—he'll probably stay in school and earn an MBA. I think his girlfriend is hoping they'll get married after he graduates, but we've promised to cover his master's degree if he continues his education. He's practical enough that I think he'll see the light."

A smile tugs at the corner of Rose's mouth. "He's a lot like you, huh?"

"What do you mean?"

"He's practical. Maybe a little bit driven and ambitious."

I fold my arms. "My son is logical, intelligent, and loaded with common sense. Aren't those good things?"

"If you say so."

I'm not sure what Rose is getting at, but I've a feeling her meaning is far from complimentary. I would have asked for further explanation, but I have to let the matter slide because the snap and pop of gravel tells me that another car is coming down the lane.

Penny.

"Hey"—I elbow Rose—"what color do you think her hair will be today?"

Rose presses her lips together. "It was red last time, right?"

"I thought it was strawberry blond."

"Then I vote for brunette."

"And which Penny will we see—heavy, normal, or stick thin?"

"She's been married for a while now . . . so I'm thinking normal-to-heavy. She's been relaxed enough to eat."

"Maybe you're right."

Rose and I lean forward, eager to learn the answers to our questions.

PENNYROYAL

"The easiest way to feel at home," Grandma often said, "is to stay there." So why did I ever leave St. Simons Island?

I cross the bridge and drive onto the island only two and a half hours after leaving Gainesville, but I have a feeling I'll be the last to arrive at Grandma's house. Ginger will be the first, of course, and Rosie, who can't bear to disappoint anyone, will be next. I don't think tardiness is a conventional middle-child trait, but I always seem to be two yards behind my sisters and completely out of step.

My throat tightens as I drive down the narrow street that leads to the shopping village. The cars on the road with me are filled with families—mothers and fathers up front, kids in the middle seat, dogs in the back. When I stop at the Mallery Street intersection, I glance to my right and see crowds of tourists clogging the sidewalks outside the brightly painted shops and restaurants. These people, too, are grouped in family units—a mother with her daughters, a father with his son, an elderly couple holding hands as they take in the sights.

The couple reminds me that I ought to call Bob to tell him I've arrived—otherwise he'll worry and undoubtedly pick an inconvenient time to call me. I reach into my purse and fumble for my phone, but I can't find it. Alarmed, I pull the purse onto the divider between the seats and toss out my wallet, my glasses case, my hairbrush, and my makeup bag. No phone. I can't call Bob to tell him anything, but neither can I call Miller to tell him when I'll be free to meet him on Jekyll Island. I can always use Rose's phone or Ginger's, but still . . .

I chew on my thumbnail and growl through a wave of irritation. I left the phone charging on the kitchen counter, and Bob didn't remind me to unplug it. He probably didn't even see it.

But neither did I.

A horn blares behind me, informing me that the light has changed, so I drive forward and search for the turnoff to Fish Fever Lane. Live oaks shade the road here, providing a lush canopy decorated with curling gray moss. These blocks, all near the village center, consist of narrow lanes lined with pastel gingerbread cottages that remind me of birthday party cupcakes. Tall trees rise to guard the charming homes, while picket fences keep traffic and camera-carrying voyeurs at a respectable distance. St. Simons may be a trendy tourist destination, but popularity has not killed the charm of this established community.

Traffic slows around a young tourist couple on a rented three-wheeled bike. I wait until the oncoming lane is clear, then I pull around the bicycle and make my left turn.

Fish Fever Lane is still unpaved and close enough to the sea that we should be able to close our eyes and hear the waves once the island traffic has stilled. I pull up to Grandma's cottage and put the car in park. After turning the key, I sit back and listen. A chorus of crickets rushes in to fill the silence, accompanied by birdcalls and the rustle of the wind in the trees. A rhythmic creaking draws my attention to the front porch, and when I spy two figures in the porch swing, unexpected tears blur my vision.

How many hours did my sisters and I spend in that swing? More than I could ever count. In our teen years, we sat and waited for boys we'd met at the ice cream store or down by the beach. We'd walk to the village, and when we finally made it back to the house, we'd find Ginger on the porch, her eyes narrow and her voice sharp.

But the keenest memory that surges forward to greet me is of that first summer, when I held a diaper-clad Rosie in my arms and rocked her for hours, watching and waiting for a mother who never came.

I swipe the tears away from my eyes and gather up the scattered items from my purse.

I will not cry this weekend. Grandma's been gone for nearly a year, and I said my good-byes ages ago. She was my mother's mother and I loved her, but half the people on St. Simons thought Grandma was crazy and the other half considered her scandalous.

I lift my head and squint as the figures on the porch stand. One of them steps out of the shadows and begins to descend the stairs. It's Ginger, looking determined and in control, as usual. Rose moves to the porch railing and leans on it, searching for me.

I breathe deeply and feel a jab of memory, a sharp shard from our shared past. Undeniable tragedy tainted our childhood, yet in this cottage we enjoyed carefree summer days and went to bed with sand between our toes. Despite the frequent application of Ginger's iron grip to my upper arm, I was happier in this island community than in any other place I've lived.

Overcome by the unexpected surge of nostalgia, I blink wetness from my eyes. Then I force my lips to part in a smile, grab my purse, and push my sunglasses to the top of my head.

I step out of the car and stride toward the house, arms open wide to greet my sisters.

GINGER

Penny, to my surprise, has stopped coloring her hair—at least I think she has. It's been so long since I've seen her natural color that I'm not sure what natural is.

Her hair is a soft brown now, with touches of gray at the temples and a widow's peak. She's wearing it a bit longer than usual, and she's in better shape than I expected. Not plump, but not anorexic either. So she's either been on a diet or she's finally figured out how to maintain a healthy weight.

The former is far more likely.

After exchanging greetings and hugs, depositing our luggage in bedrooms, putting the matter of central air to a vote (because Penny and Rose are fresh-air freaks, I lose), we Lawrence girls throw open all the windows and then settle at the kitchen table to discuss what we have come here to do.

I take my usual place at the head of the table. Penny and Rose sit across from each other and fall silent, waiting for me to kick off the discussion. Fortunately, I came prepared.

I lift my canvas tote bag from the floor and pour its contents onto the table: three pads of colored Post-it notes, felt-tipped markers, and several rolls of packing tape.

"Before we get started," I begin, "I know lots of families get into silly arguments over knickknacks, but Grandmother wouldn't want us to squabble. So I thought we'd take turns so each of us will have an equal opportunity to select items from the house. We'll divvy up the larger furniture first, then we'll move on to things that might have sentimental value. Whatever we don't want, we'll divide into two piles: one for the trash, one for the thrift store. I've already contacted a waste disposal company; they're bringing a Dumpster out this afternoon. The thrift store will send a truck on Monday."

Rose squints at me. "You got someone to come out on Labor Day?"

"I promised the trip would be worth their while. Apparently our donation—plus the promise of an additional financial contribution—was motivation enough."

Penny gestures to the kitchen cupboards behind me. "You expect us to have this house completely emptied by Monday? I remember how much stuff Grandma crammed into her cabinets and closets. She never wanted to throw anything away."

"If we put our minds to it, we can get the job done," I insist. "I figured we could empty everything today and tomorrow. Monday we can focus on cleaning." I slant a brow at Penny, noting her chic shorts and matching top. "I hope you brought clothes you won't mind getting dirty."

"Don't worry about me." She straightens her spine. "My wardrobe is the least of my concerns since I started working at Macy's. But if you expect us to be done by Monday, that doesn't give us enough time to figure out what's worth keeping. Some of that old porcelain could be valuable, but we'll need to look up manufacturers and dates—"

I cut her off with an uplifted hand. "We won't have time for research. If you want something, take it. If we stick to my schedule, we ought to be able to go out for dinner at Barbara Jean's before we drive home Monday night. It'd be nice to spend some time relaxing together, wouldn't it?"

I had hoped the promise of Southern home cooking would tempt them to linger, but a dubious look crosses Rosemary's face.

"I'm not sure I can stay that late. I wanted to drive home in daylight."

"Then we'll do lunch together," Penny says, clearly thinking about something else. "Let's cut to the chase." She leans forward and places both palms flat on the table. "Never mind the dishes and whatnots, let's talk about the money. The house sold, so how much did we clear and how much do we each get?"

I smile, eager to deliver the good news. "After paying sales costs, this year's property taxes, and the Realtors' commissions, the sale earned a profit of over six hundred thousand. That's two hundred thousand and change for each of us."

Penny and Rose stare at each other, their mouths agape.

"Two hundred thousand dollars," Rose whispers. "Wort won't know what to do with all that money."

I stare at her. "I think you can help him figure it out."

Penny inhales as if to say something, then clamps her mouth shut.

I lean back in my chair, grateful that neither of them has whined about the sale not bringing in more. "I know the lot is prime real estate, but the house is old and it's been vacant a long time. The kitchen needs updating, and the floors could use a good sanding—"

"Thank you, Grandma Lillian." A smile lights Penny's eyes. "I never dreamed this place could be worth real money."

"You haven't priced island real estate lately," I answer, distracted by movement at the edge of my field of vision. I look down in time to see Rosemary's sad-looking terrier wobble over to the tote bag I'd dropped on the floor. After taking a perfunctory sniff at the canvas, he opens his mouth and barfs up whatever he had for breakfast . . . all over my bag.

"Rosemary!" While Penny peers over the table and giggles, I glare at my animal-loving sister. "Are you aware of what that dog just did?"

The tip of Rose's nose goes pink as she pushes her chair back and hurries to clean up the mess. "Sorry." She rips a length of paper towel from the holder on the kitchen counter. "Something must have upset his stomach."

I shake my head. "I'll never understand why you had to bring that dog."

"I brought him because he needs me."

"You could have left him at home. Isn't Wort taking care of your other animals?"

She lifts her chin and meets my gaze straight on. "He's my dog, not Wort's. Besides, I don't think he likes Wort very much."

"That doesn't surprise me." I murmur my remark sotto voce, but Penny hears me . . . and snickers.

Rose walks out from behind the kitchen bar and looks at me with accusing eyes. "What'd you say?"

"Nothing important." I lift my hands in a *don't shoot* pose. "But when you're done fooling around with that animal, maybe we can talk about our plans for the weekend."

"We've already talked." Rose picks up my sullied tote bag with two fingers. "Clean up and throw out. What's so complicated about that?"

I watch, disbelieving, as she turns my bag and wipes a trail of brown slime from the canvas. "For heaven's sake, surely you don't expect me to use that tote again. Just throw it away."

Rose looks as though she might argue the point, then she crosses to the front door, opens it, and tosses my bag into the viburnum hedge on the other side of the porch railing.

She's *so* melodramatic. Sighing, I slide a pad of Post-it notes toward Penny. "Make a note—Rose needs to go outside and pick up trash in the yard, paying special attention to the hedges."

Penny looks from me to Rose, then she closes her eyes and shakes her head. "Can we get started? I'd really rather not spend the entire weekend refereeing bouts between you two."

"I'm not fighting with anyone this weekend." Rose drops into her chair, then picks up a felt-tip marker and grabs one of the Post-it pads. She flashes me a brilliant smile. "I'm happy. Go ahead, start the auction. I'll be fine with whatever y'all decide."

Her expression—determined, defiant, disturbed—kindles a vague memory, and for an instant I am twenty-one again and Rose is fourteen. We are at home in Valdosta and I am juggling the roles of student, employee, girlfriend, and sister, but I am *mother* to Rose and she doesn't like me very much. I don't like functioning as her guardian, but with a mostly absent father and nobody else to play the mother's part, what am I supposed to do?

Because the memory edges my teeth, I release the strings of time and let it float back into the past. Rose and I are mature women; so is Penny. Since our arrival, we've had a tendency to slip back into roles we've outgrown, but we are not the girls who lived here with Grandmother Lillian.

Those girls are nothing but sepia-toned ghosts.

FIVE

GINGER

Penny stands, a marker and pad of sticky notes in hand. "So how is this supposed to work? I see something I want, so I just stroll over and sticker it?"

"That's not quite what I had in mind." I push my chair back and step toward the living room area and the piano. "It'll be more fair if we take turns according to birth order. I thought I'd start things off . . . to demonstrate how the selection process will work."

When neither Penny nor Rose protests, I brace myself for resistance and cross the room in three steps. I slap a pink sticker on the top of the piano, and just in case my sisters forget who carried the pink pad, I scrawl my name across the Post-it.

"Wait a minute." Penny walks toward me, head shaking. "That piano is probably worth more than anything in the house. It's not fair for you to claim it right off the bat."

"If you want something else—"

"I could take *everything* else in the house and probably not find anything as valuable as that piece. I don't know much about pianos, but I know that thing's an antique, and it was valuable when Grandma bought it. So it's not fair for you to take it just because you were born first."

"This *thing*"—I enunciate each word with care—"is a Steinway square piano, five and a half octaves, with a mahogany case, six legs, and two music drawers. Completely restored, it might sell for five or six thousand dollars. But to restore it, you'll need to find someone willing to work on an antique piano, and then you'll need to pay him—a *lot*—for his time and trouble. When he's done, you'll have an instrument that can't measure up to a modern piano and won't match anything in your house." I give my sisters a steady smile. "I want it because this instrument means something to me—apparently I inherited Grandmother's musical talent, and without that I don't think I'd be a choir director. I know I wouldn't have majored in music or earned a graduate degree in music education. But if you really want the piano, you can have it."

Penny crosses her arms. "Since Grandma couldn't even play the dang thing, I don't see how you could have inherited her 'musical talent'—"

"She sang. Don't you remember? She'd invite that woman from church for lunch, and after we ate, she'd play while Grandmother sang."

"Miss Josie." Rose bends to pick up her dog. "The lady's name was Miss Josie. All she could play was hymns, but she ate everything on the table."

"Grandma bought that piano because she wanted to play for her boyfriends," Penny continues, her brows knitting together as she scowls at me. "She thought she'd be able to figure it out after a few weeks, but she couldn't. So don't give us that song and dance about Grandma's musical talent when we all know she didn't know middle C from a hole in the ground."

"She had a lovely voice. A lot of her talent was . . . latent." Pride prevents me from arguing further.

Penny's face twists into a puzzled look, and I know she's trying to figure out what *latent* means. She probably thinks it's a type of paint.

Rose strolls into the living room and drops onto the faded sofa, the dog tucked under her arm. "So? Who won?"

I drop my hand to the piano cabinet and look at Penny. "So . . . are you claiming it?"

THE FINE ART OF INSINCERITY 67

"No, thank you. I don't want it, but I still don't think your method's fair."

"Then . . . suppose I give up my next several turns so you and Rose can select anything you like. I'll sit out a few rounds, and then we can call it even."

Penny looks at Rose, who shrugs and rolls her eyes.

The tight line of Penny's mouth relaxes. "I guess that'd be okay."

"Fine." I cap my marker and drop my pad of sticky notes into my pocket. "So now it's your turn, Penn. Choose whatever you want."

PENNYROYAL

Ginger and Rose both turn to me, waiting to see what I'll choose from the house, but I don't give a hoot about antique furniture or dusty bric-a-brac. All I really want out of this place is money, but if I were to say that out loud, Ginger would call me crass. But she's never had to face the future with nothing between her and starvation but an anorexic bank account.

Because Ginger's waiting—and I'm in a hurry to get this finished so I can slip away and call Miller—I walk over to the corner cupboard, another sagging antique from heaven knows what era. I open the door and recoil as an odor rolls out of the confined space—scents of dust and heat and the faint aroma of tobacco. One of Grandma's boyfriends must have smoked a pipe.

I bend and examine the crusty hinges as if I actually know what I'm doing. How much would an antiques dealer give me for a smelly old corner cabinet?

If there's one thing I've learned in my forty-five years, it's how to appreciate a healthy bottom line. I've also learned that Florida isn't a community property state, so when Bob and I split, he won't automatically be entitled to half of whatever's in my checking account. My inheritance can remain solely my inheritance, and the less Bob knows about the sale of Grandma Lillian's house, the better.

With two hundred thousand dollars in a new account, I could

hire a divorce lawyer—a good one—and start over in a few weeks. I could buy a decent condo and keep it as a rental property when I'm ready to marry again. Unlike the uncertain months following some of my other divorces, I wouldn't feel pressured to find a husband to help pay the bills. I could even take time to travel if I wanted to do a little exploring.

Miller Conrad is terribly tempting, but he's not the only available doctor in Florida. I could date him for a while, let him introduce me to some other physicians, play the field for a few months. With the help of Grandma Lillian's estate, I could even make myself into more attractive bait—maybe even go blonde again. I don't have many wrinkles yet, but I wouldn't mind having a little work done for insurance.

Grandma always said that money can't buy true friends, but it can lease a few fine acquaintances.

I close the cupboard door and shift my gaze toward the kitchen. "Okay. I'd like to have the kitchen table and chairs. Do I really have to plant a sticker on it?"

Ginger releases a small moan of disappointment, but I'm playing by her rules.

"That huge table?" Rose frowns. "Will it even fit in your kitchen?"

"Doesn't matter," I tell her. "The table is solid, the wood looks great, and it's big enough to seat eight."

Rose's brows rush together. "When have y'all ever had eight people over to your house?"

"It's all right; Penny can have the table." Ginger folds her arms. "But if you get the table *and* the chairs, I want Grandmother's brass bed. The mattress is shot, but the headboard is lovely. With a little elbow grease and some polish, it could look spectacular."

"Not so fast." I point at our younger sister. "You forgot Rosie. It's her turn to choose something."

A deep flush rises from Ginger's neckline, leaving her complexion blotchy. "Sorry, Rose. Your turn."

Rose jerks her thumb toward the kitchen. "I'll take the Romper Room cookie jar. It'd be a cute container for dog biscuits."

I can't *believe* what I'm hearing. "You should be going for bigger pieces, Rosie. You can't settle for that stupid cookie jar, not yet."

She shrugs. "I don't need anything big."

"Ask for the armoire in the bedroom. An antiques dealer would love it."

"I'd rather not mess with hauling it back. Besides, I don't have any place to put a big piece of furniture."

I don't want my baby sister to be railroaded, but if she's not gonna stand up for herself—

"Rose wants the cookie jar," Ginger says, her words clipped. "Maybe she knows Romper Room cookie jars are valuable."

I hesitate, realizing that Ginger has a point. Rose makes ceramics in her spare time, and she used to exhibit her work at local art fairs. I know the cookie jar is old, but if it's also rare, Rose might be stealing a treasure right from under our noses. Grandma's cookie jar looks plain enough from here—white, with a painted clown on the side and a bee on the top. Heck, if that's a priceless treasure, I'll eat my kitten-heeled sandals.

"Okay, Rose takes the cookie jar." I settle back on the sofa and look at Ginger. "And you want the brass bed. But you were gonna skip a couple of turns, remember?"

Ginger's flush deepens. "You took the pine table and chairs. Together they're worth more than this old piano."

I'm tempted to argue, but every minute I spend debating with Ginger is a minute I can't spend with Miller. "Okay, then. Can't we speed this up by making a list of things we want?"

Ginger glares down her nose at me like an offended princess. "Are you in some kind of hurry?"

"Well"—I flap my hand at the door—"I thought I might slip away to do some sightseeing. No telling when I'll be able to get back up here after the house is sold."

"You grew up here. You've seen everything there is to see."

"I thought I might drive over and check out Jekyll Island."

Lines of concentration deepen under Ginger's eyes. "*Who* did you want to see on Jekyll Island?"

I paste on an expression of shocked innocence. "What are you talking about? I don't know anyone over there."

"Enough." Rose interrupts us with the referee's signal for time-out. "Ginger, can you fit that brass bed in a trailer?"

"You bet I can." Ginger scrawls her name on a pink Post-it note and marches back toward Grandma's room. A moment later we hear her call, "I'm taking the quilts on the bed, too, okay? I'll need them to pad the piano. We'll throw the mattress out."

I'm not happy with the way she's handling this, but I can't help smiling at the thought of Ginger polishing that humongous head-board. My older sister's nails are manicured, and I can't see even a trace of gray in her auburn hair. High-maintenance women don't usually relish elbow grease and the odor of brass cleaner. She might tackle the job once or twice, but I'm betting she'll either learn to live with tarnish or end up dragging that bed frame to the curb.

With Ginger out of the room, Rose looks at me with a question in her eyes. "You *do* know you can't fool her . . . right?"

"Why would I try to fool her?"

"Even I can tell you're meeting a man."

So . . . my baby sister's on to me. "What makes you think that?"

"You've got that sparkle in your eye."

I want to tell her that she's right, that there's a man and I may be falling in love again, but this isn't the time or the place. So I shrug. "I'm a grown woman. I can come and go as I please."

Rose snorts. "Right. And when did you start liking antiques?"

"I like the cash they could bring from an antiques dealer. I'll be needing cash soon because I'm leaving Bob."

Rose snaps her mouth shut, then slowly shakes her head. But what's her problem? She's been divorced twice herself, so she certainly ought to understand why I'm making plans.

Financial security is a single woman's best friend.

GINGER

My organized plan has disintegrated into a discordant free-for-all, but I'm not going to let my sisters' lack of cooperation upset me. I press a pink sticky note onto the oblong chest containing Grandmother's silver-plated flatware, then turn to consider digging through the pantry. I don't think she kept anything of value in the kitchen closet, but she used to keep nail polish in the fridge and flour in the freezer. The woman was anything but predictable.

I sigh and drop my phone back into my purse. I've been calling Michael all morning, but my calls have been going straight to voice mail. The thought of that two-thousand-dollar check is niggling at the back of my mind, distracting me from the work I've come here to do. I've imagined a dozen possible scenarios— Michael bought me jewelry, an early birthday present; Michael has developed a gambling problem; Michael wrote a check to Ross or Ryan because one of the boys had an accident and didn't want to tell me about it. Each possibility is more disturbing than the one before, but Michael could put me out of my misery if he would only return my calls.

I blink as Rose wanders by, her eyes abstracted and her yellow pad in her hand. In the past five minutes Penny has swept through the living room, tagging the fireplace andirons and the coffee table with blue Post-its, but I don't think Rose has claimed anything but that silly cookie jar. Either she's feeling melancholy and missing

Grandmom . . . or she got everything she wanted before our grand-mother died. After all, Rose visited her in the retirement home a lot more often than Penny and I ever could. Grandmother could have given her a boatload of jewelry and who knows what else.

When we stayed with her, Grandmother was always pulling one of us back to her bedroom, where she'd festoon us in costume jew-elry and paint our lips and cheeks. She treated us like living dolls, and though I quickly outgrew the ritual, Penny and Rose seemed to enjoy it. Since Grandmother became even more childlike when she lived in the retirement home, how do we know she didn't dress Rose up in jewels . . . and Rose didn't decide to keep them?

The idea sounds plausible, but I don't think Grandmother ever owned any jewelry of real value. Her frugal nature wouldn't allow her to enjoy such extravagance, so she preferred cut-glass beads and rhinestone earrings. I'm fairly certain that the only significant pieces she ever owned were her wedding rings, none of which have surfaced yet.

I lean against the kitchen counter and study my youngest sister from across the room. Rose has put on a few pounds since I saw her last, and I can make out a definite gray stripe at her hairline—she's overdue for an appointment with her colorist, if she even has one. She's wearing denim shorts and a T-shirt, neither of which is particularly flattering, and earlier today I noticed a scabbed cut on her hand and a half moon of dirt beneath her fingernails. What has she been doing, mending fences?

What happened to my little sister? Penny still takes pains with her appearance, but Rose looks like a woman who's lost the battle and surrendered the war.

Rose has never made her appearance a priority, though I sup-pose I can understand why. As long as she keeps her motorcycle chaps handy, her husband doesn't seem to mind how she dresses. Her animals certainly don't care, and since Rose spends more time with animals than people, why should she worry about letting her-self go?

I shift my gaze when Rose turns in my direction, but she only glances at the clock, then runs her fingers over the stacked volumes on Lillian's bookshelf.

When Rose wanders toward me, I open the refrigerator door as if expecting to find our lunch ready and waiting inside. But the fridge has been unplugged, and all it offers are clean shelves, a box of baking soda, and a faintly musty odor.

I stick a pink Post-it on the fridge and label it *Thrift Store*, mainly because I can't think of anything else to do with the old appliance. Since the new owner wants to redo the kitchen, maybe the thrift store can use this old machine. I'll have to point it out when the pickup crew arrives on Monday.

I turn to find Rose leaning against the counter, a slack look on her face. I gesture to a lower cupboard. "Do you need any Tupperware? That's where Grandmother kept it, right?"

A lopsided smile curls on Rose's mouth. "I don't need another piece of plastic in my kitchen. I have plenty."

"I don't need any, either."

"What about your boys? Don't college men survive on leftovers and takeout?"

I nod and smile in a silent touché. Rose turns to the sink, then fills a glass with water. As she drinks, I sink to the kitchen floor and open the cupboard, then peer over the top of the door. Lines have etched Rose's face, creases I don't remember noticing when I last saw her. The woman is seven years younger than I, so why does she look ten years older? I'd blame her wrinkles on the sun or smoking, but Rose is as pale as cream and steadfastly anticigarette.

So what's up with Rose? She and Wort might be having problems, but if that's the case, I don't think she'd still be with him. After all, she didn't hesitate to divorce Todd after only a year of marriage, and she kicked Jonah out after five. So if she's not fed up with Wort . . .

I bite my lip as a sudden thought occurs—could grief have done this to Rose? I know she went through a rough patch when she lost a baby a couple of years ago. She and Wort had been over the moon about the pregnancy, but, as often happens, something went wrong.

Michael and I drove to Jacksonville the weekend after we heard the news. I went armed with statistics about how many pregnancies end in miscarriage, but Rose never said a word about the baby and I didn't dare bring the subject up. That was one of the oddest weekends we've ever spent together—the four of us wore fake smiles and talked in generalities; we asked about her ceramics, Wort's bikes, and the horses, but I never found the courage to ask about the baby.

Why didn't she and Wort try again? If that wasn't possible, they could have adopted, though Wort would probably have to take off his leathers, hide his tattoos, and shave his beard to win a social worker's approval. But if she really wanted kids, Rose could convince him to do it.

But she hasn't. This leads me to conclude that she has chosen to remain childless, preferring to pour her life into that dilapidated ranch and taking motorcycle trips, crisscrossing Florida while they bake on their bikes. Harley people are crazy that way.

I shake my head and prepare to dive into Grandmother Lillian's stash of mismatched Tupperware. Sometimes I don't understand Penny or Rose. If my sisters and I didn't look so much alike, I'd swear I was adopted.

ROSEMARY

Why is it we never really *see* certain things until it's time to say good-bye? Looking out Grandma's kitchen window, I'm struck by the magnolia outside. The towering tree has to be at least thirty years old, but only now have I noticed that the shiny green leaves are bronze on the underside. The two-toned effect is stunning, yet I never realized it until today.

"Appreciation," I can hear Gran saying, "is like an insurance policy. You have to renew it now and again."

"I love that magnolia tree."

"Hmm?" Ginger doesn't look up.

"Never mind." I lower my glass and step away from the sink, uncomfortably aware that I seem to be distracting Ginger as she rummages through the Tupperware lids and containers. I wash my hands, which feel gritty with dust from the bookshelf. My brain seems only half-aware of what my hands are doing, so maybe my higher consciousness has already checked out. But I have to get a grip; I have to end this chapter well.

I never realized dying could be so complicated. Before leaving the house, I had to make sure my will and the life insurance policy were in easy reach. Now I have to think about the money I'll be inheriting from Gran.

When Ginger told us how much we'd each be inheriting, I could have sworn I heard a circuit breaker trip in my head. More than two hundred thousand dollars? I never dreamed I'd be worth so much. Or—minor correction—that Wort would.

I've never had access to so much cash in my life. Never touched a check that large. Wort is likely to faint when he hears the news. Even if he's grief-stricken, the first thing he'll probably do is go down to Watson's bar and buy a round of drinks. Maybe he'll even lift a glass in my memory.

I wonder . . . maybe I should leave him a few hints about money management and good investments. That's what smart people do, isn't it? They invest their cash and live off the interest. I have no idea how much interest two hundred thousand would bring in, maybe not so much. Maybe I should let Wort know that this inheritance is not gonna land him in the same league as Bill Gates.

I could tell him personally, of course. I could call with news about the inheritance, listen to his big plans, and remind him that the money could last a long time if he'll invest it wisely. Or maybe Ginger knows a financial planner, someone I could ask to call Wort after the checks are in the mail.

"Hey, Ginger."

She pulls her head out of the Tupperware cupboard. "Yeah?"

"Do you know any good financial planners? Someone trustworthy? I'm thinking Wort and I might like to invest the money, you know, for the long term."

An expression of pleased surprise breaks across her face. "That's a great idea, Rose."

She doesn't have to verbalize her unspoken thoughts; I can read them in her eyes. I'm the one who never went to college, the one who doesn't read newspapers, the one who could care less about politics or world affairs. But I'm not stupid, and I'm not as silly and thoughtless as she thinks I am.

"Sure, I know a couple of financial guys. Rick Duff attends our church; he's wonderful. Michael and I have known him for years."

"Have y'all invested with him?"

Ginger's smile turns rueful. "Honey, we haven't had a spare dollar since the boys started thinking about college. But after we get some debts paid, we might consider investments"—her mouth quirks—"if there's anything left to invest."

"I'd love it if you could get me that guy's number," I tell her. "I'd like to arrange a telephone appointment or something . . . later this month, I guess. How long do you think it'll take to get our checks from the sale?"

Ginger straightens and rubs her lower back, her eyes growing thoughtful. "Closing is scheduled for the fifteenth, so if that goes according to plan, we should have money available that day. But the Realtor will have to mail the checks to us . . . unless you want to drive all the way up here to pick it up."

"No," I answer, my voice flat. "Mailing it will be fine. I'll just set up the appointment for later in the month."

That will give Wort time to get through the funeral, settle my estate, and hand over the operations of Racehorse Rescue to my assistant, Marisa Coloney. Though Wort tolerates my volunteer work, the horses are primarily my passion. But Marisa is a kindred spirit, a selfless volunteer, and she will be more than capable of managing the payout from my life insurance policy and carrying on with my rescue work. Wort can sit on the board and hold Marisa accountable, but I know she loves those animals as much as I do.

I had begun to think I'd need to set part of the insurance payout aside for Wort, but Grandma's bequest will provide enough to keep him from resenting the money I've designated for the horses. With two hundred thousand dollars, he'll be able to pay for some decent advertising for his motorcycle shop. He might even erect a new garage, something closer to the highway, so bikers won't have to come roaring down the driveway at all hours of the day and night.

I find a tattered dishtowel in one of the drawers, so I pull it out and dry my wet hands. Penny stomps in from the porch, finds Ginger, and launches a heated discussion about the china from Gran's first wedding. Did she sell those dishes, or what?

"The red and white dishes are in the buffet," Ginger says.

"Those are the plates she used with Arthur Carey," Penny answers. "I'm looking for the antique dishes."

"I haven't seen them."

"Well, they have to be here somewhere!"

I slink out of the kitchen and drift back to the dining table, where I dropped my pad of Post-its. I could pick it up and stake my claim to a few little things, but what does a woman living out her final days care about knickknacks and furniture?

At this moment, all I care about is saying good-bye . . . and not leaving too big of a mess behind.

GINGER

By noon, every major piece of furniture in the house has been plas-tered with a Post-it. My system disintegrated so completely that the color of the sticky note is now meaningless, but every large item has been designated either for one of us, the dump, or the thrift shop. Once we settled the matter of the piano, the process went surprisingly well, evoking no major debates—except for Penny's insistence that Grandmother had valuable antique china stashed somewhere. "If it turns up," she warned, looking at me through slitted eyes, "that china is mine."

I expected my sisters to argue with each other at some point—Rose can be as stubborn as kudzu, and Penny has a tendency to hoard things—but Rose spent most of her time marking selections for the thrift store and Penny seemed more interested in resale values than in keeping items for herself. Since I worried that our morning would end with a declaration of war, I am nearly giddy with relief when my stomach reminds me that it's time for lunch.

"Hey." I step out of the downstairs laundry room and yell down the hallway. "What if we order a pizza before we get into the dirty work of hauling things out? We could have lunch delivered."

Penny looks up from the sofa, where she's been compiling a list of tax-deductible items for the thrift store. "I'd like that."

"Sure," Rosemary calls from the kitchen. "Anything's fine with me."

Penny pulls her purse to her side. "You want us to chip in?"

"I'll get it," I offer. "Thanks to Grandmother, I can afford it."

I use a cell phone application to locate the nearest pizza restaurant and am pleased to learn they'll deliver anywhere in the vicinity of the village. I dial the number, then cover the mouthpiece with my hand. "What kind of pizza do we want? Pepperoni?"

Rose's head swivels toward me. "I won't eat anything that had to die so I could eat it."

"Don't forget," Penny calls. "Tomatoes are living things too."

Rose makes a face while I groan and turn to Penny. "Don't tell me you've gone vegetarian."

"Shoot, no. I'll take whatever you want to put on it."

I sigh and resume my conversation with the restaurant. "One large pizza, please. Half veggie, half loaded with everything but anchovies." I give him the address and hang up.

"How long until lunch?" Rose asks.

"About an hour. While we're waiting, I think I'm going to check in with Michael."

"I'm goin' upstairs to unpack a few things." Penny sets her list aside and moves toward the stairs. "My clothes are gonna be as wrinkled as Grandma's neck if I don't get them out of that suitcase."

"Why should you care about a few wrinkles?" Rose asks, looking toward the stairs. "It's just us girls here. Ginger and I don't care what you look like."

"Because you never know"—Penny taps her nails over the banister as she climbs—"who you'll run into on the street."

I sink onto the sofa and dial Michael's cell phone again. While the phone rings, I glance at my watch to confirm that I'm calling during what should be his lunch break. I try not to bother Michael when he's away at conferences, but he has to eat no matter where he is.

Though I let the phone ring several times, my husband doesn't pick up.

"That's odd." I slip my phone back into my pocket. "I've been trying to reach Michael all morning, but he doesn't answer his cell."

"Isn't he at home?" Rose asks.

"He's in Atlanta." I turn toward the window and look out at the quiet street. "I think his entire department went to a conference. The university is struggling; everyone is in a tizzy over declining enrollment and budget cuts."

"So a bunch of professors packed up and went to Atlanta?" Rose lifts a brow. "I'm no expert, but that seems like a crazy way to save money. Atlanta's one of the most expensive cities in the South."

I frown as her point strikes home. "I'm not really sure what the conference is about, but I'm sure the money was budgeted a long time ago."

"I wouldn't worry about it. Or him."

"Oh, I'm not worried about Michael. But it's not like him not to answer his phone."

Rose's mouth pulls into a thin-lipped smile. "Maybe he set his phone to vibrate during a meeting and forgot to turn it back on."

"But then he'd *feel* it, right?"

"Not if he left it in his room, or put it in his jacket and then took the jacket off. Or maybe he left it in a briefcase or—"

"Never mind. I get the picture."

I stand and go into the kitchen, where Rose has been emptying cupboards for the past half hour. She's found an assortment of cleaning supplies under the sink and lined them up on the counter like soldiers readying for battle. "We're in pretty good shape here." She taps a crusty can of powdered cleanser. "Some of this stuff is pretty old, but it should still work."

I survey her collection. "Toilet bowl disinfectant, cleanser, soap scum dissolver, lime remover. Did you find any window cleaner?"

She bends to peer into the cabinet beneath the sink. "Um . . . no. Before we start cleaning in earnest, one of us should make a list and head to the grocery store."

"As long as we go before sunset. I worry about getting lost after dark."

"Would you look at this." From the back of the cabinet, Rose pulls out a small ceramic planter that once must have held a florist's arrangement. A woolly black lamb stands on two hind feet, his front hooves planted on the edge of an empty pink cup.

She places it on the palm of her hand, and her faint smile holds a touch of sadness. "What do you want to bet Grandma got this when Mom was born?"

"It certainly looks old enough." I take the vase and examine it. No ceramicist's mark on the bottom, but someone etched a date: 1940, the year our mother was born. The vase is probably worthless, but it *is* cute. And if it is connected to our mother, it's one of the few mementos of her we have.

I set the little vase on the counter as Penny's heels tap on the stairs. She comes around the corner and looks askance at the array of cleansers. "I can tell my hands are gonna be raw by the time this weekend is over. We could use some help."

"We don't need help," I assure her. "Three grown women can clean one little cottage with no problem."

"Still, I've half a mind to call in some reinforcements. And speaking of reinforcements, Ginger, how is my favorite brother-in-law these days?"

I ignore the implied insult to Rose's husband. "If you mean Michael, he's fine. I'll tell him you said hello. I just tried to call him, but he didn't answer."

She moves to the sink and gasps in pretend horror. "Didn't he psychically sense that you were about to call?"

"Don't tease," I tell her, not in the mood for foolishness. "We're not as connected as you seem to think we are."

"Could have fooled me. The perfect man, the perfect marriage . . ." Her voice trails away while she washes her hands, then she nods at the row of cleaning supplies. "You're not really serious about us scrubbing this place, are you? We could hire a maid service. We have money coming to us."

I blow out a breath. "Of *course* we have to clean. Once we get the furniture out of here, I'm afraid we're going to see all kinds of grime on the walls and the floor."

Rose tugs on a hank of her hair as she surveys the kitchen. "It might be easier to paint the walls than scrub them."

"No way," Penny says. "I'd rather clean than paint. Painting will ruin a perfectly good manicure."

"Either way," I point out, "you can wear rubber gloves. So stop griping and let's get to work."

Penny ignores my suggestion and dries her hands on a dishtowel. "Gingerbread, can I borrow your cell phone? I left mine at home."

Though I can't imagine how anyone could forget her cell phone when preparing for an out-of-town trip, Penny has never been detail oriented. I pull my phone from my pocket and hand it to her. "Just tell me if Michael calls while you're talking, okay?"

Penny snatches up my phone, then announces that she's taking it outside, where the signal is stronger. But she dials as she walks toward the door, and when whoever she called picks up, her "Hello, you" vibrates with warmth.

I wait until the front door closes, then I pick up an empty garbage bag and toss in half a dozen plastic lids without matching containers. "I'm glad Penny and Bob are getting along so well. She sounds like a newlywed."

Rose snorts. "You're being sarcastic, right?"

"Or ironic."

Rose pulls an old pair of plastic gloves from beneath the sink, then peers into them as if she expects to find a spider—or worse— inside. "So who do you think she's talking to?"

"I have no idea, but I'd bet he's on Jekyll Island." Curious, I leave the trash bag on the counter and tiptoe toward the open front window. Penny is bent over the porch railing, leaning on one elbow while she holds the phone to her ear. I can't see her face from this angle, but I can hear her voice rippling as she banters with someone on the line.

I turn to Rose, then point toward the porch. "Can you tell me who that is?"

She lifts one shoulder in a shrug. "I don't know."

"You don't know . . . or you don't want to tell me?"

Irritation flashes in her eyes. "Could be anyone. Except Bob."

"How do you know that?"

Rose presses a finger across her lips and tiptoes toward the couch. Together we sink into its sagging cushions and turn toward the window, studying the arc of Penny's spine like two spies.

I listen as Penny laughs, then I whisper an innocent question: "How long have Penny and Bob been married?"

Rose tightens her lips into a straight line. "Four years."

"Not so long, then."

"Long enough for Penny to get bored."

"Is she? Bored?"

Rose shrugs. "You should ask her."

And there it is, the wall that comes up whenever I quiz Penny or Rose about something the other one is doing. Those two are closer to each other than either of them is to me, probably because they've always thought of me as chief nag and rule enforcer. I had hoped we'd grow closer through the years, but time, distance, and The Wall have kept us at arm's length.

I sink a little deeper into the sofa. "She doesn't really talk to me."

"Maybe I'm easier to reach than you are . . . or less intimidating."

I blink, hearing a note of accusation in her tone, but this isn't the time to get into an argument about reality versus perception. At the moment, I'm far more interested in the potential drama playing out on the front porch. Bob Jensen, Penny's fifth husband, is a nice guy, but I've always thought he seemed a little geeky and not her usual taste. I was stunned to learn that he's younger than Penny, but maybe she was attracted to his youth. Penny's maintained her figure and good looks, but she's on the verge of discovering that the

season of unlined skin and a waspish waistline eventually draws to
a close.

When Penny laughs and drops into the porch swing, Rose and
I pull back from the window and face the fireplace, guilt flaming in
our cheeks. After a long moment, Rose and I turn again, trusting
the thin lace curtain to conceal us.

"I don't know who she's talking to," Rose whispers, "but I'd bet
my last dollar it's not a woman. Penny's never that animated when
she's talking to a girlfriend."

"Or to a husband." I prop my arms on the top of the sofa cushion. "I don't think she displayed that much enthusiasm over Bob
even when they were first dating. Of course, I wasn't around her
much in those days."

"I remember when she was a teenager"—Rose's voice brims
with nostalgia—"and I saw symptoms of this same delirium. Whoever she's talking to, I'd bet the ranch that he's male and she's interested."

I strain to hear Penny's murmured half of the conversation, but
she's softened her voice and her accent is heavier than usual. I shake
my head. "What *is* she doing?"

"Following in Grandma's footsteps." Rose heaves a heavy sigh.
"Already looking for a greener pasture."

Penny giggles and glances toward the window, so Rose and I
jerk away and sit properly on the sofa. I feel as guilty as Cain, but
I'm not sure why. Penny learned to flirt in kindergarten, so why
should her behavior surprise me?

Rose startles when her cell phone rings. Her hand darts to her
pocket and she pulls out her phone, then leans over to show me the
caller ID. "Bob Jensen." She smiles without humor. "Now, why do
you suppose Penny's husband would be calling me?"

Mystified, I lean against a stiff sofa pillow as Rose greets our
newest brother-in-law. She listens, then gives me a knowing look.
"Yeah, Penny arrived a couple of hours ago, and she's fine. I think

I know why you've been getting her voice mail—it's because she forgot her phone. She's outside now, but I'll tell her you called."

She listens again and smiles. "Nice to talk to you, too. Bye-bye." She snaps her phone shut and looks at me, speculation in her eyes.

I voice the question uppermost in my mind. "You really think Penny's done with Bob?"

"I do—and I think Bob senses that something's up."

I know better than to argue with Rose's conclusions. She may not have a college degree, but she has nearly infallible instincts about people. When I glance over my shoulder, Penny is sitting sideways on the swing, one leg curled beneath her as she croons into the phone. The woman could teach Scarlett O'Hara a thing or two about charm.

I prop my chin in my hand. "Will y'all go to her next wedding?"

Rose gives me a wry smile. "Wort and I quit after number four. She wanted me to be her matron of honor at the fifth, but I couldn't do it."

"Three was enough for me. And I had to attend the last two alone because Michael refused to go. He said he's had hiccups that lasted longer than some of Penny's marriages."

Rose barks a laugh, an abrupt sound that causes Penny to cast a sharp look at the window. Rose and I slink down in the sofa, then Rose jabs my ribs with her elbow. "Well, talking about Penny isn't gonna change anything . . . or get Gran's kitchen cleaned out." She stands, then extends her hand to help me out of the sagging cushions. "Do you want to empty the cupboards or the drawers?"

Relieved that at least one of my sisters shares my work ethic, I take her hand. "I'll take the drawers. I'm less likely to find dead cockroaches there."

She pulls me upright. "Last one to the kitchen has to sort out Grandma's underwear."

SIX

ROSEMARY

"A small house," Grandma used to say, "will hold as much happiness as a big one." This is a small house, but I'm amazed at how much stuff Gran managed to shove into it.

After pulling stacks of dishes, dusty candles, and rows of empty Mason jars from several kitchen cupboards, I press my hands to my lower back and stretch, trying to remember how the cottage looked when Grandma Lillian lived here. Though someone has walked through and done a light decluttering, no one has changed the furniture or emptied the closets and cupboards. They are still crammed with the stuff of Gran's life . . . which makes me wonder what people will think when they go through *my* personal belongings. They won't find Mason jars in my kitchen, but they will find bone-shaped treats, Bag Balm, bottles of glucosamine, and flea shampoo.

Despite the familiar furnishings, the cottage in my memory is much cozier. When we stayed here, women's magazines and mail-order catalogs stretched like ivy over every surface in the living room, including the floor. A sea-colored Lava lamp burned in the window until Penny knocked it off the ledge, and a "check your lipstick" mirror hung by the front door. Gran would sooner go naked than without lipstick, and in no time at all we learned to follow her example.

She may have been flirtatious, but Gran also had a knack for filling a room with light and laughter. Sunlight filled the summer days of my childhood, and when we sat on the porch swing and the cool night air threatened to send us indoors, Grandma's embrace drove away the chill. She'd rock and sing, her voice harmonizing with a chorus of crickets and the steady rhythm of the clanking swing. She cared for every living thing that crossed her path, even the stray cats that wandered up from the village. Her favorite pet, though, was a blue parakeet, a bird she called Ricky. His cage stood over in the corner, between the two dining room windows. She used to purse her lips at the bars of his cage, saying, "Gimmie sugar!"

The bird would come over and peck her lips, repeating, "Gimme sugar, gimme sugar!"

I snap my fingers. "I thought of something I want," I announce to anyone who's listening. "Grandma's bird blanket. It has to be tucked away somewhere."

Ginger steps out of the hall closet, her face a map of confusion. "Her *what*?"

I know my request is silly and I don't have any real plans for the blanket. I didn't even remember it until a minute ago. But the old thing is a tangible link between Gran and me—it represents our love for animals, a trait she shared with me alone. I'm not exactly sure *why* I want it, but I know I won't be satisfied unless I leave with that tattered blanket in my car.

"Don't you remember?" Since Ginger's drawing a blank, I look at Penny, who's coming out of the hall bathroom. "Grandma made a blanket to cover the birdcage every night. It was edged in green, I think, and made of quilt squares. Every other square had the bird's name embroidered on it."

Penny's bewildered expression softens to one of fond reminiscence. "Her bird—you mean Petey."

"Ricky." I nod with certainty. "That was one of the first words I learned to read because his name was all over that blanket. His name was Ricky, he was blue, and she had him for years."

Ginger's mouth twitches with amusement, and Penny's smile ripens into a chuckle.

"Did I say something funny?"

Ginger throws her head back and explodes in laughter. I stare at both my sisters, perplexed, until Penny wipes tears of mirth from her eyes and Ginger gains control of herself. "I hate to break it to you, kiddo, but Grandmother didn't have that bird for as long as you think. Her parakeets—well, she loved animals and she wasn't cruel, but she was terribly forgetful. She lost three or four because she'd leave them out in a draft or forget to feed them—"

"But she had Ricky—"

"She gave them all the same name." Penny gives me a rueful smile. "Reusing the name was a lot easier than making a new quilt for every bird. Maybe we should have called them Ricky One, Two, and Three, but they were different parakeets. We never told you when they died because we knew you'd get upset and cry."

Ginger fans herself and sinks onto the loveseat. "We were always terrified that you'd notice. But you never did."

I lower myself to the couch, my shoulders slumping. Penny sits by my side and drapes her arm around me. "Sorry to burst your bubble, Rosie. Honestly, I thought you'd figure it out eventually."

I release a choked, desperate laugh. "I should have. But as a kid, I thought for sure that bird would live forever."

"Some birds do live a long time," Ginger says. "But those dime store parakeets weren't very hardy."

Penny releases me and pats her knees. "If we find that quilt, it's yours. Want me to help you look for it?"

"Later." Ginger stands and moves toward the door. "Right now it's time for lunch. I spy an adolescent boy bearing pizza."

While Ginger picks up her purse and steps outside, Penny goes into the kitchen and grabs three plates. My gaze falls on Justus, who is panting on his pillow and blinking, probably wondering what all the commotion is about.

Grandma's bird blanket may be long gone, or it may be threadbare and stuck in a closet. But if it's here, I want to fold it into a seat-sized square, and I want Jussy to rest on it when we head out for our final drive.

I'm not sure Gran would approve of my intentions, but I know she would understand how I love that dog.

GINGER

Why do these women push my buttons? When I am home, I know who I am—wife, mother, choir director. Neighbor and friend. But here, with Penny and Rose in Grandma's house, I find myself slipping back into a role I thought I had shed long ago.

As my sisters gather around the pizza box on the table, I pull diet sodas from my cooler and toss one to each of them. They don't seem surprised that I remembered to pack snacks, ice, and sodas, but I've been the responsible one for so long they were probably expecting me to take care of details such as food and drink. But my responsibility to care for them involves more than inviting them to Grandma's house, overseeing the property division, and ordering their lunch. I care about them as people, too, and I especially care about their families. Neither Penny nor Rose seems very happy in her current marriage, and neither of them has a praiseworthy matrimonial record.

If our parents were still living, over the past twenty-seven years they would have found themselves dealing with three adult daughters and nine sons-in-law, and I'm responsible for only one of those sons-by-marriage. Apparently I'm the only Lawrence sister who believes in marrying for life. Or maybe I'm the only one who didn't inherit our grandmother's tendency to marry one husband after another, a quality I've begun to think of as the "grandma gene." It's my duty to guide my sisters, to encourage them to love more deeply and be more patient with their husbands.

But as I slide into my chair at the end of the table, I can't help remembering Michael's distant expression as he left the house this morning. Maybe I ought to talk about the work involved in a relationship to remind myself that with patient effort, the storm will pass from above *my* head. From my own marriage.

I nibble on a slice of pizza as Rose and Penny make small talk about someone they knew in school. Because I left Valdosta long before they did, sometimes I feel as though we grew up in different generations.

When they exhaust the subject of where Penny's first boyfriend is currently living, I clear my throat. "So tell me more about your families," I say, taking pains to keep my voice light. I look at Penny, who is busy picking the olives off her pizza. "How's Bob doing these days?"

"Mr. Mensa is fine." She bites the pointed end of a pizza slice, swallows, and finally meets my gaze. "Still dependable, still into computers, still a bit of a geek." She takes another bite. "Can you believe he reads a book a week?"

"By the way"—Rose hands Penny a paper napkin—"Bob called a while ago."

Penny stops chewing. "What'd he want?"

"I think he was just checking to be sure you made it up here. He didn't leave a message."

"Figures." Penny snorts. "He's always checking up on me."

I peer at her. "You two doing okay? And how's your son?"

"Reese is fine. He moved out of his dad's place a few months ago and now he's got his own apartment. He's working for a computer company in Indiana."

My sisterly intuition picks up on something in her voice, but Penny is no longer looking at me. She's shifted her gaze to Rose, and the two of them are smiling at a secret joke. I don't understand—wasn't Rose also wondering about Penny and Bob a few minutes ago?

"What?" I look from one sister to the other. "What's so funny?"

"You." Penny waves at me with her free hand. "You're still trying to mother us. At our age."

I lift my chin. "I am *not* trying to be your mother. I'm simply making conversation."

"Is that what you call it?" Rose snorts. "Every time we get together, you try to stick an emotional thermometer under our tongues. You may not have noticed, but we're grown up now." The spark of mischief in her eyes vanishes as her gaze moves into mine. "No matter what happens, you're not responsible for us anymore."

"I don't feel that way," I protest, but my words are a halfhearted lie. Rose is right, but how can I help it? I've looked after these two for so long that I don't know any other way to relate to them. If only they knew how desperately I wish I didn't have to feel accountable for them.

"Have it your way." I fold one arm across my chest. "From now on I'll pretend not to care about either of you. I'm sorry I ever cared at all."

Penny groans. "Oh, can the melodrama, will you? I don't blame you for being bossy—and when I was growing up it was kinda nice to know somebody would notice if I went missing. You were okay as long as you weren't on my case about something."

"I don't remember being really hard on y'all about anything."

Penny fizzes with laughter. "Your memory must be slipping, Gingerbread. You'd have chained me to the bedpost if you'd known I was climbing out the window. Sometimes I think you'd still like to lock me in my room and throw away the key."

"I wouldn't—"

"Yes, you would." The friendly tone evaporates from Penny's voice, replaced by the chilliness of steel. "Don't you think I know you're dying to tell me what you think of me? Every time I have to end a marriage, the first thought that flashes through my mind is *Ginger's gonna hate me for this.* I know I shouldn't care what you think, but I do. You're like an old habit I can't outgrow."

Despite my best efforts to remain stoic, Penny's words make me flinch. My sister has just made me feel about as welcome as Attila the Hun, but she has to be speaking from a place of pain I know nothing about.

Because she's never been willing to talk to me as a friend.

I fold my hands and try to answer Penny's criticism with reason. "I'm sorry you feel that way, but since you left home, when have I criticized you? Through five marriages and four divorces, I've never said a thing."

"You don't have to." Penny bares her teeth in an expression that is not a smile. "I can feel your disapproval across the miles. I know you think I'm a skank—"

"I never said—"

"You don't have to say it; I know what you're thinking. And for your information, I don't sleep around. I marry the men I love, and I can't help it if the marriages don't work out. Grandma's marriages weren't terribly successful, yet she wasn't an awful person. You loved her, didn't you?"

"Grandmother Lillian"—I hesitate, dismayed to hear a quaver in my voice—"was like a child in many ways. She didn't have much of an education. And after our grandfather died she had to feed, clothe, and shelter two little kids. Marrying again was her only option."

"Well, I'm not exactly from the Ivy League," Penny answers, drawling, "and I don't make much above minimum wage. So if Grandma can be excused because she wasn't wealthy, why can't I?"

I blink at her, completely at a loss for words. Ten minutes ago I wanted to talk to my sisters about their families. I had hoped to share a little wisdom, perhaps give Penny and Rose some insight into what makes a marriage work and suggest how they can keep a husband for more than a decade. Clearly, they're not willing to listen.

I shift my gaze from Penny to Rose, hoping to spot some evidence of understanding in my youngest sister's expression, but Rose is wearing her face like a mask. When she senses my eyes on her, she lowers her gaze and her chin wobbles . . . signs that convince me Penny has spoken for her as well.

"I'm not judging either of you." I turn the catch in my voice into a cough and press on. "I care about you, that's all, and I want you both to be as happy as Michael and I have been—"

"Maybe you don't think you're judging us," Rose says, cutting me off, her voice low and intense. "Maybe you don't intend to, but sometimes I feel your disapproval too. Maybe that's why we're not close. When we do talk, if I even hint that things aren't going well at home, you get that disappointed tone in your voice—like I've done something to let you down. Not everyone is lucky enough to marry Mr. Wonderful and have a perfect marriage and family, you know."

A thick silence falls among us. I want to tell my sisters that luck has nothing to do with it, that marriage is equal parts faith, friendship, perseverance, and hard work, and that even my marriage hits the occasional rough spot, but if I voice that thought they'll say I'm preaching at them.

I offer my sisters a peacemaker's smile. "Why don't we simply consider the subject closed?"

My appetite gone, I push my chair back from the table, then pause. "We came here to clean out Grandmother's house, so let's get back to work. I'll tackle the upstairs bedrooms. Rose, why don't you box up the pots and pans while Penny empties the pantry and rips out the old shelf liners. If you want anything you didn't sticker earlier, set it aside. If you find something that's worthless or ruined, toss it into a garbage bag and later we'll haul the bags to the Dumpster." I grip the arms of my chair, aware that I'm giving orders again. "We can do it this way," I add, shrugging, "or not. It's up to y'all."

"Aye, aye, Captain." Penny grins at Rose as she touches her temple in a mock salute. "One plan is as good as another."

PENNYROYAL

I luck out when the queen mother assigns me to the pantry. Because I don't think any of the staples in the narrow kitchen closet are less than ten years old, I fill a couple of heavy-duty trash bags with cereal boxes, dusty cake mixes, and soup cans, then drag them to the edge of the front porch. The Dumpster Ginger promised hasn't shown up yet, but we'll have plenty of garbage to feed it when it arrives.

I linger on the porch, where a cool sea breeze is sweeping away the sticky heat of the afternoon. Above the canopy of the oaks, the sky is a beautiful blue, a perfect day for walking on the beach . . . or playing hooky.

I glance back at the living room window, afraid I'll see Ginger's disapproving scowl; then I skip down the stairs and go out to my car. Ginger can be a slave driver and isn't likely to take a break for anything short of a national emergency. But the younger sisters' union has just declared that all workers deserve a fifteen-minute break every hour.

And I'm starving. The single slice of pizza didn't fill me up, and I desperately want a snack, something not covered by tomato sauce.

I open my car's trunk and pull a crisp green apple from a grocery bag. As I perch on the bumper and savor the first bite, I wonder if Miller has left for Jekyll Island. He said he planned to arrive at the golf resort by late afternoon, so if I could get away for dinner . . .

Against my will, my thoughts turn toward home. Right now Bob is probably sitting at his computer, playing one of his games or helping another Mensa member solve a problem that has stumped mathematicians for centuries. Bob may be boring, but he *is* sweet, and if he weren't so set on having children, I probably could live with him for years. But he wants a baby. I don't, and if I explain why I can't have kids, he'll leave me.

So I should leave first. Ginger may believe I'm apathetic about marriage, but I really don't like divorce. Sometimes, however, a woman can get backed into a corner from which there's no other way to escape.

I take another bite of my apple and close my eyes, enjoying the afternoon quiet. Whispers of traffic drift around the houses between us and the main boulevard, and from far away the whine of a siren stretches toward me. The pastel beach houses around me are quiet, as if they are listening for the sound of change on the air.

"Change comes to everything," I announce to the empty road. The oak leaves flutter in applause, and an engine growls in the distance. The rumble grows louder by the minute, and soon I realize that a truck has turned off the main road and is coming closer. I stand and consider calling for Ginger, but then a big blue truck turns the corner, its huge wheels crunching the pebbles that carpet Fish Fever Lane.

Our Dumpster has arrived.

I fold one arm across my chest and lean against my car, grateful that I now have a legitimate reason to loiter outside. Ginger can't accuse me of goofing off if I'm talking to the driver.

The truck rumbles to a halt in front of Grandma's house, then the driver hops out of the cab. "Afternoon," he says, doffing his hat in a charming display of chivalry. "Is this Seven Hundred Fish Fever Lane?"

I hit him with the sort of smile that makes old men wish they were younger. "Sure is."

The driver returns my smile in full measure. "Then I have a delivery for you. Where would you like this container?"

I really don't care where he puts the Dumpster, but if I get this wrong, Ginger will never let me hear the end of it. She'll want it someplace close, but not so close that it blocks the sidewalk or our cars—

Speak of the devil. The screen door slams as Ginger comes flying out of the house, her cheeks pink. "Oh! Thank goodness, we're about to drown in trash."

The driver smiles again, but his expression holds only a smidgen of the warmth I glimpsed a minute ago. "Yes, ma'am. Where would y'all like this thing?"

"How about over here, at the end of the drive? Thanks so much for bringing it out on a Saturday."

"No problem, ma'am."

The man hops back up in his truck, but he winks at me as he puts the vehicle in gear and backs the giant garbage bin into position. Too bad I'm not staying longer on St. Simons; Dumpster Dan seems like a nice guy. He looks a little like Bob. I doubt he's Mensa material, but appearances can be deceiving.

Dumpster Dan lowers the trash container on the back of his vehicle, releases it, and puts the truck in drive. Before he pulls away, though, he taps the horn, catches my eye, and waves goodbye. I grin and wave back, happy to know I haven't lost my appeal.

As the truck rumbles down the lane, Ginger leans on the porch railing, her lips puckering into an annoyed expression. "What are you doing out here?"

I toss my half-eaten apple beneath an oak tree so the squirrels can finish it. "I came out to get something from my car."

She turns to go back inside, but I can tell she's unhappy with me. "There's still an awful lot of work to be done in the house," she calls over her shoulder.

"I'll be there in a jiff."

She charges back inside and I sit for another couple of minutes out of sheer spite. I'm a grown woman, but Ginger still orders me around like I'm twelve. I'm tired of her bossiness, I'm tired of cleaning, and I'm tired of my husband—

The front door opens again. I stand, about to assure Ginger that I'm on my way, but Rose plows through the doorway, dragging two bulging trash bags. She struggles to maneuver them onto the porch, then kicks them, one by one, down the steps.

"Hey, let me help you." I hurry to her side, but before I can help her hoist the bulky bags into the Dumpster, I have to lift the plastic door that covers the opening.

The sharp stink of decay, urine, and sweat rolls out and assaults us.

Holding one of the bags, Rose crinkles her nose and tries to bury her face in the bend of her elbow. "Son of a gun, that stinks."

"What did you expect?" I help her tip the bag over the rim of the boxy container, then I run up the steps and drag down the bags I hauled out earlier. One of the overloaded bags rips at the last minute, so Rose scrambles to chase cans of mushroom soup and pork 'n' beans while I heave the trash into the container.

When we have gathered all the garbage and cleared the bags off the porch, Rose's eyes flick to the front door. I follow up by jerking my thumb toward the house. "What's the reverend mother doing in there?"

"She's in the front upstairs bedroom," Rose says. "Throwing away board games, I think."

"You ready for a break?"

"Do you think we can get away with it?"

"Last time I checked, she hadn't mastered the art of being in two places at once. Besides, we need fresh air to clear the Dumpster stink out of our nostrils."

Rose laughs, but her laughter has a sharp edge. I lead the way to the swing and sit, waiting for her to join me. Once she's aboard, we push off in unison.

For a while we rock in silence, hearing only the creak and clank of the swing, accompanied by a mockingbird practicing his scales.

I could have enjoyed the quiet a long time, but apparently Rosie has something on her mind. "About what happened at lunch . . ." she begins.

I probably should feel guilty about jumping on Ginger like I did, but at the moment I'm feeling too good to feel bad. I release a deep sigh and tug on the ends of my hair. "Yeah?"

"Sometimes I think Ginger hates me. Do you ever get that feeling?"

I want to assure Rose that she's wrong, but shock causes the words to wedge in my throat. Truthfully, while I've never felt that Ginger hated me, there have been times when I picked up on an odd vibe when Ginger talked about Rosemary. But I can't tell Rose about *that*; I don't want to make her feel worse than she already does.

"You think Gingerbread hates you?" I widen my eyes in pretend surprise and force a laugh. "Sweetie, she has no reason to hate you, but she's got plenty of reasons to be mad at me. I've annoyed the fire out of her more times than I can count."

The pink line of Rose's mouth clamps tight for a moment, then her throat tightens as she swallows. "Maybe I've been imagining things."

"Of course you have. Ginger's bossy, but she's our *sister*. And you know what Charlie Brown says about big sisters."

"What does he say?"

"'Big sisters are the crabgrass in the lawn of life.'"

Rose's mouth twists in an expression that's almost a smile, then we rock some more. "Will you tell me"—Rose crosses her arms—"why you want to leave Bob?"

I brace myself, preparing to get defensive, but I see nothing but honest curiosity in her open face.

So I grip the chain of the swing and look out over the porch railing. "I thought he'd be The One," I tell her, my voice low and steady. "When we met on the Internet and he wrote me such sweet letters, I thought he'd be the love of my life and our romance would never die. I thought we'd spend our lives together, just the two of us."

"So . . . what happened?"

"The romance shriveled up and blew away. He stopped being attentive, he stopped saying sweet things, he stopped . . . well, I'm pretty sure he's stopped loving me. And I need a man who'll love me like there's no tomorrow."

"Oh." Rose stares straight ahead, her gaze becoming vacant as her thoughts wander away. I leave her to her silence and think about the man waiting for me at home. Sweet Bob . . . dependable, dull Bob. If he can't cope with the real me, maybe Miller Conrad can. People may mislead one another on the Internet, but hands never lie. Miller Conrad's broad hands have seen at least forty-five years, maybe even fifty, and mature men are beginning to appeal to me. Miller seems stable, nurturing, and kind. I can't quite figure out why, but in some way he reminds me of Daddy.

"Well"—I lower my foot to stop the swing—"if we're gonna get this job done, we'd better get back to work."

Rose gives me a mute nod but makes no effort to move. I leave her alone and go back into the house, heading toward the kitchen and the unfinished cupboards.

As I rip old shelf paper from the cabinets, I consider my own predicament—earlier today, on the phone, I told Miller Conrad that I'd try to slip over to Jekyll Island tonight. But at the rate our cleanout is proceeding, I'm not likely to get away without a major confrontation, and I'm not sure I want to rouse Ginger's ire this early in the weekend.

Away from Ginger, though, I will be in charge of my own life. And when I get home, I'm telling Bob our marriage is finished. I'll tell him the truth about my age, and I'll explain why I can't have any more children. He'll probably be upset and he may storm out of the house, but eventually he'll see that someone else would be better suited for him. Then when he's ready to talk about settling our affairs, I'll have his lawyer call mine.

Our marriage was good while it lasted. But Grandma Lillian met seven grooms at the altar before she found her Prince Charming, so I'm not yet giving up hope.

SEVEN

GINGER

By the time I've cleaned out the front bedroom closet, I've become reacquainted with the board games of my youth—Candy Land, Chutes and Ladders, Sorry!, and Life. All of the boxes have cracked corners and some of the pieces are missing, but the sight of those games is enough to carry me back to hot summer days on the porch, when Rose, Penny, and I lay belly-down on the painted planks and rolled dice.

I drop the games into a box intended for the thrift store, then walk over to the open windows, where a warm breeze is ruffling the faded curtains. From here I can hear the creak of the front porch swing, so at least one of my sisters is taking an extended break. I sigh, wishing we shared the same work ethic. How can three girls spring from the same parents and be so different in temperament?

While I hungered for higher education, neither of my sisters graduated from college. Penny enrolled in community college right after high school graduation, but she dropped out to marry Ted Thacker. Rose nearly completed a program that would have qualified her to be a veterinary technician, but a man also interfered with her plans.

What *is* it with my sisters and men? Rose isn't nearly as flirtatious as Penny, but neither of them has had any trouble finding husbands—especially Penny, who seems intent on establishing a world record for signatures on marriage licenses. She cleans up nicely, but since we all share the same facial structure I can't credit her attractiveness to looks alone. She speaks with a heavy Southern accent—and hers is more pronounced than anyone else's in the family—but surely men aren't stupid enough to be charmed by honeyed tones and a knack for shoehorning an extra vowel into every one-syllable word.

I remember the flirtation I observed between Penny and the man who delivered the Dumpster—Penny has no designs on him, she doesn't even know him, but he winked and waved at her before he left . . . and he called me "ma'am." Twice.

I'm not that much older than Penny. Any stranger observing the three of us in a lineup would be hard-pressed to guess who was the eldest. So why are men drawn to Penny like flies to honey?

I lean my elbows on the windowsill and search the sky for answers. Maybe Penny attracts men because of the way she treats them. I see other men as workmen, deliverymen, other women's husbands, coworkers. Penny, on the other hand, looks at them like Grandmother did—like no matter what kind of uniform they're wearing, beneath it they're all knights in shining armor and she's an innocent damsel in distress.

Penny attracts men through vulnerability.

The realization rises from a place miles beyond political correctness and feminism. I straighten and pull away from the window, relieved to discover an answer and astonished to find it so distasteful.

I don't suppose I can blame her for her antediluvian approach. After all, Penny doesn't read, she hasn't allowed herself to be exposed to much culture or current political thought, and she'd consider philosophy a foreign tongue. Ditto for Rose.

So if playing the part of a helpless female is what allows my sisters to remain happy and married, maybe I shouldn't criticize their choices. But that would never be my choice. I'm too strong to play that role; I've been "the responsible one" my entire life. It never will be my choice if, heaven forbid, something should happen to Michael and I find myself dating in the coming years.

I go downstairs and wash the dust from my hands and forearms. Because dinnertime has drawn near, Rose suggests McDonald's. I can think of a dozen things I'd rather eat than fast food, but we're a long way from being finished with the cleanout. We're also dirty, disheveled, and sticky with perspiration—in short, none of us is presentable enough to step into a restaurant, and I'd rather not stop working to clean up. And so, as usual, I volunteer to pick up dinner.

Because there is no McDonald's in the picturesque village area of St. Simons, I have to drive several miles before I finally spot a pair of golden arches. I pull into the drive-through and wait my turn, my thoughts wandering until my cell phone rings. Ross is calling, which means he must need something important enough to discuss. If he simply needed gas money, he'd text an SOS.

"Hey, son." I rub my temple, anticipating the start of a headache. "What's up?"

"I need a financial aid form signed today," he says without preamble. "Can I e-mail it to you? You could fax it back."

"Sorry, I can't help you now—I'm nowhere near a fax machine. You'll need to send it to your father."

"I tried calling Dad, but he doesn't answer his phone."

"He's at a conference, but he'll be your best bet. His hotel should have a fax machine." I squint at my reflection in the rearview mirror and try to remember if Michael told me the name of his hotel.

Ross snorts in my ear. "So why isn't Dad answering his cell? If we ever ignored one of *his* calls, he'd give us all kinds of grief—"

"He's not ignoring you. I've tried calling him too. He probably left his phone in his room because he's sitting in a lecture. Try his office. The department secretary should know which hotel he's in. You could have someone from the hotel pull him out of the meeting."

"It's Saturday, Mom. No one's in the office on Saturday."

Of course not. I'm so out of my routine I can't remember what day it is.

"Why do you need this form signed on a Saturday? What happens if it isn't?"

"It was due yesterday," Ross says. "The dean is giving me a break, but if I don't have the form waiting in his fax tray on Monday morning, I lose my scholarship. Without that, y'all have to pay my tuition fees."

I tighten my grip on the steering wheel. Michael and I have struggled to pay for Ross's room, board, and car expenses; his academic scholarship was the one saving grace in our son's list of educational costs. I ought to scold Ross for waiting until the last minute, for not thinking about how costly this mistake would be for us, but this is not the time or the place for a lecture.

"Let me see if I can find Dad for you," I tell my son, careful to keep my voice steady. "I'll call you once I've found him."

The blue Volvo ahead of me eases forward after Ross hangs up, so I lift my foot off the brake and scroll down the list of names in my phone's address book. Marlo Hemmings is the history department secretary, and she knows everything going on within the hallowed walls of Savannah State University. She'll know where Michael and the others are staying. She may even be in Atlanta herself.

Fortunately, I have her cell number. I stop short of the Volvo's bumper and dial. The phone rings twice, then I hear Marlo's voice: "Hello?"

"Marlo? Are you in Atlanta?"

She releases a low, throaty laugh. "All right, who *is* this?"

"Sorry, it's Ginger Bishop."

"Mrs. Bishop?" Confusion fills her voice. "Why would I be in Atlanta?"

I blink. "Um . . . never mind. Listen, I've been trying to reach Michael all day, but he's not answering his phone. Do you know how I could reach him? Maybe the name of his hotel?"

"Um . . . I might be able to help."

Why did she hesitate? I frown at the resulting silence and wonder if I've done something to offend this woman, but she's probably looking for the hotel's contact information. After all, this is the weekend, and she isn't likely to have the conference schedule at hand. Or she might not like being disturbed on weekends. . . .

"I'm pretty sure you can find Michael at this number," she finally says, then she rattles off a string of digits. I grab a pen from the dashboard and jot the numbers on the palm of my hand. "Thanks," I tell her. In an effort to end on a light note, I add, "So you didn't go to the conference?"

"I don't know anything about a conference," she says, her voice tight. "But the professors usually don't tell me much about what they do on the weekends."

"But—but there's a conference," I stammer. "In Atlanta. Something to do with grant writing—"

"Don't know anything about it. But try that number. You might reach your husband there."

I disconnect the call, then glance up as the line of cars surges forward again. I've finally reached the menu, so I lean out the window and call out our order: two quarter-pounders, two large fries, and a large garden salad.

"Pay at the next window," the girl says, so I drive until I'm nearly kissing the Volvo's bumper.

Maybe this conference has something to do with the two-thousand-dollar check Michael wrote. Maybe it's an independent event only he and a select few were invited to attend. The university should pay for any approved educational expenses, but perhaps Michael learned of this conference only recently and he didn't have time to file a requisition or get the expense approved.

My spirit lightens. If all goes well, the university will reimburse us and I won't have to mention the matter to Michael. I'm not likely to get the overdraft fees reimbursed, though, and he should have told me about the check before sending it off.

I dial the number I've jotted on my palm and wait. The phone rings once, then a woman answers. Because I'm expecting to hear someone announce the name of a hotel, I'm caught off guard when all she says is "Hello?"

"Um . . . I'm looking for a guest, Dr. Michael Bishop."

I have no idea whose phone I've dialed—my brain imagines a matronly professor on the line, a scholar annoyed because I've interrupted her lecture on the importance of grant writing in a technological era. But she'll look around and pass the phone to Michael, who has once again played absentminded professor and placed himself out of reach. . . .

My imagination may be off base, but I nailed the annoyance, because the woman's response is curt: "I knew you'd find us."

I frown as the matronly professor morphs into a woman twenty years younger and infinitely more confusing. "Excuse me? I'm looking for my husband, Michael Bishop. Is he—"

"He's right here." I hear muffled sounds, a murmur of conversation, and finally Michael's voice. "Ginger? Is something wrong?"

I have found him . . . so why do I feel like I've tumbled down some kind of rabbit hole? I blink as my mind tries to sort confusing conversations into a logical form. Marlo knew I could find Michael at this number—which was answered by a surprisingly youthful-sounding woman. What did she mean about *me* finding *them*?

Who's *them*? And what is going on with my husband?

"Michael?" My greeting emerges as a strangled whimper.

"Are you okay? Are the boys all right?"

I shake my head. "Michael, whose number did I call?"

"Um . . . Theresa's. Professor Guzman's."

In that instant of guilty hesitation, I hear the unspoken truth. My husband has no reason to be so attached to another woman that Marlo knew I could find him with her on a Saturday afternoon. The history secretary has been privy to things I have not seen; she's heard comments and observed flirtations; she may have witnessed the small, affectionate touches a man and a woman give each other when they're testing the waters. . . .

My mind flies through the facts and settles into one inescapable conclusion: Marlo gave me this number so I'd *know* what my husband is doing in his off-hours.

The pieces fall into place with an almost audible *click,* and suddenly I can't bear to hear another word. I fling the phone away; it cracks the passenger window and drops into the seat like a dead thing. The Volvo pulls away from the drive-through and I stomp on the gas pedal, roaring past the delivery window and into the parking lot. I drive around the boxy Volvo, pull to the edge of the highway, and slam on the brakes, dimly aware that I will be risking innocent lives if I venture into traffic now.

Trembling against the steering wheel, I see one truth clearly: my husband of twenty-seven years has been lying to me. He's been sneaking around with another woman, blithely betraying me. He is having an affair . . . and apparently paying for it with our family's hard-earned money.

He has showered me with red roses . . . and every petal was a lie.

ROSEMARY

I remember sitting in this kitchen as a kid and asking Grandma about death. I was thinking about my mother, but Gran said only, "Depending on how a woman lives, she can die old at thirty or young at eighty."

As a child I wasn't quite sure what she meant, but now I can see that she thought Momma died old at twenty-nine. I can attest to the fact that Lillian died young at ninety-five. She would be shocked if she knew I was preparing to die at forty-two. But once a family becomes acquainted with the unimaginable, things unthinkable become possibilities, and possibilities become options.

I came here to look for Gran's secrets of survival, but so far I've found nothing but dust and the detritus of a life well lived.

As the minute hand sweeps across the face of Grandma Lillian's kitchen clock, Penny stops moaning about scrubbing the oven long enough to ask what could be keeping Ginger.

"She doesn't live around here, remember?" I turn on the kitchen faucet to rinse out the sponge I used to clean the microwave. "She may have had to look for the McDonald's."

"I'm liable to be skin and bones by the time she gets back. I'm starving, and these fumes are making me queasy."

I shake my head and wash the sponge, then toss it into the dish drainer. I'm not at all worried about Ginger. She can take care of herself, and she'd call if she had car trouble. But since Penny is likely to complain until Ginger pulls up with food, I decide it's time to take another break. "Justus needs to go outside," I tell Penny. "I'll be back in a few."

Because my old dog could never manage the stairs, I scoop him up and step onto the porch. I jog down the steps and set him on the lawn, where he wags his tail and begins to sniff, searching for the perfect toilet spot.

Knowing he'll be safe inside the picket fence, I slink away and head for the gate. Before I know it, I'm striding down Fish Fever Lane, my escape accompanied by the rattle of oak leaves and the crickets' steady churring.

I fold my arms and look up to the majestic tree canopy. After Monday, I will miss these greens and blues . . . if the dead miss anything at all. If they don't, surely oblivion holds charms of its own. Not to feel, yearn, or suffer loss . . . after enduring the ache of empty arms, insensibility has a definite appeal.

Still, if the dead can yearn for things they knew before, I will miss nature. I'll miss birdsong, and the way soaring live oaks draw my gaze to the limitless arc of sky. I'll miss my animals: the light in my dog's eyes and the caress of a horse's velvet muzzle against my palm.

I won't miss seeing my animals grow blind and feeble. I won't miss stroking their heads while the vet runs an IV into a shaved leg so my beloved pet can painlessly be put to sleep.

I won't miss mourning my infertility month after month and seeing the blood that appears from my most private place as evidence of a wound that has never healed.

Grandma always said that death is not a period, but a comma in the story of life, but Grandma had more faith than I do. She also said that the nearer the time comes for our departure from life, the greater our regret for wasting so much of it—but I have no regrets. I've lived long enough to realize that I'll never accomplish what I want to do; I'll never right the wrongs I've committed. And I have no one to blame but myself.

I keep walking, my footsteps crunching the graveled drive, but I slow my pace when I spot an orange tabby cat peering from beneath a salmon-pink house. I stop and bend, then lower my open hand to the animal's level. "Here, kitty, kitty."

The cat hesitates only an instant, then jogs toward me, darting beneath my hand as if she's afraid I'll withdraw it. "That's a surprise," I tell her. "The last cat I called wanted nothing to do with me."

When I squat to examine the tabby, she begins to purr, performing a feline figure eight beneath my outstretched palm. Her spine feels bony against my skin, and her green eyes glint in gratitude . . . or is that feline superiority?

"Do you live around here, ginger cat?" I scratch between her ears. "You look like you've missed a meal or two."

I look up when another cat calls, then another. Four cats appear from the dark space beneath the house, then all of them rush toward me. I find myself squatting in a small sea of felines, all of them apparently desperate for human affection. Since most of them are marked with variations of orange stripes, I wonder if they are the ginger cat's kittens.

"Whoa." I laugh as a tomcat presses against me with such force that I nearly topple over. "Easy there, big fella. You're stronger than you think."

They swim around me, some of them seeking the steady touch of my hands, others rubbing against my jeans. Like most cats, they seek contact on their terms, so by some miracle I must be providing what they need at this moment.

Imagine me, meeting a need. I clench my jaw to strangle the sob rising in my throat. Wort has needs, and so do I. We needed a child; we needed to give our love to a baby. But our baby died before it ever took a breath.

And no one wanted to talk about the unfairness of it all.

If it's possible to long for someone after death, I'll miss Wort. And maybe Penny. And though I have always missed my mother, I imagine I'll miss her in eternity too.

I cup my hand around a cat's chin and watch as he closes his eyes in feline bliss. Such small things can bring such happiness. Like a touch. Or believing in God.

Grandma Lillian believed. I think she was fulfilling her social duty when she dragged us to church as girls, but when she knew her years were numbered, she clung to Jesus like a drowning woman.

What did my mother think of God? What did she say to him when she passed from this earth into the afterlife, whatever it looks like? Might be helpful to know, since I will soon be following in her footsteps.

Does heaven exist? Do guards stand at the gate to prevent suicides from entering? Or maybe it's not how we die that matters, but how we live.

I don't really understand what heaven's all about, but I hope God will forgive what I've done because I've been hurt so much. If he is love, surely he will understand.

But will he forgive?

Without warning, the ginger cat tenses and her purr stops rattling; then she darts off, dashing toward the safety of her lair beneath the pink house. The other cats flee with her, none of them stopping for so much as a parting stroke.

I glance around, but I can't see anything that might have spooked them. Yet cats are flighty creatures, and I accept that. I can't blame them for being exactly what they are.

I stand and wipe tears from my cheeks, hoping that God will accept me as easily.

GINGER

I'm not sure how much time passes—maybe twenty minutes, maybe an hour. Numb and shivering, I bring my arms up to shield my head and tell myself that the events of the past few minutes are impossible; I did not just dial a strange woman's number and find my husband at the other end of the line. A husband who is supposed to be in Atlanta for a conference. A husband who may not be in Atlanta at all, and for whom the word *conference* has surely taken on a new and more intimate meaning.

My husband—my lover, my soul mate, and my closest friend—is spending the weekend with another woman.

"Truth," Grandmother liked to say, "is like a sandspur in a dog's tail. The harder she tries to shake it off, the closer it sticks."

I've just stumbled across a painful truth . . . and as much as I want to deny it, I can't.

I lower my arms as the realization slowly sinks in, accompanied by remembered fragments of the conversation. The triumph in the woman's voice—*I knew you'd find us.* The shock in Michael's words, followed by the guilty hesitation. If the situation had been innocent, if Michael and this woman had been sitting next to each other at an educational seminar in Atlanta, I would have heard surprise from her and mild concern from him. But if the situation had been innocent, Marlo wouldn't have given me the other woman's cell number. And Michael wouldn't have spent the day ignoring my calls.

Theresa . . . Theresa Guzman. The name conjures up an image of a Latina beauty, lustrous lashes, long brown hair, rounded hips. I don't believe I've ever met Professor Guzman, but I can see her sitting in the passenger's seat, smiling at me with victory in her brown eyes.

Somehow my senses recover so that I am able to pick up my cell phone, ascertain that it still works, and redial the number smeared on my palm. Michael answers this time—of course, caller ID forewarned them. Though I hope he will greet me with a hurried explanation and protestations of innocence, my husband's tone is resigned.

His quiet acceptance ratchets up my fear.

"I'm glad you called back," he says, his voice distant. "We have to talk."

Somehow I choke out a question: "Are you in Atlanta?"

Another hesitation—has he forgotten where he said he'd be?

"Good grief, Ginger, what does it matter?"

"It matters." I clench my fist, unable to explain why I need to know the extent of his lies. "Don't I have a right to know where my husband is?"

"I'm in Savannah, at Theresa's place. If you can meet me—"

"You forget, I'm on St. Simons, where I said I'd be. I can't meet you, not today, not tomorrow. But our son needs something from you, so call Ross right away, will you?"

"You want me to talk to Ross *today*?"

"You're his father and he needs you. It's important."

"Yes, but we need to sit down and—"

"Not now, we don't. I'll talk to you later . . . after I've had some time to think."

I disconnect the call and turn off my phone, then rest my elbow against the driver's door as I gulp unsteady breaths and focus on the blazing western horizon. The sun is steadily disappearing, its rose-colored rays setting the sky afire in a stunning farewell performance. I watch, bite my lip, and try not to scream.

As the sky beyond my windshield burns, a dull anger begins

to bubble and boil beneath my rib cage, sending heat through my veins. I'll never look at a sunset in the same way again. Is this a blazing farewell to what I considered a happy marriage? How long has Michael been dissatisfied with me? How long has he been seeing this other woman? Did they fall helplessly in love, or has he been chasing other women for years? What does he see in her—or in *them*—that he couldn't see in me?

I catch my breath when other questions arise in my head: What sort of woman has my husband been with? If she's the type who sleeps around, will I have to be tested for STDs? How can I face my doctor and ask for that kind of test? A shiver of revulsion contracts my flaming skin. What if Michael has given me HIV?

The questions keep coming, each more intrusive and painful than the last, and at this point I have no answers. I need advice, someone who can tell me what to do. I have no one to turn to . . . except Penny and Rose. My two sisters, neither of whom has been able to sustain a happy marriage.

Then again, neither have I.

I tilt my head, watching a mother and her two scampering little girls as they make their way back to their car. Without knowing them, I would say they are part of a happy, middle-class family, with a husband and a dog waiting at home.

An hour ago, anyone watching me would have said I was a successful middle-class wife, with nearly grown children and a devoted husband. But now . . . everything's changed. I'm not the happy wife I thought I was. I'm not the contented mother. I've become a betrayed woman, a woman who's been cast aside . . . like my grandmother. Like my sisters.

The abrupt revelation reminds me of the reason I'm at McDonald's—Penny and Rose sent me out for dinner. Feeling as though I've been badly beaten, I get out of the car, stumble into the restaurant, and place another order at the counter. I suppose I could ask for the food I bought and never claimed, but I'm too embarrassed to explain why I drove away.

As I wait for my burgers and salad, the girl working the drive-through window strolls over and looks at me, her eyes searching my face. "Blue Honda CRV, right? I wondered what happened to you. Do you want me to replace that order?"

"Forget the other order. I had to deal with a family emergency." I accept a bag from another girl and check the contents, then nod my thanks and shuffle back to my car.

Family emergency? Family catastrophe would be more accurate.

EIGHT

GINGER

"God, you've got to help me. Please help me. Please."

I scarcely know what I'm saying, but I find myself babbling as if I've developed a sudden case of Tourette's. I shiver behind the wheel, wondering how the drivers around me can be so blasé when my world has exploded. The skies ought to be weeping, traffic should be creeping along like a funeral procession . . .

I pull up to a stoplight and brake as the light turns red. In some dim recess of my mind, among neurons not occupied with pondering the demise of my family, my primary choir begins to sing:

> *When we don't know what to pray—the Spirit prays for us,*
> *come what may.*
> *If you groan—He'll pray! If you moan—any day!*
> *He knows you better than you know yourself.*

I didn't cry when talking to Michael, but the sweet memory of those childish voices draws tears that spurt down my cheeks. A few months ago I wasn't sure the song was appropriate for fourth and fifth graders, but the catchy tune quickly became one of their favorites.

Now, apparently, the song is going to haunt me.

With that melody playing in my head, my hands and feet manage to guide the car back to Grandmother's cottage. I park my vehicle, pick up the bag of fast food, and open the car door. My feet move toward the house while my brain marvels that I can still place one foot in front of the other. I can almost believe that a benign force has entered my body, allowing me to carry on while my heart huddles in a heap, shivering beneath a fatal blow.

Rose rises from the porch swing, her arthritic dog in her arms, and meets me at the top of the stairs. Because I don't want her to see my watery eyes, I lower my head and trudge to the front door.

"We were beginning to worry," she says. "Penny thought you might be lost."

"Not lost. I had to . . . stop and make a couple of phone calls."

"No big deal." She opens the screen door and holds it for me. "It's not like either of us is starving. Except Penny, of course."

I lead the way into the house. We're greeted by Penny, who has covered the kitchen table with gadgets of all sorts: flatware, utensils, pens, papers, and other gewgaws from Grandmother's drawers.

"I was about to call the police," Penny says, then her smile pulls into a puzzled expression. She looks intently at Rose. "Did something happen out there?"

Why is she looking at Rose? I turn to stare at our younger sister and am amazed to see tracks of tears on *her* cheeks. For an instant I'm convinced she's become aware of my emotional crisis through some sort of sisterly empathy.

"Rosie." Penny steps toward her. "Are you okay?"

"I'm fine." Rose swipes at her cheeks and summons up a wavering smile. "I went for a walk and got a little nostalgic, that's all. This place . . . has always meant a lot to me. It's like I can almost hear Grandma's voice as we're working."

I'm hearing Grandmother's voice, too, but I no longer have the energy for nostalgia. I toss the McDonald's bag onto the crowded table. Silly of me to think Rose is intuitive enough to pick up on my tortured state. Neither she nor Penny has ever tried to understand or even know me outside my role as the oldest sister. They think of Michael as "Mr. Perfect," and of Michael and me as a slightly dull, completely married couple.

I still think of myself that way. So how am I supposed to adjust to this new reality?

If I were home, I'd lock myself in the house and wear my pajamas for seventy-two hours, eating and crying until I had cleaned out the refrigerator and used up several boxes of tissues. I wouldn't tell anyone about Michael's affair until I learned how to tell the story without breaks in my voice.

But here I don't have that luxury. I can't even go to pieces in private, because this cottage is small and the walls are thin. I'd rather not say anything to my sisters, but I have to share this burden with someone. Who better than Rose and Penny? They've been through similar situations, and neither of them lives in Savannah. They're not likely to share my secrets with my neighbors.

Once Penny and Rose have claimed their food, I brace myself on the back of a dining room chair.

"By the way"—my voice tightens—"I learned something while I was out. Something truly . . . terrible."

Rosemary looks at me, her brow arched. "Did you have a fender bender or something?"

I lower myself into the chair and cover my face as fresh tears fill my eyes. Behind my protecting fingers, I wrestle with the idea of keeping silent. I don't want to talk about this, not now, not ever. I don't want to cry in front of my sisters.

Yet I feel positively saturated with disaster; I have to release these feelings or I'll burst. Maybe putting Michael's betrayal into words will force me to face the truths I've been struggling to accept for the past hour.

"It's worse than a fender bender; just look at her." Penny slides into the chair across from me. "Talk to us, Gingerbread. What happened?"

Slowly, I lower my hands. Not knowing where to rest my gaze, I focus on a rusty potato peeler. "Ross called while I was getting dinner. He needed a signature on some kind of form, so I told him he'd need to talk to Michael. When I tried to track him down, Marlo—she's a friend—gave me a number to call."

Rose squints as she sits next to me. "Is Michael all right?"

"He wasn't in Atlanta where he said he'd be. He's in Savannah . . . with another woman."

"You mean"—Penny leans toward me—"*with* another woman? Like an affair?"

A whooshing noise fills my head, and I feel as if all the air is being sucked out of the room. I cling to the edge of the table, Rose's hand comes up to cover her mouth, and Penny's right eye narrows in a sudden spasm.

Penny is the first to recover. "Wait a minute. Surely the situation isn't as bad as you thought. I'll bet Michael has an explanation."

"I didn't want to think anything at first. Then I realized why Marlo gave me the number. It's Saturday. So she wasn't acting as Michael's secretary, she acted as my friend. She wanted me to know that he's been unfaithful."

"That's impossible. Michael's not a louse."

"I spoke to Michael, and he didn't deny it. He didn't explain it away, either."

Penny shakes her head. "I would never have imagined this. Not of Mr. Perfect."

"I still don't believe it." Rose reaches for my hands and holds them in a tight grip. "There has to be a logical explanation. Maybe Michael couldn't talk without ticking the woman off. Maybe she's crazy and she's been stalking him. Wait a while, then call him back. Listen to his side of the story."

"I don't want to talk to him."

"But he's your husband." Penny pats my arm. "You have to talk to him; y'all ought to talk. No matter what happened, you're married, and married people are partners."

I stare at my sister in disbelief. Penny has married five husbands and is apparently scouting for number six. None of her marriages has lasted more than a few years, so what does she know about healthy relationships?

"Excuse me"—a frosty note chills my voice—"but what gives you the right to talk like some kind of marriage expert?"

Penny throws up her hands and surrenders the field, but Rose draws closer and slips an arm around my shoulder, whispering the only words I want to hear: "I'm so sorry."

I'm sorry too. Sorry I ever put this weekend together, and sorry I ever thought I could trust Michael long enough to let him out of my sight. For twenty-seven years I have believed that loyalty and stability were part of Michael's personality, that he'd be the last husband on earth to cheat in marriage. He doesn't like conflict, he avoids messy confrontations, and he is downright dense when it comes to picking up emotional cues.

So how in the world did another woman manage to attract him?

I bury my face in my hands again. I had thought this weekend would be a good thing, and I'd hoped the money from the sale of this house would take the strain off our marriage. I'd thought I could solve our problems by making life easier for him.

But at this particular moment, I'm sorry I ever met my husband.

PENNYROYAL

After the shock of Ginger's announcement, I realize I'm not gonna be able to meet Miller Conrad tonight. Even if poor Ginger decides to go to bed and cry herself to sleep, Rosie would never forgive me if I went on a date during a time of family crisis.

I still can't believe Ginger is actually crying. I'm not surprised she cries, since every woman does, yet I can't remember *ever* seeing her cry in front of us.

But Ginger has lowered her head to the table and is quietly sobbing while Rosie rubs her back. Since both of them are occupied, I walk over to Ginger's purse and pull her cell phone from its pocket. I tap in Miller's phone number, then send a text message: *Can't meet you tonight. So sorry. Family trouble.*

I close the phone and drop it back into Ginger's purse, realizing that Miller is probably on Jekyll Island by now. I'm sure he can amuse himself on the golf course, but if that resort is swarming with single women, Miller isn't likely to be dining alone for long. Which means I *have* to find a way to see him tomorrow.

But tonight, I have to help my big sister. From the stricken look on Ginger's face, I can tell she's in shock. But she needs to think clearly—and for the first time in her life my older sister needs to listen to me and Rose. We've been through this before. We've shed those bitter tears ourselves.

"Okay." I return to the table, where Ginger's staring into empty air like a woman suffering from posttraumatic stress syndrome. "So you put some incriminating facts together and came up with the conclusion that Michael is cheating—and may have been cheating for a while. But that doesn't mean your life is over. It doesn't mean your sons' lives will be ruined. Hold your head up and listen to me; Rose and I are gonna help you get through this."

"He brought me roses," Ginger murmurs, studying a spatula as if she's never seen one before. "Two dozen red roses, just the other day."

Rosie murmurs another consolation and pats Ginger's shoulder, but sympathy is the last thing Ginger needs right now. She needs practical advice, and the sooner she gets it, the better off she'll be.

"Ginger." I bend to meet her vacant gaze. "You need a good lawyer. Do you know one?"

She blinks and drops the spatula. "I know a couple of attorneys from my church. One of them did our wills a few years ago."

"You don't need an estate attorney, you need a divorce lawyer. One who knows Georgia law. Do you know anyone who fits that description?"

She shakes her head, so I grab her purse and again pull out her phone. "I'm gonna call the woman who handled my last divorce. She's bound to know someone in Georgia."

Ginger's eyes fill with fresh tears. "Isn't it a little soon to talk about divorce? I know it's ironic, but I was hoping—I thought my inheritance from this house would help our marriage. We've been under a lot of financial pressure."

"You think Michael cheated because y'all are short on *money*?" I say, catching a warning glance from Rose. I force myself to slow down and ease up. Ginger needs time, I get that. I can't expect her to be used to this sort of thing.

I soften my voice. "I'm not saying you have to talk about divorce now. But what if Michael makes the first move? What if he empties your bank accounts when you're not looking? You need to be prepared, Gingerbread. Y'all are no longer partners; y'all are adversaries. You have to outthink and outwit him, starting now."

Ginger flinches, but she's never stood between battling lawyers in divorce court. I have, and I know even the nicest ex-husband can turn vindictive when it's time to divide the dishes and decide who gets the dog.

"In any case, your life is far from over," I tell her, sitting next to her. "How old are you, fifty?"

Her blank look twists into a scowl. "Forty-nine."

I'm grateful to see she hasn't completely lost her spirit. "Forty-nine is still young. Grandma Lillian was fifty-three when she married Walter, so she went through six marriages before she found the man who was perfect for her. And she and Walter were happy, weren't they? What'd they have, twenty-five years together?"

Ginger closes her eyes. "Thirty. They were married thirty years before he died."

"You see? It's never too late. Divorce Michael and move on. You raised his kids and helped put him through grad school, but you've also established a career of your own. That was smart; now you can teach music anywhere you like. And you'll soon have a tidy bankroll to get started with, money that's all yours. Michael can't touch a dime of your inheritance from Grandma Lillian."

Ginger remains motionless for a moment, then a shudder shakes her shoulders. "This all feels so . . . sudden. I'd like to talk to Michael before I do anything. I need to know what made him do this."

"Doesn't matter." I cross my arms and look at Rose, daring her to contradict me. "Midlife crisis, stress, hormones, male menopause— men blame their infidelity on all kinds of things. He may confess anything; he might deny everything. If he confesses, he'll blame his affair on stress, your career, or *your* midlife crisis. But no matter what he says, the bottom line is he cheated and you didn't. The failure of this marriage is on him, so take your half of everything and get out while you can."

"Or not." Rosemary's eyes flash. "Good grief, Penny, she just found out what's going on. Give her some time to sort through her feelings before you send her into divorce court."

I send Rose an *are you kidding?* glance, but hold my tongue. I don't know why she's being all sympathetic and understanding when what happened is as obvious as the devastated look on Ginger's face. In all the time I've known my older sister, I don't think I've ever seen her look so defeated and helpless. My always-in-control and ultra-responsible sister's world has just turned inside out.

I know that feeling; I've experienced it more than once. But after my second divorce, I swore I would never again let a man leave me. From that point on, I vowed that the moment I could tell a relationship was heading south, I would pack a bag and walk toward the door. And that's one vow I've managed to keep.

Before tonight, Ginger would have called my attitude *callous*. I don't think she'd say that now.

I wouldn't wish a situation like the one Ginger's experiencing on anyone, but I'm glad I can be here to help her . . . even though this development has ruined my plans with Miller. Maybe tomorrow I can help Ginger and Rose clean for a while, then slip away for a couple of hours. Surely my sisters won't mind if I take off for a little sightseeing with a new friend.

I leave Rose to continue soothing Ginger while I scoop up a handful of utensils from the table. "I'm assuming nobody wants any of these gadgets," I say, speaking to Rose's and Ginger's bent heads. "If you don't holler, I'm fixin' to throw them all out."

My only answer is a muffled sob, so I grab a trash bag and begin tossing the worn-out items away.

If only we could get rid of husbands as easily.

GINGER

I look from Rose to Penny and again wish I'd never suggested this weekend get-together. If I hadn't arranged this trip, I'd be at home, where I'd be able to fax Ross the signed financial form he needed. I would never have called Michael, so I'd never have found him with another woman. I could maintain our happy family facade for only God knows how long, living in blissful ignorance.

But God, or fate, or life itself has conspired to unite me with my sisters and expose Michael's betrayal and my heartache. Penny and Rose ought to understand me better than anyone else on earth, but I'm not sure they've ever met the woman behind the big-sister mask. Usually we are aligned against one another, me explaining the right thing to do and one or both of them dead set against me.

Yet Rose is right about one thing: I need time to think. I can't decide the fate of my family in an hour, and I can't decide if I should end my marriage while sitting at my grandmother's cluttered kitchen table. I need time to sort things out, even though I doubt time will teach me how to forgive and forget. One day I might be able to forgive Michael, but forget? Impossible, unless God strikes me with dementia.

Because I think better when my hands are occupied, I steel myself to finish the work we came here to do. I straighten my back, blow my nose, and look up to meet my sisters' eyes. "Thanks for the advice," I tell them, "but I've got a lot to think about, and I may as well think while I work. Go ahead and eat your dinner before it's ruined."

Penny picks up one of the burgers and offers it to me. "Aren't you hungry?"

I brush my hands on my slacks. "Since we don't have a lot of time, I think I'll clean out Grandmother's bookcase while you two eat."

I catch the look Penny shoots at Rose, but I'm too tired to try to interpret it.

"Are you sure you want to stay?" Rose says. "You could drive home if you want. Penny and I can finish this up."

"I could even load the piano into a trailer," Penny offers. "I'm gonna need one for the table and chairs, anyway. Maybe Bob could drive the piano to Savannah next week—"

I shake my head. "I don't want to put anyone through any trouble. Now go on, you two, eat. Don't worry about me."

While my sisters eat their meals, I move toward the bookcase and consider the task in front of me. I feel robotic, like my hands and legs are moving independently of my brain, but the bookcase is a concrete object, a piece of furniture I can empty without much mental effort. The case contains three shelves, each loaded with books, some stacked horizontally, some vertically. The frayed edges and corners of yellowed papers jut out from the dusty piles.

I drag over a brown vinyl footstool and settle in front of the bookcase. "Either of you want any of these books?" My voice sounds as brittle as old paper, but my sisters don't seem to notice. I lift the first couple of volumes from the shelf: two novels, their endpapers speckled with age, both of them published in the early sixties. Unable to toss out even used paperbacks, Grandmother must have read them and kept them.

"Thrift store," Rosemary answers. "People love old books. Some even buy them to resell online."

Penny waves my offer away. "Take all of them."

I set both books on the floor, mentally establishing the "thrift store" pile, then reach into the bookcase for a bulky stack of papers and books. On the top is a poetry collection; beneath it, a biography of Abraham Lincoln, a worn copy of Dale Carnegie's *How to Win Friends and Influence People*, and a nice copy of *Jane Eyre*.

I set *Jane Eyre* aside for my own library. At least Jane managed to find lasting love.

The biography and poetry book go into the thrift store stack, then I briefly consider the Carnegie. I read *How to Win Friends* in college, but perhaps I ought to brush up on the basic principles. My influence didn't have much of an effect on my husband, did it? I struggle to remember whether Dale Carnegie dispensed any marital advice, then decide that he didn't. I place the book in the thrift store pile.

The next item in the stack is a newspaper clipping, a wedding announcement. I stare at a black-and-white photo of an attractive bride and groom before realizing that I'm looking at my own face—twenty-seven years younger, blonder, and leaner. Michael and I are smiling for the camera, and our expressions appear genuine. Surely they were. In those days we were desperately in love, though now I'm amazed at how little we knew of life. How could we be so ignorant and so mad about each other? After sharing a home, two sons, thousands of kisses, and countless intimate nights, shouldn't we be more in love than ever?

I look up, half expecting to see Grandmother Lillian standing in the hallway, a purposeful look on her face. If she were still living, I'd think she slipped this clipping into this stack on purpose, so I'd find it and be reminded . . . of what? Of the holiness of wedding vows? Of the solemnity of marriage?

Michael promised to love me faithfully . . . and I should have known better than to trust his word. After all, mothers are supposed to love their children, too, and my mother obviously didn't love me enough to stay.

The familiar feeling of abandonment surfaces like a strong undertow, a riptide that drags me into the abyss of grief and loss, the cluttered fragments of my derailed childhood. Loneliness billows at the door and presses against the windows, threatening to seep through the cottage, but I mustn't let my sisters see, mustn't let Penny and Rose know how close I am to drowning in anguish.

When I reach up to brush a traitorous tear away, Penny's voice slices into my thoughts. "Ginger"—her practical tone dispels the fog of fear—"you don't have to stay here. Go home and take care of yourself. Rosie and I will be fine; we promise to leave this place looking like new."

I shake my head and drop another book onto the thrift store pile. "I promised to be around when the Realtor stops by with the papers."

Truthfully, though the idea of crying in private is appealing, I can't imagine being home with only my despair, grief, and a cat for company. Though being with my sisters is often frustrating, at this moment, being alone would be far worse.

ROSEMARY

At the kitchen sink, I wash my hands with an ancient sliver of soap and glance over at Penny. "Except for mopping the floor, we're about done with the kitchen, Penn." I keep my voice low. "Do you think we should move into the living room and give Ginger a hand with that bookcase? She might want to talk."

"Good idea. Just let me haul this trash bag to the Dumpster." While Penny secures a huge garbage bag, I dry my hands and go into the living room, where Ginger has been working in silence for more than an hour. She has stacked a mountain of books by her knee, set a couple of books on the sofa, and piled a huge collection of papers, booklets, and other printed materials against the wall.

I know I ought to comfort her, but I've never known how to approach Ginger. Earlier, when I was rubbing her back, I felt like I was soothing a cactus.

"Grandma Lillian was quite the pack rat." I pick up a theater program for *Guys and Dolls.* "Anything interesting in all that stuff?"

Ginger barely lifts her head. "A couple of things. Found my wedding announcement, along with yours and Penny's. Your first weddings, that is."

Not knowing how to take that remark, I sit on the edge of the couch. "I didn't even send out invitations when Wort and I got married. I e-mailed a couple of close friends who promised to stand up with us, and that was it."

Ginger's eyes narrow. "I wondered why you didn't invite us."

"Would y'all have come?"

She snorts softly. "I don't know. But I thought you'd at least send an announcement. We are sisters, after all. And Michael and I did take you in for a year."

So . . . she's reminding me that I owe her one, or chiding me because I've apparently forgotten that fact. "I'm sorry I didn't invite y'all to my wedding," I say, trying to appear nonchalant. "But if it'll make you feel better, I want you and Michael to come to my funeral."

"Very funny."

"I'm not kidding."

"Then don't hold your breath. I'll probably croak long before you do because I've got a seven-year head start. Add the stress from taking care of you two all these years, and it's a wonder I'm not already in the grave."

I study Ginger's expression, but her gaze is pinned to a newspaper article and her voice is stony. Here I am, being far more open about my plans than I ever intended to be, and Ginger only hears what she wants to hear.

She'll probably beat herself up when she learns that I'm gone, but she has no reason to feel guilty. Penny and I keep telling her that we're accountable for our own mistakes, but Ginger never seems to listen. Doesn't matter, though. If my plan is a big mistake, I'll be the one responsible for making it.

Unwillingly, my mind drifts back to my junior year and the nine months I lived with Ginger and Michael. By the time I hit seventeen, I had lost interest in school and almost everything else, dropping out of church, art, and my part-time job. When I got involved with a boyfriend who sported cigarettes, shaggy hair, and glassy eyes, Daddy sent me to live with the newlyweds . . . a decision that didn't please anyone at first. But moving to Savannah gave me a fresh perspective, and after an initial rough start I learned how to give Ginger and Michael the space they needed.

Ginger and I got into a few skirmishes that year, but I think she took comfort in ordering me around because she was more familiar with the role of big sister than wife.

Michael proved to be an understanding friend . . . and at seventeen, a girl appreciates protective male friends. By the end of the school year, Ginger decreed that I had recovered from my inappropriate love affair and sent me off to Gran's cottage on St. Simons, but I wouldn't have minded staying in Savannah.

I haven't seen much of Michael in the intervening years, but I'll always be grateful to him for making me feel like a real sister and not an annoying intruder. I can't imagine what he was thinking if he cheated on Ginger, but I know he is usually tolerant and easygoing. If he strayed, something significant must have happened between those two.

But do we ever know what *really* goes on in other people's homes?

I probably shouldn't blame Ginger for not picking up on my secret—her elder sister's intuition has been numbed because she's still in shock about Michael. Despite her apparent attention to the dusty books scattered around her, she's wearing the dumbfounded look I wore when I discovered my first husband cheating on me. I clutched at all kinds of reasons for why Todd would be taking his secretary out to dinner when he was supposed to be fishing with his best friend, but in the end it came down to one thing: the man was a cheating dog and I never should have trusted him.

Still, the betrayal felt like a punch in the stomach and left me breathless. I went to pieces during those days, so this state of shock may be a blessing for Ginger. She'll fall apart later . . . maybe in an hour, maybe next week.

"If you want to talk"—I push the words through the empty space between us—"I know what it's like to find out your husband's cheating. So I'm here. If you want to talk."

"I'm fine," Ginger answers, each word like a splinter of ice. "I don't need to talk."

To you.

She doesn't speak the last two words, but I hear them all the same. Ginger has never confided in me, never let me peek behind her calm and polished exterior. I'd be surprised if she confides in Penny, which means she must not talk to anyone in the family . . . except Michael.

So this betrayal must be doubly difficult.

I know she's on a collision course with despair, but I've a feeling Ginger will handle this disaster like any other event on her schedule. One day, when she has no other engagements planned, she'll crumble in her quiet, controlled way, then steadily pick up the pieces and arrange them in some kind of defined order. She must have been forged of iron and steel in the womb.

Unlike me. I am made of tissue paper. But when I say my final good-bye, no one will blame my exit on a particular crisis. People will believe I died in an accident. Even if some suspect otherwise, they'll never be able to prove anything.

I'll be firmly in control when I check out of this world. I have my affairs in order, my life firmly in hand.

In that moment, I will be as much like Ginger as I have ever been.

Because we've allowed ourselves to be sidetracked from our declared mission, when Ginger stands and turns as if to deliver an announcement, I brace myself for a rebuke or a new plan involving charts and Post-its. Instead, she yawns and gestures toward the stairs. "If you two don't mind, I'm going up to bed. Driving always wipes me out."

It's not the drive that exhausted her, it's the calamity that followed, but I'm not about to verbalize that distinction. I glance at Penny, wondering if we share the same thought, but Penny's waving Ginger up the steps.

"Go on, get some rest. Rose and I will finish up here so we can tackle the bedrooms and closets tomorrow."

Ginger shuffles toward the stairway, her stockinged feet moving soundlessly over the pine floorboards. I watch until her shadow disappears from the stairwell, then I turn to Penny. "Do you think one of us should sleep in the room with her tonight?"

"I wouldn't want company. You take Grandma's room and I'll sleep in the blue room."

"But she'll be alone. And she's not used to being alone."

"Maybe she *wants* to be alone tonight. What if she wakes up crying? Would you want someone else hearing that?"

"But we're her *sisters*."

"We're not her friends. Think about it—would she have told us about Michael if we hadn't been here? I don't think so."

I stare at Penny, then realize she's probably right. The three of us are not friends. Though we are bound by shared experiences, we are separated by beliefs, distance, and years. At times the gaps between us feel almost unbridgeable.

I release a deep sigh. "I guess I'll go to bed too. I'm beat, and I'd like to call Wort before I go to sleep."

"Tell him hello for me, will you?"

"Okay."

"And, Rose"—Penny waits until I look at her before she continues—"are y'all really doing okay? You seem . . . kinda *down* this weekend."

I summon up a bright smile. "I'm fine. Wort's good. Everything's great . . . except for my sick dog, that is. The little guy has seen better days."

"Better *years,* you mean."

I stop by the cushion, where Justus has been sleeping, and wake him with a gentle scratch behind the ears. "Hey, buddy, are you ready to go to bed?"

"It's not like he hasn't been sleeping all day," Penny says, chuckling. "In fact, you'd better take him outside before you put him to bed. Ginger will have a fit if that dog pees on Grandma's floor."

"Good point." I slap the side of my leg and whistle softly. Justus pulls himself up and follows me out into the humid Georgia night. He's hanging in there, and so am I. And so, apparently, is Ginger.

As I watch Justus root around in the soft grass of the front lawn, I lean against a porch post and consider my plans for Monday. I want Ginger to be okay; I want her to weather this crisis. As sorry as I am to see her marriage implode, I hope she bears up under her grief and remains strong.

Because if she's still shell-shocked on Monday, I don't know if I can proceed with my plans. Ginger may never want or accept help from me, but she's my sister and I have a feeling I should stick around in case she needs me.

Though the idea of Ginger needing me makes me laugh.

NINE

PENNYROYAL

Why did we enjoy staying up so late when we were kids? I click through the television channels, but standard cable has little to offer, and the picture on Grandma's old TV looks more pitiful than I remember.

Just before midnight, Rose brings her sorry-looking terrier back inside and tells me good night, then trudges down the hall to Grandma's room. I've heard nothing from the bedroom upstairs, so I assume Ginger has dozed off—either that or she's crying into her pillow.

I turn off the porch light and wander into the kitchen for a drink. The water from the tap doesn't taste like the water at home, but it eases the tickle in my throat. My throat is a bit sore, probably the result of talking more than usual. I don't talk much at work, and I talk even less at home. These days Bob and I seem to have little to say to each other.

To keep from bothering Ginger, I brush my teeth in the downstairs powder bath, then tiptoe up the steps and change into pajama bottoms and a T-shirt in the blue bedroom. I know I ought to go to bed, but I'm too awake, too restless, so I go back downstairs and open the door to the hall closet where I know I'll find a pillow and a blanket. Grandma always kept linens handy in case we girls fell asleep watching *Saturday Night Live*.

When I yank on a folded square, a smaller blanket on the same shelf falls and lands at my feet. I blink in astonished silence when

I recognize the embroidery on the quilt shapes—this is Grandma's bird blanket, the quilt Rose wants. Just as she remembered, it's edged in green and *Ricky* is embroidered on each hand-pieced square.

Delighted with my discovery, I set the blanket on the love seat, then return for my wool blanket and pillow. I make myself a cozy nest on the couch, power on the old TV, and adjust the volume to a whisper. I know I ought to be thinking about how I can get over to Jekyll Island, but my brain feels sluggish. A talk show host is interviewing a blonde starlet I've never heard of, but I do adore her pixie haircut. I spend a few minutes trying to imagine my head with her hair, then I lean back and close my eyes. The televised conversation is dull enough to calm my thoughts and help me relax.

I've been dozing for about an hour when I wake to the sound of crunching gravel outside the house. Night noises are nothing unusual here because the wildlife on St. Simons comes out to play after dark—in Grandma's yard we've seen raccoons, possums, and even the occasional armadillo playing in the moonlight. But none of those creatures walks heavily enough to crunch pebbles, and none would tramp with such an even tread.

I roll off the couch onto my hands and knees, careful to stay low so the open window doesn't reveal my silhouette against the light of the flickering TV. I look around for a weapon and grab a fireplace poker, then I shimmy over to the door and stand. I flatten myself against the wall and listen.

The footsteps continue across the gravel drive where our cars are parked. I close my eyes and try to imagine what the intruder is seeing—three cars, all of them littered with the debris of travel. The house looks like dozens of other rentals in the area, but three cars might tempt a thief. Is the night crawler here to steal our car radios, or does he have designs on the house?

Sweat slicks my grip on the poker, so I wipe my hands on my pajama bottoms and try to steady my breathing. I hear nothing for a brief interval, but a chill climbs the ladder of my spine when the footsteps begin to ascend the porch stairs, each tread groaning beneath a heavy weight. Now the intruder squeaks the porch flooring while a flashlight shines through the glass panes in the front door.

Nervy burglar!

Someone jiggles the door handle, but all I hear is the pounding of my heart. I grip the poker with both hands and move it to the right, ready to swing with every ounce of force I can muster. I hear another sound, a *whisst* and more doorknob jiggling, and then I realize someone is trying to slide a credit card between the edge of the door and the locking mechanism.

I gulp back my fear as nausea churns my stomach. How should I strike? If he breaks a windowpane and puts his hand through the opening I could whack his arm with a downward blow, but what if he steps through the doorway? His midsection would be a bigger target, but maybe I ought to aim for his head. A blow to the gut might slow a man down, but a blow to the head could take him out. I'm sure of only one thing: I don't think I'll get a second chance to stop this guy.

The latch clicks, the handle turns, the door moves forward half an inch. I gather my resolve and tighten my grip on the poker, again realizing how heavy it is, and the door swings open. A man's body fills the space; I aim for his midsection and am halfway through my swing when my gaze rises and I recognize my brother-in-law's salt-and-pepper beard.

Michael?

Fortunately, my cry of startled recognition provides an instant's warning. Michael retreats, but though I try to halt my blow, the poker catches Michael across the arm. He winces as the iron strikes against bone, then a stream of vowels erupt from his mouth and an overnight bag falls to the floor. All I can do is drop the poker and stare at my brother-in-law in horrified silence.

"Why'd you do that?" he finally asks through gritted teeth. "Didn't you see it was me?"

"I didn't look." Teetering between astonishment and alarm, I stare at the overnight bag. Did he honestly think Ginger would let him spend the night? The man has lost his mind.

"I'm sorry I hit you." I grip his wrist and guide him into the house, then gesture to a chair at the kitchen table. "You want some ice? Never mind, the ice maker's not working. I could give you a wet towel, though."

He gapes at me, his brows lowered. "I knew you'd be upset, but I didn't think you'd try to kill me."

I swallow a burst of hysterical laughter. "Be glad I didn't hit you on the head. I thought you were a burglar."

"Would a burglar walk up and let himself in?"

"Why didn't you call to tell us you were coming?"

"I couldn't. All my calls have been going straight to voice mail. Ginger must have turned off her phone."

Oh—and that explains why I didn't hear from Miller after I texted him. I file that mental note away to concentrate on the matter at hand.

I can feel a dozen questions bubbling up, so I drop into a neighboring chair and ask the one that's been uppermost in my mind: "Why did you cheat on my sister?"

He gives me a blank look, with only a wary twitch of the eye to show that he knows he's sitting behind enemy lines. "Believe me, I never meant for it to happen."

"You were just having a good time when *oops*, you ended up in bed with a friend?"

He presses his lips together and shakes his head, body language I interpret as *something like that, but I can't admit it now.*

I lean forward and pick up the poker on the floor. "Maybe I *should* beat you up. Ginger's too civilized to do it herself."

"Please." Michael holds up his hand. "I came here to talk to my wife. I've had a long drive and a longer day. So if you'd just let me talk to Ginger—"

"I don't think she wants to talk to you. You broke her heart, you know."

A sudden spasm knits his brows. I watch, noting that he does appear to be gripped by genuine sorrow. "Since you've driven all this way . . ." I sharpen my gaze and pin him in a more intense scrutiny. "Actually, I'm impressed you came. Ginger's in a bedroom upstairs; turn right at the landing and walk toward the front of the house. She's not armed, but I'd recommend that you approach cautiously and talk fast."

"Thanks, Penny, you're a pal."

"Well, you're my brother . . . at least that's what you've been for the past twenty-seven years."

Michael stands, but keeps his injured arm bent and close to his chest. Before he reaches the stairs, he turns and looks at me. "Any chance of getting a cup of coffee around here?"

I can't stop a smile. Any man who'd mess up like he did and then willingly drink his sister-in-law's coffee must have a trusting heart. "Go on up and face the music, Michael. I'll see what I can do."

GINGER

A hand touches my shoulder.

I swim up through a fitful sleep and sense a presence in the bedroom with me. When I open my eyes, I know I'm dreaming because Michael, bathed in silver moonlight, sits on the edge of my bed. His hair is uncombed and disheveled, his shirt rumpled, his beard sparkling with gray flecks. He looks so much like an apparition that I gasp at an unexpected conclusion: *Michael's dead and his spirit has come to say good-bye.*

Then the ghost speaks in a broken whisper: "Why wouldn't you take my calls?"

I blink, wondering if my dead husband has decided to haunt me, and the illusion shatters when my visitor stands to turn on the bedside lamp. Michael is here, obviously alive and well, though the relationship between us is dead. And of all the things he could say to me, he wants to know why I don't want to talk to him?

The crazy thing is I *do* want to talk. Some demented part of me wants to know how, and when, and why, and how often. How he touched her, where they made love. My marriage has been invaded, and I want to hear every grisly detail so I can learn how I was fooled into believing everything was fine.

But not now. I'm not ready to hear specifics now. Right now I could happily claw out his eyes.

Striving to free myself from the lingering tendrils of sleep, I struggle to sit up. "I didn't answer"—I cross my legs beneath the quilt—"because I didn't want to talk to you."

I grab the pillow and bury my fists in it as he sits again, this time on the edge of the matching twin bed. I peer across the distance between us and see that his eyes are puffy and his face haggard. "Good grief, what time is it?"

"Nearly two."

"In the *morning*?" I blow a clump of hair out of my eyes, then focus on him again. "Why on earth did you drive all the way down here in the middle of the night?"

"We have to talk. You didn't let me explain anything this afternoon."

He thinks he can *explain* this? His answer fans the resentment smoldering inside my chest. "I'm not interested in explanations, Michael, because I've had time to think and I've already reached the appropriate conclusions. Let me see—this afternoon you were with a woman instead of being at a conference in Atlanta. When confronted, you didn't deny having an affair, which leads me to believe this thing has been going on for at least several months. Furthermore, the woman felt confident enough to speak to me when I called. She wouldn't be so self-assured unless you'd made promises to her; so apparently you've not only made promises, but you've also given her two thousand dollars of our family money, maybe to buy her silence or something. Did I get any of that wrong?"

I lean against the headboard and study my husband, who seems to be contemplating the pattern in Grandmother's chenille bedspread. "I wanted to explain . . . how it happened."

I shake my head, warning him off. "What makes you think I want to hear that now? What matters at this point is how we explain things to our children, how we help the boys cope with what they'll hear from our friends and neighbors."

He grimaces as if I'd slapped him. "I'm sorry, Ginger. I didn't mean for it to start, and I certainly didn't intend for things to go this far—"

"How far have they gone?"

He stands and turns toward the window, his shoulders slumping. "Past the point of no return, I'm afraid. Theresa's pregnant. She showed me the report from her doctor's office this afternoon, just before you called. She's . . . going to have my baby."

I confess—until that instant I had enjoyed Michael's suffering. Hurling the accusations, watching him cower and confess and apologize brought me extreme satisfaction. Because despite everything, I still believed Michael loved me. He cared deeply for our sons. He might have a fling, but he would never end our marriage or destroy our family.

But a pregnancy would change everything.

I close my eyes and when I open them I see him again at the window, his posture softening as he tells me about the pregnancy. He may have adopted that defeated pose with me, but I wonder if he slumped when he first heard the news. Michael has always loved children. He might have smiled when he heard about the baby— oh, privately he would have felt guilty and he would have worried about the repercussions, but he wouldn't have slumped in defeat. News of the baby actually might have made him *happy*.

But that child is a rock dropped into the pool of my heart, sending ripples of panic in all directions. My eyes sting and tears spill onto my cheeks, an overflow of dread. The other woman has dealt my marriage a fatal blow. I have no defense, no weapon to use against her. Michael is responsible; Michael will want to do the right thing. If he wants to keep his job, his *identity*, he will quietly divorce me and marry this pregnant professor. The university officials will barely bat an eye if he handles the situation discreetly. And Michael is a man of utmost discretion.

My stomach drops like a hanged prisoner.

"That's why I gave her the money," Michael says, his attempt at objectivity marred by a catch in his voice. "She needed a bigger apartment, something with two bedrooms. She needed money for the move."

"So . . . you've known about this baby for a couple of weeks."

"We—I—suspected. I didn't know for sure until today."

How could he have kept this news to himself for so long? How could he have kept up appearances, pretending everything was fine and normal—

"You brought me roses," I remind him, my voice a mere whisper. "Red, the color of love. You said you loved me. You lied."

"I didn't lie, Ginger. I *do* love you. And . . . I know you love red roses."

"A man who loves his wife doesn't sleep with other women. He doesn't betray her."

"I do love you," he repeats, his voice breaking with huskiness. "But I never said I was perfect."

I lift my left hand and stare at my wedding band, feeling as if sections of my body have been torn away. My husband, my lover, the father of my children, and the man I have trusted with my heart and my life—that man has vanished. My soul mate. My other half.

I bite my lip until it throbs, then I crumple and begin to sob. Michael moves to take me in his arms, a gesture probably more reflexive than heartfelt, yet I can't bring myself to turn away. I ball my fists and pound his chest, but he's holding me so closely I have no room to strike with real force, no way to hurt him the way he's hurt me.

My only weapons are these scalding tears, so I open the floodgates and let them flow. Michael bears the touch of my tears, my pounding on his chest, my racking sobs, and my anguished protests. Finally he relaxes his grip so I'm able to pull away. Immediately, I slide back to the security of the headboard.

He, being a man, will never know the blow he's dealt me. He should grow old along with me, he should glory in our nearly adult sons, we should face retirement together. Instead, he has fulfilled every tawdry stereotype, surrendered to a base hormonal urge, and abandoned his premenopausal, dried-up, increasingly unfruitful wife for someone younger and more fertile, someone who can give him a new lease on life.

Why does he get to start over when I've finally reached the home-stretch? I look at him, trembling with unasked questions and unmet needs. His handsome face and dark eyes, which would attract most women even from a distance, are full of frustrated sadness and his voice is hoarse. "I made a mistake, Ginger. And I'm sorry. If I could rewind the clock and make different choices, I would. Believe me, I never meant to betray you or hurt our family."

I command my hand not to tremble as I reach for the box of tissues on the nightstand. "Too late."

"But it's not too late to talk things out. Can we—can I stay here tonight, so we can go out for breakfast in the morning? Things will look better after we've had a good night's sleep. Tomorrow we'll be thinking more clearly, so we can decide . . . what we need to do next."

Our marriage is barely dead. Is he already hinting that he's ready to divide up the spoils? I shake my head, repulsed by the idea. "I don't want you here. I need to be alone."

A frown line settles between his brows. "But you're not exactly alone here. I know your sisters, and I know what they'll tell you to do. But they wouldn't know a good marriage if it hit them between the eyes."

I rub a finger over my lips, quelling an inexplicable urge to laugh. "That's another reason you should go—my sisters are liable to eat you alive if they find you here."

He winces and rubs his forearm. "That's not exactly true. I survived talking to Penny."

"Only because Penny adores anything with a Y chromosome. Go home, Michael, see your girlfriend, take a long walk down a short pier, stick your head in a gas oven. I don't care what you do, just don't be here in the morning."

He stands, a look of inexpressible distance in his eyes. "You sure?"

"Good grief, would you *go*?"

The obvious exasperation in my voice drives him a step closer to the door. "One more question," he says, his jaw wobbling. "When you get home . . . should I not be there?"

Is he asking if he should move out? I am tempted to shout *yes*, but once he leaves he may never come back.

I have to slow down. My answer will affect not only Michael as my husband but also as the father of my sons, a professor at the university, and my partner in life and business. There's something dreadfully public about the act of moving out.

"I don't know," I answer, and in my voice I hear a note halfway between disbelief; and pleading. "I don't know what I want you to do. Go home; wait for me. When I can think clearly, I'll come home and we'll talk."

A brief smile flits across his face, a smile that says he's glad to see I'm thinking rationally. "Good."

"Go," I repeat, hugging my pillow closer. "We'll talk . . . when I get home."

PENNYROYAL

"Conscience," Grandma often said, "keeps more people awake than coffee." Though Michael asked me for coffee, something tells me his conscience will keep him awake for the long drive home.

The kitchen has filled with the aromatic scents of vanilla and coffee beans by the time I hear footsteps on the stairs. I turn, not sure who I'll find on the landing. A smile tugs at my mouth when I see Michael, but the tortured expression on his face forces me to look away.

So . . . Miss Perfect Example of a Model Marriage isn't ready to forgive and forget. Something in me wondered if she would sweep the incident under the rug and choose denial rather than to confront the truth about her perfect husband.

I should send her an official invitation to the Betrayed Wives Club.

I catch Michael's eye as he stops at the bottom of the stairs and rubs the back of his neck. "I'd offer you a place on the couch, but I don't think you'll want to be here when Ginger gets up tomorrow morning. I did make you some coffee, though."

He gives me a rueful smile. "Did you sprinkle it with rat poison?"

"You're in luck—we cleaned out the kitchen drawers today. Not a spoonful of rat killer to be found in this entire house."

Michael moves to the bar and perches on a stool as I open a thrift store box and pull out a mug. "Do you take cream and sugar?"

"I think I'd better take it black. It's going to be a long night."

I pour the steaming liquid into the cup, then slide it across the bar. He lifts the mug, then raises a brow. "Why are you still speaking to me?"

I lean against the counter and cross my arms. "I always liked you, Michael. And believe it or not, I understand that marriages can get stale. I'm not happy about you cheating on my sister, but there's no sense in pretending that these things never happen." I shrug. "I might even be a little relieved because now Ginger will have to step off her soapbox and stop preaching to me and Rose. But we'll take care of her. You don't have to worry about that."

A halfhearted smile flits across his face, then he sips from his mug. "This is good. Aren't you having any?"

"I shouldn't. I need to sleep tonight. Ginger can be a slave driver, you know."

"Oh, I know." He takes another sip and lowers the cup back to the counter. I suspect Michael is stalling because he wants to talk, but I'm not sure he should be talking to me. Even though we've been family for twenty-seven years, I've always suspected that Michael doesn't take me seriously because I never finished college and I don't like to talk about politics and world affairs.

But at the moment, I'm the only person around.

"Did, um"—he turns his coffee mug by the handle—"did Ginger say much to you and Rose?"

"Enough to understand the situation."

He grimaces, and his dark eyes brim with threatening tears. "I hate that this is happening. I didn't mean to hurt her. If you knew how I've agonized—"

"You weren't thinking about *her*; that's the point. And you know what Grandma always said about a man who takes fire into his hand—eventually he's gonna get burned." The quote isn't Shakespeare, but it's enough to make him wince.

"I don't want to lose my wife, Penn. It was a mistake, an infatuation. Theresa kept after me, waiting for me after class, coming to my office for advice, managing to meet me in the parking lot every morning. I was . . . flattered. She was attractive and quite intelligent. She's brilliant, actually."

"Your wife isn't exactly chopped liver."

"But you know how it is—marriage gets comfortable after a few years. And this woman was so . . . exotic. She *listened* to me. She said she needed me. And now she's pregnant."

This news slams into me with the force of a blow. Michael has been caught in a trap, complete with iron bars and a pickproof lock.

His face transforms, the handsome and detached veneer peeling back to reveal the misery underneath. "I don't know what to do." He folds his arms on the counter and casts me a look of helpless appeal. "Ever since I heard that Theresa might be pregnant, I've been thinking about my options. I've considered the problem from all angles, and the best solution isn't what I want to do. But it's the only way I can own up to my mistake, keep my job, and continue providing for my sons. I have to walk away from *someone*, but if I walk away from Theresa, she'll destroy me. And then I'll have nothing to offer anyone."

"I wonder"—my voice sounds as dry as sandpaper—"what made this woman think you had so much to offer in the first place."

Michael drops his head onto his folded arms, quietly and thoroughly going to pieces. The sound of his contrite sobs strikes me as surreal—I feel like I'm watching a *Star Trek* rerun, and Spock has just collapsed in a crying jag.

After a few minutes, I prop my elbows on the counter and look my brother-in-law directly in the eyes. "Get ahold of yourself and listen to me. Have you seen a genuine pregnancy report? Something from a doctor's office?"

He blows his nose, then wearily props his chin on his hand. "Yeah. I have. And I hate to admit it, but I almost found myself hoping that she'd miscarry or choose—you know, not to have the baby. But I've accepted it and she's determined to keep this child."

"Of course she is. So don't you dare think of this woman as innocent, because she's obviously clever enough to get you where she wants you. Let me guess—she said you wouldn't need to worry about birth control, right?"

When his eyes close, I shake my head. "You're such a man, Michael. You're smart, but your brains go right out the window when your hormones get stirred up. Face it, this other woman played you, and now Ginger and the boys are fixin' to pay the price."

His lips tighten. "Do you think Ginger will—"

"Divorce you? I don't see any reason for her to stay with you."

The tension on his face dissolves into a tortured expression of relief. "I never thought I'd be asking Ginger for a divorce, but I can't see any other answer. Theresa could make things miserable for me at the university if I don't marry her."

"I thought you couldn't be fired. That you had immunity or something."

His mouth twists with bitter humor. "Tenure doesn't mean I couldn't be fired for gross misconduct. If I abandon Theresa, she could claim sexual harassment. I'd be fired in a heartbeat."

"Would she make that kind of claim?"

He considers a moment. "Yeah, she would."

"What about your family? Can you just walk away from them?"

"Would I really be walking away? Ross and Ryan are practically grown, and I'm sure most of their friends have divorced parents. I could stay in touch with them and with Ginger; there's no reason this has to spell disaster. Ginger's always been independent and capable. She'll be fine on her own. She doesn't need anybody's help."

Overcome by sheer disbelief at his matter-of-fact summary, I can't speak. Ginger has always said that Michael lives more in his head than in his emotions, and now I see the proof of it. He speaks like a true professor, a man who regularly turns problems into logical solutions. I can't disagree with his argument; his sensible conclusion sounds like something I might have come up with on a good day. Being the man he is, Michael will want to marry the other woman. He can even cloak himself in responsibility, claiming that his unborn child needs a father.

But what about the wife and sons he will abandon? Though I can appreciate the practical aspects of his proposed solution, how can he rationalize the misery he will cause? The Betrayed Wives Club requires a stiff membership fee: one broken heart.

"I don't understand," I say, the words hurting my throat, "why this other woman can't see that a man who'd cheat on his wife will also cheat on her, but maybe she only wants you for a couple of years." I catch his gaze and hold it until he flinches. "So drink your coffee, brother-in-law, stiffen your spine, and go back to Savannah. Ginger will come home when she's ready."

Michael looks at me, his eyes soft with pain. "It's the best thing, you know. Ginger will want to divorce me. No one will blame her for doing it."

"You may be right," I answer, "but that doesn't mean she'll be happy afterward."

Michael stares at the counter for a long moment, then gulps his coffee down. He lowers the mug and runs the back of his hand across his mouth. "I never thought I'd be grateful that you were around to talk to Ginger. You're more experienced in these matters, so I know you'll give her good advice."

For some reason, the compliment stings.

"If Ginger wants to talk," Michael continues, "tell her to call me. I'm not going to bother her anymore, but I'll keep my phone on."

"And you'll answer it this time?"

A guilty look flashes across his face. "Yeah. I'll answer."

I nod. "Good-bye, then."

He moves toward the door, picks up the overnight bag he dropped on his way in, and steps onto the front porch. He casts a look at me, a wordless plea for mercy or sympathy or understanding, but I send him on his way with a curt wave. "Drive safely, Michael. Have a nice life."

GINGER

There's a baby.

My husband is having a baby. With another woman. A difficult situation involving one interloper has become an impossible situation involving two.

Michael's latest confession has left me anxious and bewildered, too agitated to sleep. I'm still awake when I finally hear the front door close, followed by the roar of a car engine and the pop of tires over gravel. I'd heard voices from downstairs, so one of my sisters must have talked to Michael before he left. I can't imagine what was said.

I hope he thinks about what he's done to our family on the drive home.

Still . . . in the solitude of my room I have to admit I had hoped Michael would say something that would help me make sense of this situation. At first I'd clung to the hope that he'd tell me the woman was going through a divorce of her own, so he'd been a friend and counselor, nothing more. But he and this woman have created a baby . . . and, knowing Michael, he will want to do the best thing for all concerned. Which leaves me to do . . . what, exactly?

I lie in the darkness, staring at the moonlit walls while my imagination cobbles together possible outcomes: obviously, I could divorce him, release him to marry his lover and be a father to her child. I would be left alone and our sons would lose a lot of respect for their father. They're old enough to understand what Michael did, and they might not want to forgive him.

If Michael and I divorce, I would be asked to resign from my job at the church. St. Paul's is a conservative congregation, and Reverend Howe has often stated that divorced people shouldn't fill leadership positions. Though not everyone would agree with my termination, I wouldn't want to be the center of a public debate.

With no job and no husband to hold me in Savannah, maybe I could move somewhere else . . . to Jacksonville, to be near Rose, or to Gainesville, to be near Penny. The boys might complain about me leaving their childhood home, but once they heard my reasons, they'd understand. Soon they'll be establishing their own families, so without the old homestead to keep them close, our family will scatter to the four winds.

And who says I have to live near my sisters? I could move to Ireland, a country I've always loved. Or Italy, where I could imitate Frances Mayes and create a new life for myself under the Tuscan sun. I'm young enough to start over; I could go to some city where no one knows me and teach music while I build a new network of friends. My life doesn't have to end just because my husband couldn't keep his pants zipped.

A blush rises to my cheeks. How tawdry it all is! The story will spread around the college, our neighborhood, our church. People who love Michael might hear the rumor and grant him the benefit of the doubt, but the baby will be proof of his guilt. And as our friends whisper over dinner tables and cell phones, people will speculate about what I might have done to drive him away. Did I neglect him? Was I frigid or overbearing? People who know me will assume it's all my fault, that my organization and list-making drove bookish Michael straight into another woman's arms. What they don't know is that Michael *appreciates* my organizational skills— they're responsible for keeping our family stable.

My sweet choir kids—what will they think? What will they hear? Children are familiar with divorce these days, but for years my choirs have heard me sing songs about forgiving one another and trusting God to work things out. Will any of them wonder why I couldn't forgive or trust God to work out the problems in my family?

I don't think I did anything to drive Michael away, but my opinion doesn't matter. People will talk. The only way I can preserve my reputation is to remain steady and behave as normally as possible. Since I didn't cheat, why should I suffer?

Nothing about this is fair.

Perhaps I shouldn't surrender the high ground. Michael's the one who strayed, so he should be the one to leave the house. But when should he leave? If I tell him to leave until we settle the situation, where will he go if not to the other woman? And once he's ensconced in her house or apartment, how am I to get him back . . . if I *want* him back? Do I? Do I want him at all?

Right now I can't imagine ever wanting him again. My brain, which has always benefited from a fertile imagination, is supplying me with all sorts of unpleasant mental images: Michael walking with a leggy young professor on campus, driving her home in his car, entering her apartment, falling into her bed. It takes no effort to imagine him in her arms, skin against skin, to hear the endearments he might have whispered in her ear.

I grit my teeth and roll over to face the wall, dropping the curtain on my dark visions. My husband has been with another woman. Why? Was I not enough for him? Am I no longer attractive? I'm not the waif he married, but I've borne him two children. I've stood by Michael's side for twenty-seven years, fretting with him over employment cuts at the college and family financial crises. I've stayed up with him while we struggled to figure out how we were going to finance two boys in college. I've spent half a dozen nights in a hospital easy chair, watching over Michael's son as he recovered from an emergency appendectomy. I've put miles

on this body for Michael and his children, and I've done my best
to hold back the ravages of time.

Obviously I didn't do enough. I faced a competitor I didn't even
know existed, but now she's standing between me and my husband, between Michael and our sons. She's bringing a new life into
the world, a life Michael will be responsible for. . . .

I groan at the thought of adding child support payments to an
already-stretched budget. And college! And orthodontia and education expenses and a regular allowance—all the things children
want and need. If Michael sets up his own place, he will not only
have to pay for an apartment and utilities, but he also will have
to pay child support to the other woman. He might be forced to
move into her apartment simply for financial reasons.

Yet the alternative is inconceivable. How can I stay with a man
who abused our marriage vows? Who betrayed me? Whose actions
will tell the world that I didn't satisfy his needs? Staying with
Michael might mean I would be forced to endure this woman's
child in my home on weekends, summers, and alternate holidays. I
would have to open my heart and life to the child of a woman who
stole what belonged to me, the right to enjoy my husband's body.
The right to occupy first priority in his heart.

I close my eyes as the irony becomes painfully clear—I came
to St. Simons to empty my grandmother's house, hoping that the
resulting financial windfall would ease the strains on my marriage.
But now I'm not even sure our marriage will exist by the time I
walk away from Grandmother's cottage.

I bury my face in my pillow as a rush of angry tears bubbles up
from an untapped well within me. I wish I could cry prettily, but
I have never been able to manage it. Hollywood actresses seem to
weep effortlessly—tears flow from their mascaraed eyes and roll
down perfectly sculpted cheeks. My tears spurt like geysers, accompanied by a red nose, a stuffy head, and labored breathing. In seconds I am such a sniffling, blubbering mess that I have to employ
a dozen tissues to keep my airways clear.

Finally I fall back onto the bed, exhausted. I still don't have any answers, but at least I don't have to handle the shock of this discovery at home. Few people know me on St. Simons, so no one will care if I burst into tears in the middle of Fish Fever Lane or the Harris Teeter grocery store. Here I don't have to face my neighbors, my coworkers at church, or my friends. Here I won't have to face Michael . . . and I'll be able to process my thoughts without interference.

My sisters already know the best and the worst about me, and they've been through this sort of thing before. As had Grandmother Lillian.

I roll onto my side and bury my fists in my pillow. Knowing that Grandmother, Rose, and Penny survived the heartbreak of betrayal and divorce ought to make me feel better, but it doesn't.

As I close my eyes, a new thought strikes: for twenty-seven years, Michael and I have stopped what we were doing and headed to bed at eleven o'clock. I have drifted off to sleep with him by my side.

So if he's gone . . . who's going to remind me to go to bed?

TEN

PENNYROYAL

I wake at 7:00 A.M., then close my eyes and groan when I remember it's Sunday. Finally, a morning on which I don't have to get up and get ready for work, but Ginger will be handing out chores as soon as she's up. Except—the events of the previous day come rushing back at me—maybe she won't be up for a while. Still, if I know my big sister, she won't let anything, not even Michael, derail her plans.

I roll off the bed and head toward my suitcase. In the hope that I'll be able to drive over to Jekyll Island later in the afternoon, I pull out a pink knit top and a short green skirt. After picking up lingerie and my toiletries bag, I stumble toward the hallway bathroom. If I'm lucky, Ginger and Rose may sleep for a while—Rose has always slept like a stone, and I wouldn't blame Ginger if she stayed curled under the covers until noon.

I shower, brush my teeth, and change into my new outfit. The top fits like a second skin, and short skirts always make me feel young and flirty. By seven thirty I'm in the kitchen, freshly styled hair tucked behind my ear as I search for my purse. I'm going out for coffee and doughnuts, figuring that we could use a sugar high to help us get through the rest of this job. Ginger is usually careful about eating too much sugar, but I don't think she'll give me any grief today. And I'll get religious about my diet as soon as I get home.

I finally find my purse behind an empty cardboard box. I'm heading out the door when Rose emerges from Grandma's bedroom, her sad-looking terrier trailing behind her.

"Morning," I say, opening the door for her and the dog, who seems to be panting more heavily than usual. "How'd y'all sleep back there?"

"Good." Rose yawns as she pushes on the screen door. "Come on, Justus, let's go water the lawn."

I follow them onto the front porch and watch as Rose scoops up the dog and carries him down the steps. She sets him down, then leans against the stair railing as he sniffs the sidewalk. He lumbers toward the fence, then runs into it and heads off in another direction. I laugh when he finally moves onto the grass and lifts his rear leg.

"That dog's like a mechanical windup toy," I tell Rose. "When are you going to admit his time has come?"

"When I know it has," she says, her lower jaw jutting forward. "Just because he's blind and nearly deaf doesn't mean he's not fit to live."

"Whatever you say." I jog down the stairs, then stop and look at her. "I'm going for doughnuts and coffee."

Rose had been in the middle of another yawn, but at this news she snaps her mouth shut and her eyes fly open. "You're going out in public dressed like *that*?"

Poor Rose. Stuck out on that ranch the way she is, the girl wouldn't know fashion if it bit her on the behind. "Don't you like my outfit? It's new."

"I'd like it on a teenager, maybe. I don't think tops like that are designed, you know, for women with breasts."

"Rosie, Rosie, Rosie." I shake my head and jangle my car keys as I walk toward the gate, but some of the spring has gone out of my step. Leave it to Rose to deflate my self-confidence on this of all days.

"By the way," I call, pausing by the gate, "you'd better let Ginger sleep—she had a visitor late last night."

"A visitor?"

"Didn't you hear Michael?"

She shakes her head.

"He drove all the way down here." I lower my voice. "I don't know what they said to each other, but they talked, then she sent him on his way."

"At least they talked." Rose crosses her arms and shivers in the early morning air. "That's good."

"I don't think much good came out of it. Michael's girlfriend is pregnant."

Even across the lawn, I can hear Rose snatch a breath. "She's *what*?"

"Don't mention it to Ginger. She doesn't know we know the whole story."

I twiddle my fingers in a wave and walk to my car, taking care that Rose's decrepit terrier doesn't follow me out of the gate.

With a frown puckering her brows, Rose watches me get behind the wheel, then she bends and whistles for her dog. I put my car in gear and drive away, asking myself where a doughnut shop might logically be located.

Not everything in life makes sense, but most things do.

As I maneuver through the narrow, tree-lined streets, I keep remembering bits and snatches of my conversation with Michael. Though I'm shocked and horrified by what he did, I understand why he thinks a divorce is the best solution for Ginger. She will probably think her entire world has collapsed, but I know better. I've learned how to guard my heart, how to mask my secrets, and how to escape the kind of devastation Ginger is about to face.

Maybe I'm more like Michael than either of us ever realized. After all, I'm going to divorce Bob within a few weeks, and though he may be crushed, later he'll see that I did what was best for both of us. He wants things I simply can't give. Once he's settled with a more appropriate woman, he'll figure out that I never meant to hurt him.

I spy a doughnut shop in the village, so I pull into one of the diagonal parking spaces and run into the shop. I order three cups of coffee and a dozen assorted doughnuts, then tuck the box under my arm and carefully balance the tray with the three covered coffees. Fortunately, an older gentleman sees my awkward burden and gallantly offers to hold the pastry box while I open my car door and set the coffees on the floor of the passenger side. I thank him with a smile and send him off to join his frowning wife.

And while I sit in the car, adding sweetener and creamer to my steaming coffee, I look up and spot the ice cream shop that has been part of the village strip for as long as I can remember. On hot summer afternoons, if we'd been good and not squabbled too badly, Grandma would put on her lipstick and take us to that shop for ice cream cones. Ginger would hold my hand and Rose's while Grandma walked up to the counter and placed her order.

I remember twisting around to see others waiting in line, women who saw us and whispered behind their cupped hands.

That Lillian . . . Though Grandma was happily married to Walter by the time we arrived, I always heard *Lillian* and knew they were talking about her. One woman who didn't bother to whisper once announced that Lillian had had as many husbands as Elizabeth Taylor. Grandma turned around, smiled, and said she'd actually had *more* husbands, because Liz had married the same man twice. "But"—Grandma arched a brow at the other woman—"at least I married my men before I slept with them."

I looked from Grandma to the gossip, not sure why the woman had gone red-faced, but Ginger practically yanked me and Rose out of the store, muttering under her breath as she dragged us out to the sidewalk. Ginger muttered a lot at Grandma Lillian's house, and not until years later did I understand why.

By that time I was beginning to see the same smug smiles on women's faces when I went to the ice cream counter alone. Only they weren't whispering Lillian's name, but mine.

GINGER

Feeling as empty as a church on Monday morning, I climb out of bed and shower in the small bathroom adjacent to my bedroom. After changing into tattered shorts and a paint-spattered T-shirt, I pull my laptop from my travel bag, grimly grateful that I remembered to bring the computer. Grandmother's house doesn't have wireless Internet, but with any luck, one of the neighbors might.

My laptop discovers four wireless signals, and one of them is wide-open. Using a neighbor's bandwidth (and hoping my intrusion doesn't slow their computer), I do a quick search for lawyers in the Savannah area. Though several of my choir kids have parents in the legal profession, Penny is right: I need a good divorce lawyer, not a friend who feels obligated to do me a favor. If I see a listing for *Brutal Bob Hatchett* or *Killer Karl Pounder* under "divorce attorneys," I'll call those numbers first.

My search turns up half a dozen names, none of which would instill terror at first glance. I examine several of the lawyers' websites, but I can't help seeing Michael's anguished face superimposed over the slick photos. Could he truly be sorry for having betrayed me, or is he only sorry he got caught? Was this his first affair, or has he been cheating for years? Does he love this other woman? Does he still love me? Does he care anything about the family we've established?

Within the first year of our marriage I realized that Michael tends to live in his head; it didn't take me long to learn that I would have to specifically explain how I needed him to meet my emotional needs. I learned not to expect lavish dinner dates, romantic cards, or a cake on my birthday . . . unless I told Michael to get them for me. At Christmas, I wasn't beneath buying myself something special, wrapping it, and writing "To Ginger from Michael" on the gift card. Sometimes Michael was so distracted by December exams, holiday parties, and student papers that he probably assumed he actually ordered the gifts in question.

What I can't understand is how another woman managed to get inside his head . . . something I've never really been able to do. Did she worm her way into his heart as well?

I set the disturbing thought aside and study my computer screen. Attorney Jo Edwards has a twenty-four-hour emergency number, which I dial on my cell phone. Though I don't expect anyone to answer on a Sunday morning, I may be able to leave a message. If Michael empties our accounts or tries to take my name off the deed to the house, I'll be left with nothing. At my age, starting over with an empty wallet is not a viable option. I'm not sure it's even possible.

My call puts me in touch with an answering service, where a nice woman speaks in soothing tones and takes my number. "I'll have Ms. Edwards return your call," she says. "I know this can be a confusing time, but we'll want to set up an appointment as soon as possible. Can you come in Tuesday morning?"

I think of the Realtor I still need to meet with, the work to be finished at the cottage, and the drive home. I could quit early and head back to Savannah tomorrow afternoon, but then I might have to spend several hours with Michael at home before I see the attorney.

I don't want to talk to him first. I'll sit down and hear his explanations after I've consulted a lawyer. Penny was right; I need to protect myself before I do anything else.

"I'm on St. Simons through Monday night," I tell the operator, "but I think I can make it to the office on Tuesday morning. As long as it's not too early."

"How about ten?" the operator asks. "You'll need to bring your financial records, a list of all marital accounts, and a check for the retainer."

"How much do I need for the retainer?"

"Thirty-five hundred dollars. The retainer will engage Ms. Edwards immediately so she can begin working on your case."

I draw a ragged breath. Setting an appointment, scraping up money . . . it's as though our future has already been decided and prearranged. How could a happy marriage disintegrate to divorce in a matter of days?

"Tuesday morning, then," I tell the operator. "Thanks for your help."

I thought I'd feel better after taking this important first step, but an acute sense of loss assails me as I toss my cell phone onto the bed. The downstairs quiet is broken by Penny's and Rose's voices. Then I hear a car door slam, an engine revving, and someone pulling away. Are my sisters bailing out on me?

I creep down the stairs in sock-covered feet and startle Rose, who is carrying that decrepit dog back into the house. "Sorry," I tell her, knowing I must look a fright. "I heard voices."

"Penny went for coffee." She carries the pitiful-looking creature over to his lumpy cushion, then gently lowers him to his bed. "I thought you might sleep in. Penny said you were up late."

"Technically I'm still up," I tell her. "I don't think I slept much at all."

She leaves the dog, then pulls a diet soda from the cooler and hands it to me. "It's not very cold, but it's caffeinated."

"Thanks."

She looks at me, her expression guarded. "I heard about Michael's visit."

I manage a wry smile as I pop the top of the soda can. "News travels fast."

"Ours is a small circle." Rose's smile trembles as she searches my face. "I know you're hurting, Ginger, and I understand a little of what you're feeling. But Michael's mistake isn't the end of the world, and it doesn't have to mean the end of your marriage."

"It's adultery." I spit out the word. "Even God allows divorce in the case of adultery."

"God may *allow* it, but he doesn't order it," Rose answers, gentle softness in her voice. "I'd just hate to see you throw away everything y'all have worked so hard to build. You two have a home, a history, and two fine sons—"

"Michael wants a divorce, so I've already engaged an attorney." I sip my soda, then climb onto one of the stools at the kitchen counter. "A lawyer named Jo Edwards. I'm meeting with her Tuesday morning. Somehow I have to find thirty-five hundred for the retainer." I rake my hand through my still-mussed hair and frown. "I suppose I could get a cash advance on my credit card and pay it back when we get our checks from the sale of the house."

"Think about it." Rose sits next to me, her eyes clouding. "Hiring a lawyer will send a signal to Michael."

"Isn't that what I want to do in this situation?"

Rose shakes her head. "That's a question you're gonna have to ask yourself."

Poor Rose. Even after three marriages, she still has trouble seeing the obvious. I rub my temple with my fingertips, wishing I could massage away my irritation with her useless suggestions. "Last night I learned that Michael's lover is pregnant. He's going to be a father, so if he wants to leave me and start a new family, I'm not about to stop him." My voice breaks. "And if that woman has a miscarriage, I'm not taking him back."

Rose stares at me, and beneath her blank expression I see a suggestion of struggle and passion, as though a hidden stream is trying to break through. But for some reason she won't speak up and tell me what she's thinking. . . .

"What?" I ask, exasperated. "Go ahead, say *I told you so*. Tell me I was wrong to judge you and Penny about your divorces; say I've been stupid for not understanding what y'all were going through."

Rose slides off her stool and begins to walk toward the hallway. "That's the last thing I'd ever say to you."

ROSEMARY

Safe in the shelter of Gran's room, I curl up on the tarnished brass bed and hug the spare pillow to my chest. The old wound is aching again, the empty place transmitting waves of scalding grief that burn every bone and nerve.

I swallow hard and cling more tightly to the pillow. I can't go on like this. Even in the agony of her pain, Ginger is stronger than I am. She will weather her storm and come out stronger on the other side. I don't have the energy to cope with my loss and hers too.

I wipe my streaming eyes and sit up, steeling myself to face these last two days with my sisters. Where is Penny? I need her; I need her standing between me and Ginger.

Ginger has always thought she could read me and Penny like billboards, but I don't think she ever had that ability. Maybe she could read us as children, but as adults we've developed techniques of subterfuge. We've learned how to hide in plain sight. Especially from family members.

My eldest sister ought to know me better than any other living person, but sometimes I think she can't see farther than the end of her own nose. As she ranted about how she wouldn't take Michael back even if the other woman had a *miscarriage* I struggled to keep from screaming. She glibly pronounced that awful word, and then assumed I was upset about *her*.

Where is Penny?

Knowing that Ginger will eventually come looking for me if I don't go back out to the living room, I smooth my hair and walk down the hall, finally dropping onto the couch. I glance around to see where Ginger is—staring out the kitchen window—and then I spot Grandma's bird blanket on the love seat.

"Oh!" I stand and gather the blanket into my arms, breathing in the scents of cotton and age. "Look at this! Did you find it?"

Ginger turns, her eyes widening as she recognizes the quilt. "What do you know, it's still here."

"Penny must have found it." I shake out the quilt and hold it to my chest as I run my index finger over the rudimentary embroidery that spells *Ricky* on every other square. "This is wonderful."

"Will miracles never cease," Ginger murmurs, but there's no wonder in her voice.

I bite my lip and fold the blanket into a rectangle, then set it on top of the pillow Justus uses for a bed. "Here, boy." I whistle. "Come sit on this, buddy. Doesn't that feel good?"

Jussy stops panting long enough to sniff the blanket, then he gingerly steps onto it, probably wondering why his bed feels different. "You'll learn to like it," I promise, "because this is a special quilt, made with lots of love."

Justus curls up beneath my hand and closes his eyes, ready for a morning nap. I place my hand on him, feeling the labored rise and fall of his chest, and wait for his panting to slow. When he finally sleeps, I go back to the couch.

I'm looking out the window, waiting for Penny, when my cell phone begins to ring. I'm startled, unable to imagine who'd call me this early, then I dive for my purse. Wort might have had an accident on the group ride. Or someone might have hurt one of the horses; our county has had trouble with people shooting pastured animals at random. . . .

I grab my purse, pull out my phone, and hold it to my ear, breathless. "Hello?"

"Sweetheart?" It's Wort's voice, and I'm relieved to hear him sounding strong and upbeat. "Hey, I just called to check in and tell you we're all here, ready for this ride—"

"Are you all right?"

"What? Of course." I hear the grumble of Harleys as my husband's voice drops half an octave. "I wanted to tell you good morning, is all. I miss you. And I want you to be careful on the drive home tomorrow, okay?"

For an instant I'm convinced that he's guessed my intentions. Wort is not sentimental, not the type to bring me unexpected candy and flowers. He never calls except to remind me to pick up something or to ask what it means when one of the horses won't settle in its stall.

Could my husband really be *missing* me?

"I love you," I tell him, careful not to look in Ginger's direction. I don't want her to think I'm flaunting my marriage while hers is falling apart.

"And you'll be careful tomorrow?"

I hesitate, not knowing how to answer. "If you'll be careful," I finally say, "on the ride today."

Wort's laughter—big, bold, and raucous—fills the line as I say good-bye.

I drop my phone back into my purse, my throat aching with remorse. I love that man. He has such a good heart.

How can I leave him?

A wave of guilt threatens to engulf me, but I push it back. Every decision in life means one option is chosen while another is forfeited. I have regrets about the relationships I'll be relinquishing, but those inconsistent joys cannot compare to the bliss of being pain free.

Besides, Wort deserves better than me; he always has.

GINGER

I know I shouldn't eavesdrop, but I can't help sneaking glances at Rose as she takes her call. She's obviously talking to Wort, and I'm surprised to see a blush brighten her cheeks when she tells him she loves him. Where did the blush come from? That honeymoon glow should have vanished long ago.

When Rose drops her phone back into her purse, I walk over and poke her with a fingertip. "Did you two have a spat or something?"

Rose's eyes fly open. "What? Oh, no. He just called to say he misses me."

"Must be nice."

Rose shakes her head. "I don't know what got into him. Wort doesn't usually do things like that."

We both look up when a car approaches and stops outside. A few minutes later Penny stomps across the porch and blows into the house, one hand holding a bakery box, the other carrying a tray of Styrofoam cups. She sets her burdens on the counter, then steps back and looks at us, her expression defensive above an abbreviated outfit that shrieks for attention. "What?"

I look at Rose, who presses her lips together and refuses to speak. "Nothing," I finally answer, one corner of my mouth twisting. "But seeing you reminds me of something Grandmother used to say: 'Nothing ages a woman faster than dressing to prove she's as young as ever.'"

"I don't have a clue what you're talking about." Penny opens the box of doughnuts, then glances at Rose. "Here's breakfast. And I brought coffee, if you want it."

I let the subject of Penny's ridiculous outfit drop and take one of the cups. "Thanks. Coffee beats warm soda any day."

Penny tosses a handful of sugar packets toward me. Rose takes a cup, too, and peeks into the bakery box. "Yum, doughnuts. And I'm glad you remembered napkins."

"I knew there weren't any left in this kitchen."

I prepare my coffee automatically, watching my fingers rip open a packet of sugar and dump the granules into the steaming black liquid. I'm struck by the realization that this coffee cup and I are a lot alike—we're both filled to the brim with hot liquid that will spill if jostled or shaken the least little bit. If I can get through this morning without crying, I'll feel like I've accomplished something.

"So," I say, injecting a false note of cheer into my voice as I remove a doughnut from the box, "Wort just called Rose to tell her how much she's missed. Has Bob checked in with you this morning, Penn?"

"He can't call me, remember?" Penny's wry smile contradicts the mischief in her eyes. "I left my phone at home. Now that he knows I'm safe, I doubt he'll want to bother either of you again." She picks up a glazed doughnut and takes a bite out of the sugary confection. "How do you do it, Rosie?" she mumbles around the food in her mouth. "How do you keep ol' Wort gulping at the love bucket?"

Rose makes a face. "I swan, you have a gift for making something sweet sound downright silly."

"You know what I mean." Penny flashes an unrepentant grin. "Bob never calls me unless he wants me to put something on his calendar. So how do you keep Wort so enthralled?"

Rose looks away as another flush brightens her face. "Wort actually doesn't call me much. Probably because I hardly ever go anywhere."

"He doesn't look like the sensitive type," I point out, more than willing to keep the conversation centered on Rose's husband. I'll lose it if anyone asks me about mine.

"Well, y'all know what they say about appearances," Rose answers. "You can't judge a man by his coveralls."

I smother a smile and lift another doughnut from the box. Touché, Rose. Anyone who looked at Michael would think him a dedicated and serious family man, but beneath his wool jacket and elbow patches he's as susceptible to a pretty woman's advances as any other male.

Rose finishes her doughnut and pulls a plastic container from her bag near the door, then whistles for the dog. "I'll feed Justus on the porch," she says. "Less mess that way."

The old dog must have heard her, because he staggers to his feet and shuffles to the door, picking up his pace as she rattles the kibble container.

Once Rose is out of the house, Penny glances at me. "Do you think Rose seems weird?"

I swallow another bite and shake myself out of my reverie. "Weirder than usual, you mean?"

"Yeah . . . she seems sort of detached. Like she has something on her mind, but she doesn't want to share it."

I wave Penny's worries away. "Rose always has something on her mind. If she's not worrying about Wort, she's fretting about her animals or trying to figure out how to stop us from eating meat."

"That's another thing—she hasn't tried to convert us to vegetarianism, not once. Last night she watched me eat a hamburger without saying a word."

"Last night we had other things on our minds. Or maybe she's realized you're a lost cause."

"But it's not like Rose to give up once she's set her mind on something."

I finish my second doughnut and reluctantly admit Penny has a point. Rose is doggedly stubborn, even in the face of opposition.

"Maybe she misses Grandma," Penny suggests, lifting her coffee cup. "After all, she drove up to Brunswick nearly every weekend after Lillian entered the home. Being here, surrounded by all of these things—she must be missing Grandma something awful."

"She went to Brunswick every weekend?" This announcement floods me with guilt. I didn't visit the retirement home more than a couple of times, but then I remind myself that Rose doesn't have a full-time job and she doesn't have kids, so she's the only one of us who could find the time to drive up here. Plus, Jacksonville's only an hour away, so she didn't have to drive far.

"I'm just glad she could go." Penny pushes the doughnut box toward me, silently inviting me to take another. "She told me once that she really didn't appreciate Grandma until she'd grown up and gotten married herself. That's when she started to see Lillian as a friend, not a parental figure."

Will Rose or Penny ever see *me* as a friend?

I can understand why Rose might be feeling nostalgic this weekend, maybe even a little sad. After all, as the youngest, she was the last to leave Grandma and this cottage.

But her sadness is nothing compared to what I'm feeling now. Her emotions are bittersweet; mine are raw and acrid. Rose is missing the past; I am facing a drastically changed future. The pain Rose must be feeling is a natural part of growing up and saying good-bye; my pain is unnatural and devastating.

As hard as it is to bear, at least I'm not here alone. I have my sisters, and I have . . . pastry.

When I finish my third doughnut Penny offers me another, but this time I shake my head. The last thing I need is more sugared pastry . . . for now. After all, that bakery box isn't going anywhere.

I sip my coffee and lean against the counter, taking in the painted kitchen cabinets, the scalloped trim, and the yellow and white gingham wallpaper. The dated decor now strikes me as hideous, but when I was young this cottage felt like a magical retreat. This was where we ran around in bare feet, where we danced in the

sprinkler, and carried our buckets and shovels to the beach to dig
for crabs. This is the place where I could relax and let Grandmother
be the boss, where I didn't have to worry so much about keeping
my sisters in line.

That was childhood, but like the song says, once you pass its
borders, you can never return again. No matter how much you
want to.

As something Michael said comes back to me, I set my coffee
on the counter and look at Penny. "If you could go back in time,
would you change some of the decisions you've made?"

"Are you kidding?"

"I'm just . . . curious."

Penny tilts her head and bites her lip before answering. "My
first instinct was to say yes, sure, but I don't really think so. After
all, we all do what we think is best given who and where we are at
the moment, right? Nobody goes around making stupid decisions
on purpose."

I snort softly. "Maybe some people do."

"But not most people. Not *reasonable* people. We do what we
think is right, and if we regret those decisions later, it's only because
we've learned something so we can look back and see where we
went wrong."

If I could turn back time, would Michael succumb to the
charms of his coworker again? If Penny's right, he would . . . unless
something happened to change him.

Now change is barreling down on us, whether we welcome it
or not.

"So," Rose says, leading her dog back into the house, "did you
and Michael have a good talk last night?"

I draw a deep breath. "We talked. I can't say that anything good
came out of it."

"Did he—did you—make any plans?"

"He says he still loves me. But since his girlfriend is pregnant,
he's afraid he'll lose his job if he doesn't marry her."

Rose leans on the counter, her expression soft and sympathetic. "I'm sorry to hear that. I can barely believe it."

"I couldn't believe it, either." I choke back a sob. "I've been awake all night, trying to figure out if I've suddenly become repulsive or something. Michael says he still loves me, but obviously he doesn't find me as attractive as he finds *her*—"

"Honestly, Ginger," Penny interrupts, "I have to ask. Do you even own a push-up bra?"

I stare at her, speechless.

"I mean, surely they have a Victoria's Secret in Savannah," Penny rattles on. "You ought to get yourself some luscious lingerie, sleep in something besides sweatpants and T-shirts."

I turn my gaze to Rose, who stands frozen at the counter, her eyes wide. "Rose"—my voice is choked—"are you hearing what I'm hearing?"

Penny looks from me to Rose, then frowns. "I'm not telling you anything but the bald-faced truth. Men are visual creatures; they like pretty women."

"Marriage is about loving someone because of who they *are*, not what they look like," I snap. "I wouldn't want a man who was so shallow I could keep him from straying by wearing a tacky bra."

"All right, so why not please the not-shallow man who loves you for who you are?" Penny shrugs. "This ain't rocket science we're talking about."

A single thought occurs to me: Penny is insane. No, not insane, *superficial*. Silly. Small-minded. The relationship Michael and I shared wasn't based on underwear; it was born out of mutual respect, deep concern, and the understanding that neither of us was complete without the other. His strengths called to my weaknesses; my strengths enabled him to follow his destiny. We were a team, a pair, two of a kind.

And she thinks that kind of relationship can be repaired if I enhance my bustline?

I hold up my hand, swallow hard, and inform my sisters that I'm going outside for some air.

_____

When I have recovered—and Rose assures me that Penny has promised never again to mention underwear or sex appeal—we reconvene in the kitchen. I gather what remains of my tattered dignity and stand by the table as Penny and Rose look at me, awaiting instructions. I feel more anguished than motivated, but we've come here to do a job, and I'm hoping the work will take my mind off Michael and my murdered marriage.

"The bedrooms," I say simply. "The closets. The attic. Today we need to empty those areas, so tomorrow we can clean."

"We're beginning to trip over the thrift store stuff." Penny gestures to the bags and boxes along the kitchen wall. "Can we move some of those out to the front porch?"

"I don't think anybody's going to take them if we leave them outside for one night."

"If somebody wants them, they can have them," Rose adds. "I don't care if someone steals Grandma's castoffs."

And so we split up. I go back upstairs to the front bedroom and tackle the closet again, while Penny works in the blue bedroom at the back of the house. Rose, naturally, chooses to work in Grandmother's bedroom.

I pull vintage clothing, bags of quilt squares, and several bags of yarn from the closet. Under a bed I find a box of record albums; I hope the thrift store appreciates them. Grandmother had good taste in music, so I'm sure she had a wonderful collection.

We work for two hours, and after my third trip up and down the stairs I realize that Rose was smart to work on the first floor. My thighs are beginning to burn.

Just before lunch I am at the kitchen sink, washing a layer of dust from my hands, when Penny pauses by the front window.

"We've got company," she says, looking out at the road. "Some woman with red hair just pulled up in a Mercedes. Are you expecting anyone?"

For an instant I draw a blank, then I reach for a dishtowel. "I'll bet it's our Realtor. She was going to bring papers for us to sign."

"She needs all three of us?"

"I would imagine so."

"I'll get Rose." Penny goes to the back bedroom while I open the front door. Barbara Jones, who is about twenty pounds heavier than she looks in the photo on her business card, comes up the steps with a folder in one hand, a cell phone in the other.

"You made it." She greets me with a broad smile as her stilettos tap across the front porch. "Did your sisters make the trip too?"

"We're all here. Come on in and see the progress we've made."

She walks in and breathes deeply, surveying the piles of boxes, the bulging trash bags, and the open cupboards. "Wonderful! The place looks fresher already. The new owner's going to appreciate working from a clean slate. I think he's planning some major renovations."

For some reason, my stomach tightens at the thought of changes to this cottage. "He's renovating?"

"He has good ideas," she assures me. "Granite countertops, new wood cabinets, new colors for the exterior and the porch. I think he also wants to install new carpet upstairs."

I nod. "That doesn't sound too bad. I'd hate for anyone to destroy the character of this place."

"He loves the cottage's charm, so y'all don't have to worry about that. And now"—she pulls several papers from her folder and spreads them on the old pine table—"it's time to sign the official sales contract."

I pick up the pages and skim them; everything seems in order. The buyer is purchasing the property for a determined price, he will close and take possession on the fifteenth of the month, the property is being sold "as is," and it's a cash transaction.

I tap the paragraph about the buyer's right to inspection. "I trust the inspection went okay? I haven't been here in years, so I have no idea what kind of condition the electrical and plumbing systems are in—"

"The house passed with flying colors," Barbara says. "It's in great shape for a home of this age. We found no major problems."

"That's good."

I bend and sign my name on one of the lines reserved for the seller. By the time I've finished, Penny and Rose have joined us at the table.

I make polite introductions and then gesture to the contract. "We need a signature from each of you," I tell my sisters, wishing everything in life was this simple.

"I'm going to need your signature on some closing documents too," the Realtor says, looking at Penny and Rose. "But I'll overnight those copies as soon as they're ready for the closing. I don't foresee any problems at all."

When Rose has finished signing, I gather up the papers and return them to Barbara. "Thanks for stopping by. We'll leave our keys on the kitchen counter when we go."

"That'd be fine. And oh!" The Realtor lifts a manicured index finger. "I forgot to mention this the other day, but when I first opened the house after Lillian's passing, I found a box on the front porch—I believe it came from the retirement home where your grandmother stayed. A nurse gathered what remained of her personal possessions, boxed them up, and had them delivered here. I thought y'all might like to look through those things, so I put the box in the storage closet upstairs. I thought about leaving it in a bedroom closet, but we like those spaces to look uncluttered when a property is on the market."

"Thank you." I glance at Penny. "Have we found that box?"

"No." Penny crosses her arms. "I haven't had time to look in the upstairs closet yet."

"I'm sure you'll want to go through the box carefully," Barbara says as she moves toward the front door. "No telling what sort of treasures y'all may find inside. Well, happy cleaning! And congratulations on the sale."

We tell Barbara good-bye and watch her tap across the porch, then all of us turn toward the stairs. Since I have the longest legs, I lead the way.

"You know Grandma Lillian didn't have any real treasures," Rose says, huffing up the stairs behind me. "I'm pretty sure there couldn't be anything valuable in the box."

I grab the handrail. "Then why are you running?"

"You don't know there's nothing valuable," Penny says, crowding my right side. "Maybe one of the husbands left her some nice jewelry. Or some stocks. Like Apple computers or Microsoft."

"I doubt that's true," I add, panting. "But she did have all those wedding bands—"

"They've been pawned," Rose answers. "Through the years, she got rid of all of them except Walter's, and I think she was wearing that one in her casket."

I don't remember that detail, but I'm not about to resent Grandmother's right to wear a simple gold band to her grave. I turn left at the landing and pull on the painted door of the overlooked closet. The three of us crowd into a dark and airless space.

"Oh!" Rose takes a breath and coughs. "It's awful stuffy up here."

I pull on a dangling cord and relax when light blazes from a bare lightbulb in the ceiling. The closet space is long and narrow, extending from the middle of the house to the eaves under the sloping roofline. One of the husbands walled and floored this area, but he forgot to allow for ventilation.

"There." Behind me, Penny points at a cardboard box on the floor. The box originally held canned milk, but someone used a Magic Marker to write *Lillian George* on the top. I kneel and lift the box into my arms, then stand and turn into a swaying cobweb. "Blech!"

"Let's take it out," Rose says. "It's too hot to open anything in here."

She leads the way into the blue bedroom, where the pillow still bears the imprint of Penny's head. I set the box on the bed and rip away a long strip of packing tape, then lift the flaps.

The box isn't deep, but it's filled to the brim with Lillian's final possessions. A folded note rests on the top of the collection.

Penny unfolds the note and reads aloud:

February 10, 2010
To whom it may concern:
It was my pleasure to care for Miss Lillian in her final weeks. She passed away this afternoon during her nap time. I have cleaned out her room and collected the few items she asked me to set aside for her heirs. I trust that you will enjoy looking through these things and remembering how delightful she was. She was a treasure and a blessing to all who knew her.

Liz Dorset, nurse's aide

Together, Penny, Rose, and I lean forward and peer into the unexpected box.

ELEVEN

PENNYROYAL

I don't know why we all gravitate toward that box—maybe morbid curiosity, maybe the hope of discovering some overlooked treasure. But gravitate we do, and Ginger begins to poke at items as if she's afraid a rat or a roach is fixin' to scurry out and attack her. I'm not as squeamish, so I plunge both hands into the box and lift out an armful of stuff—a faded housecoat, a pair of pink slippers, a stationery box, a pair of glasses, a worn Bible, and a journal. Ginger opens the stationery box and discovers dozens of photos, mostly shots of Lillian's husbands and us girls, while Rose sits and pulls the journal onto her lap.

"What is all this?" Ginger gives me a handful of the photos. "See if you recognize anyone. If not, I don't see why we need to keep these."

I scan several of the square photographs, many of them in faded color or black-and-white. I'm looking at beach photos of women in one-piece bathing suits, most of their faces too small and distant to be recognized. I also find several snapshots of a black cocker spaniel. I don't remember Grandma ever having a cocker when we came to visit. So either this is someone else's dog, or my memory has developed some serious gaps.

I hold up one of the dog pictures. "Anybody remember Grandma having a cocker spaniel?"

"Cinder," Ginger replies without even looking. "She had him for years."

"Okay . . . so maybe aspartame does cause memory loss. I don't remember a dog at all."

Ginger lowers the pictures in her hand and looks at me. "You were just a baby when Grandmother married Walter. That's how she got the dog—it was Walter's before they married." Her eyes soften. "I was a flower girl in their wedding; that's why I remember it. They had me walk the dog down the aisle during the ceremony."

"Are you serious?" Rosemary's eyes widen. "I never knew that."

Ginger's gaze shifts to the photo in my hand. "Yeah—I remember Momma had a fit. She kept saying animals didn't belong in a wedding, but Grandma just laughed and said this would be her last trip down the aisle so she was going to do what she wanted. By then I guess she'd figured out how to make a marriage work."

When Ginger's voice breaks I look at Rose, not sure if we should comfort Ginger or pretend we don't notice her pain.

Rose provides a welcome distraction when she pulls a battered tape recorder from the bottom of the container. "Oh, good!" she says, untangling the electrical cord. "I knew she had this at the home, but I assumed we'd never see it again."

Surprise blossoms on Ginger's face. "Why on earth did Grandmother need a tape recorder?"

"Why, to listen to audiobooks. She loved books on tape, and I tried to bring her a new one every weekend. She especially loved mysteries."

"She did a lot more than listen," I add, bringing up a handful of plastic from the depths of the box. I turn a clear bag, displaying its contents: a handful of cassette tapes, each labeled in Grandma's slanted handwriting.

"She made tapes?" Ginger cuts a look from the recorder to the plastic bag. "Who taught her how to make tapes?"

"It's not rocket science." Rose takes the bag from me. "I'd like to listen to these sometime."

Ginger peers over a cardboard flap, but there are no stock certificates at the bottom of the box, only one other item: a photo album. She crinkles her nose as if she expects it to be dusty, so I lift it out and settle on the corner of the bed to look through it. I'm gonna flip through it quickly, and if I don't recognize any faces I'll toss it into a garbage bag. Seems a shame to throw out perfectly good memories, but if these pictures are anything like those in the stationery box, they aren't *my* memories.

Unlike with the jumble of disorganized photos we found earlier, Grandma took an artistic approach with the volume in my lap. The opening page features only one photo, a formal, posed shot of an older couple holding a baby in a lace dress. The image is sepia-toned, and someone has handwritten a caption: *Lillian Irene Harper, born January 6, 1915.*

"Wow." I whistle softly. "Have y'all ever seen Grandma as a baby?"

Rosemary drops the journal she's been leafing through and peers over my shoulder. "That's a nice picture. You ought to keep it."

"We should probably keep the whole album. Looks like Grandma spent some time on this one." The second photo is as formal as the first, but years have passed between events. This photo displays a bride and a groom—the man wears a tux, the woman is dressed in a lace sheath and a tightly fitted cap. The bride's features are smooth and unlined, and in them I see traces of the grandmother I knew and loved.

"Grandma was a beautiful bride." I run my finger over the writing at the bottom of the picture. "'Mr. and Mrs. Charles Winslow, June 1931.' She was sixteen years old."

"Charles Winslow." Rose slides into the space by my side and peers at the photograph. "Husband number one. I think he's the guy who went off to war and died at the invasion of Normandy. Gran always said Charlie was a hero."

"They might have been happy for a lifetime." I peer at Charlie's face. "He looks like a good guy."

"Who's that?" Ginger leans over and taps the next page, where we see a young Lillian standing in church, a boy and a girl by her side. Lillian is dressed in black; the children wear somber expressions as they hold her hands.

I peer at the spidery handwriting. "'Donald and Ruby Winslow, 1944.' I'll bet this shot was taken at Charlie's memorial service. I don't think he ever made it back to the States."

I pause, realizing that my grandfather's body lies somewhere in France, maybe even beneath one of those white crosses that stand like silent sentinels at Normandy. I've never lost anyone in war, so I can't imagine what Grandma must have endured. And her children—Donny couldn't have been more than twelve in this picture, and Ruby's face is still round with baby fat.

"Is that our mother?" Rose asks, her voice trembling.

"Yes." Ginger looks down, her lashes shuttering her eyes. "That's Momma."

A wisp of anxiety creeps into my mood. I don't know how far Grandma went with this photo album, but if this is a complete family history, dark chapters lie ahead. We might see pictures we don't want to see or discuss.

"Is that journal still around?" I ask, hoping to change the subject. "I'd like to know how a war widow survived in those days."

Rose offers a ready answer: "She married again."

I'd like to halt this trip down memory lane, but Rose turns the page. Sure enough, we see yet another picture of Lillian in a bridal outfit, a suit. In this photo she's holding a bouquet so big it nearly obscures her tiny waistline. The broad man next to her wears a dark suit, and a hat shadows his eyes. His smile, however, is wide and toothy, and his hand rests protectively upon the arm Lillian has linked through his.

"'Joseph Goldstein,'" Rosemary reads. "'1945.'"

"So that's Joe Goldstein." I study the photograph more closely, realizing that the shot was taken at some sort of depot, probably a train station. The happy couple stands on a platform, with Donny and Ruby positioned on the stairs in front of them. Neither child is smiling, and neither has changed much since the photo taken at their father's memorial service.

"Lillian didn't waste much time," I remark, my tone dry.

Rose rises to Grandma's defense. "Think about it. Gran didn't have many choices in life. She once told me that she had to drop out of school in the eighth grade because her parents needed her help on the farm. She was always embarrassed about her lack of schooling."

Ginger lifts a brow. "They didn't have compulsory education in those days?"

"They didn't have a lot of programs we're used to," Rose says. "Grandma was pretty and smart, but her family was dirt poor. They ate what they could grow in their garden, and early on she realized that a good marriage would be her ticket out of poverty."

"Looks like she struck it rich with Mr. Goldstein," I point out. "Look at the size of those orchids."

"Gran said he was nice enough," Rose adds, "but because he was older and Jewish, his family never accepted her. Plus, he must have weighed two hundred and fifty pounds when they married, and he didn't get any thinner as time went on. He also smoked like a stovepipe—nearly everybody did in those days. He died a few years after they were married."

I struggle to remember what Grandma told me about Mr. Goldstein, but I can't recall her ever mentioning him. Either that, or my memory holds as much as a sieve. "Did Joe at least leave her a little money?"

"Some—and he left her this house," Rose continues, looking at me with an almost imperceptible note of pleading on her face. "I think he died in 1950—and I only remember that because Grandma said he passed around the time the Korean conflict broke out. Donny signed up for the air force in '51 and went overseas, but he died a few days before the armistice was declared in '53."

When Rose looks at me again, I think I know why she's so interested in these photos. All this talk about people long gone is for Ginger's sake. Rose is trying to distract Ginger from her own troubles.

But how can Ginger forget everything that's happened?

I glance at my elder sister, whose expression has darkened with unreadable emotions. She's been relatively quiet today, behaving as if she's been drained of her usual energy. I've seen Ginger exhausted, but I've never seen her like this—beaten down. Defeated. Lost.

But she's staring at the pictures, so she's at least pretending to be engaged in the conversation. I glance at Rose, then elbow Ginger. "What do you think, Gingerbread?"

GINGER

Penny's question hangs in the air, but it takes me a while to gather my thoughts and respond. "I haven't heard any of this. I thought I knew Grandmother well, but I had no idea . . ."

Rose clears her throat. "Gran didn't like to dwell on the past, but she had a hard time in her younger days. She was lonely after Mr. Goldstein died, so she married again. The next guy wasn't such a good choice." She lifts the corner and peeks at the next page, then nods and flips it. "There, that's number three, Arthur Carey. I don't know when she put this album together, but I'm surprised she included his picture. He was a complete loser."

"A history's not complete," I murmur, my thoughts drifting toward the secrets Michael has been hiding from me, "unless it's honest."

I study the picture on the page. Another black-and-white wedding shot, but this time Lillian is wearing discreet widow's colors. The man next to her is tall and thin, his face seamed with deep wrinkles.

Penny recoils from the image. "Good grief, he looks like somebody's grandfather. How old was he?"

"Not that old, I don't think," Rose answers. "But he was a mess. Grandma married him because he was besotted with her, but I think he was even more in love with his booze. A couple of years later he took a fatal dive off a hotel balcony—no one ever knew if he fell because he was drunk or if he was pushed by one of his gambling buddies. Grandma never said so, but I got the feeling she was relieved to see him go."

"How do you know so much about these men?" Penny catches Rose's eye. "Grandma never talked to me about these guys."

She shrugs. "I spent a lot of time with her at the retirement home. One weekend I helped her sort through her photos, but I didn't know she meant to put them in a book. I think she did this just for us."

Penny turns the page. Lillian is wearing her bridal suit in the next picture, but this time she's standing next to a stout, broad-faced man in baggy trousers and a short-sleeved shirt. She has slipped one arm around his waist but his hands are clasped together, almost as if he is afraid to touch her. She's not carrying a bouquet, though an arrangement of beribboned carnations adorns her right shoulder.

"Stanislaw Bobinsky," Rose says, chuckling. "Number four. Not very politically correct, but she called him her little Polack."

Even I can't stop a smile. "There's not much *little* about him. He's bigger than Joe Goldstein."

"She loved him," Rose explains, "but though he married her, he never got over his first wife. He was nice to Grandma, but never in love with her the way she wanted him to be. She tried to stick things out for the sake of the marriage, but she ended up divorcing him."

"Because he was still mourning his first wife?" Penny asks.

"I don't know why," Rose says. "Grandma didn't say. But I'm sure she had her reasons."

"No one goes through a divorce without a good reason," Penny adds, looking at me. She seems to be sending me an unspoken message, but I'm not sure I want to hear it.

She turns the page and we find another shot of Lillian with a man. She's still an attractive, vibrant woman, but touches of gray adorn her hairline, and her face has broadened with age. The rectangular man in a spiffy suit next to her is heavyset and crew cut, his face dominated by a bulbous nose.

"'Edward Gordon,'" Penny reads the inscription. "Number five, the husband of 1959."

"Look there." I tap the image of a younger woman in the background. "That's Momma. She would have been about nineteen when Grandmother married Ed."

Rose and Penny lean closer, intent upon studying the woman they barely knew. Our mother is dark-haired, lovely, and smiling, her waist as thin as a pencil. She is laughing at someone we can't see, and I can't help but wonder if she's talking to our father. She married at twenty, so it's certainly possible.

I want to ask Rose if Grandmother told her anything about Mom and Dad's courtship, but I abandon the effort when an unexpected lump rises in my throat. Instead, I turn the page and find another traditional wedding photo. A bride in a long white dress and veil stands on carpeted church steps, her wedding party fanning out to the right and left. The young groom stands next to her in a dark suit, his hair slicked into place with some kind of oil. Both bride and groom look slightly nervous, maybe even embarrassed.

Penny reads the caption: "'Ruby Winslow marries Albert Lawrence, Valdosta Chapel, 1960.'"

"Mom and Dad," I say, my voice thick. "Isn't Momma beautiful?"

"Yeah, for an old maid," Rosemary deadpans, but no one laughs. None of us can tear our eyes away from the picture. I study the attendants, searching for another familiar face, maybe a relative, but I don't recognize anyone.

"Mom's only brother died in Korea, and our father's siblings disapproved of the marriage, so they stayed away," Rose says, apparently intuiting my thoughts. "Mom wasn't Catholic, and Gran said Catholics were real set on marrying each other in those days."

Penny flips the page and we find a photo of our mother and father holding a baby. Me.

"Ginger," Rose announces. "Born in 1961—the same year Ed Gordon went to prison and the Vietnam War began."

I look up. "Remind me—why'd Ed go to prison?"

"Income-tax evasion." The corner of Rose's mouth dips. "After Gran married him, she learned that he hadn't paid taxes in years. If she'd stayed married, she could have been indicted for income-tax evasion, too, so she divorced him to save herself. The government took nearly everything they had to settle Ed's debt. She got to keep this house only because it had never been in Ed's name."

"Ouch; all these facts are hurting my head." Penny closes her eyes and presses the meaty part of her hand to her forehead. "I can't keep all these men straight. How did Grandma do it?"

"How do *you* do it?" I ask, but there's no rancor in my voice. I'm beginning to realize that not everyone can expect to find happiness-ever-after on the other side of the altar.

Penny straightens her spine as she turns another page. "I manage."

The next photo features Grandma Lillian in a deck chair, sunglasses over a bright smile, and her hand on a handsome man's arm. Even though styles have changed in the passing decades, time could never diminish the man's subtle sex appeal. Stubbled chin, strong jaw, dark eyes, tousled brown hair, broad shoulders . . .

Penny lets out a low whistle. "Please tell me this is one of the husbands and not some miscellaneous boy toy."

Rose smiles. "What kind of girl do you think Lillian was? That's Thomas James, number six. Grandma was forty-seven when she met him, but she still managed to drag him to a justice of the peace."

Penny runs her finger over the man's striking profile. "I don't think I ever heard her mention him. Why is that?"

"Because after the divorce she always referred to him as 'that no-good philanderer.' Sometimes I think she forgot he had a name."

I shake my head. "Why would a man like that get married?"

"He met her here, on St. Simons," Rose says. "Saw her sunning on the beach and assumed she was a wealthy widow who kept a second home on the island. After they were married, he realized she wasn't as rich as he supposed. So he kept catting around, and she tried to put up with it . . . until she came home and found another woman in her bed. Then she sent Mr. James packing."

The words slide easily off Rose's lips, but a sharp tone underlines her voice. By the time she finishes, I know she's no longer thinking about unfaithful Thomas James, but about Michael. Maybe she's wondering if he ever brought another woman into my bed.

"Let's move on." Penny flips the page to a color snapshot of our mother in a hospital bed with another newborn in her arms. I see my four-year-old self hanging over the bed rail, my eyes intent on the baby, while Dad hovers over the little family.

"Finally." Penny smiles as though she's accomplished something simply by showing up. "About time I arrived."

I study the picture of my younger self, searching for signs of jealousy in my childish features. My expression isn't exactly joyful; more than anything, I look . . . confused.

Penny lifts a brow. "Not sure what to think about your baby sister, were you?"

I snort softly. "Put yourself in my place. For four years we got along perfectly well without you and then—bam! Another girl in the house. I had to adjust."

The next picture is almost a copy of its predecessor—another shot of the family, with Ruby again in a hospital bed. Albert leans over her pillow, and a slightly taller version of me watches from the other side. But this time Albert holds the new infant, while a chubby-cheeked toddler—Penny—stands behind me and peers around the big sister.

"And the family is finally complete," I say, my voice flat.

I glance at Rose, but the glow of nostalgia has vanished from her face. She is focused on the photo, her eyes dark and searching.

Curious, I study the picture again—our mother is smiling, but her smile is not wide and her eyes are not smiling at all.

Did the darkness that claimed her life have its roots in that moment? Or had it begun to grow long before?

I find no answers in the picture, but the snapshot reveals other details I missed at first glance. I see a serious older sister reaching for the baby; did I feel responsible for my younger sisters even then? I see the doting father, all smiles as he beams at the new arrival. I see the vacant mother, and I see the overlooked middle child who can't seem to find her place in the family order.

Again, I look at our mother's face. Something is off, something subtle. The shot of mother-with-baby-in-bed is almost a cliché, yet my mother's arms are empty. Did she not want to hold her newest daughter? Or was Daddy so taken with his pretty little Rose that he asked for the honor?

I lower my gaze, not wanting either of my sisters to read my thoughts. Depression is no longer the mystery it once was; people recognize it as a clinical illness and treat it appropriately. But few people understood "the baby blues" in 1968, and no one expected the condition to continue for several months after a baby's birth.

Penny turns the page and I brace for what we might see, but the next picture features Lillian standing with yet another man at the front of a church. Number seven, Walter George, is the husband who would remain by Lillian's side until he died thirty years later. Grandmother finally got it right.

She is older in this picture, her hair streaked with gray, and fifty-five-year-old Walter's tummy tugs at the button of his suit coat. I am in the small wedding party, a little girl holding a black cocker spaniel on a leash.

Lillian has not included photos of our mother's funeral. Instead she left a blank page, perhaps out of respect for the myriad questions that surround a suicide. The final photo features three little girls dancing in the wave wash on St. Simons Beach.

Needing time alone to recover from his loss, in 1969 our father put us on a train and sent us off to South Georgia and our first summer with Grandmother Lillian.

Feeling as droopy and dust-covered as the blades on the ceiling fan, I stretch out across the head of the big iron bed as Rose and Penny recap the history of the husbands. Penny asks questions about people she never knew, and Rose responds with stories and conjecture she's heard over the years, mostly from Grandmother Lillian. I close my heavy eyes, noticing how carefully both Penny and Rose avoid discussing our mother's death and our father's emotional abandonment.

They chatter like magpies, probably hoping their bright conversation will engage me somehow. But I don't want to be engaged today; I don't want to talk to anyone. I really don't want to be here anymore, but I've nowhere else to go. I am . . . unattached and alone.

I open my eyes and study the ceiling and the plaster walls around me. This room used to be a magical place. This iron bed was unlike any other—I remember falling into it and rolling to the center, where I could sleep cocooned by a mountain of warm quilts. When I wasn't sleeping, I could sit on the mounded covers and become a princess as Grandmother draped me in jewels, sang for my entertainment, and assured me that she loved me most of all.

But now the room seems faded and barren. Now I know the jewels were only cut glass, the songs were outdated folk tunes, and Grandmother's assurance was only a benevolent lie.

Just like all of Michael's promises.

My attention drifts away on a tide of exhaustion, and I float on the edge of sleep.

I am walking home from elementary school on a quiet afternoon when I remember, too late, that I am supposed to go home with a friend from my second-grade class. Momma is gonna be furious with me for being at the house when I should be at my friend's, but what can I do? This isn't the first time I've forgotten where I'm supposed to go, and the other time I tried to go back to school, only to have my frantic parents search our house, my friend's house, and every inch of the highway between school and home before they found me.

"Stay put," Momma told me later that day. "If you keep wandering around we'll go crazy with worry. Get someplace safe and stay there."

So I should definitely stay put. A blanket of quiet stillness lies over the house when I slip the key from under the mat and unlock the door, but then I remember that three-year-old Penny and baby Rose are probably at the sitter's. Momma should be here, though, because she has to work tonight. She always works at the hospital on Tuesday nights.

"Momma?"

I walk into the kitchen, where the black cat clock wags its tail in time to the tick of the second hand, but there's no sign of Momma. I check the living room, where the TV is playing a soap opera, but though a laundry basket of unfolded clothes waits on the end of the couch, Momma isn't there. I go into my parents' bedroom, thinking that maybe Momma wanted to rest, but the unmade bed is empty.

Then I hear another rhythm . . . a ticking from the bathroom, but there is no clock in that room. The door is cracked, unlocked, and water is ticking, *drip-drop, drip-drop*, onto the tile floor. When I push the door open wider, I see her white shoes waiting by the side of the sink and long brown hair spilling over the rim of the claw-footed tub.

Relief washes over me. "Momma?"

Momma doesn't like to be interrupted in the bath, especially when she's tired. But she says nothing, and her arm dangles over the side of the tub in perfect stillness, like she's fallen asleep. I step closer, noticing the dark fringe of her lashes against her pale cheek. Is she taking a nap?

I feel a coldness in my tummy, the hollowness of fear, as I stare at my mother's pale face. "Momma, are you . . ."

I look down and see that Momma is bathing in raspberry Kool-Aid. The water shouldn't be this dark or so thick I can't see her legs in the tub. No matter what she's doing, she's gonna be late for work, so she'll be cross with me for sure.

I look at the floor, where the white tiles have been splashed with droplets rolling down Momma's arm and falling from her fingertips. Not raspberry Kool-Aid, but blood.

————————

I awaken as if slapped by an invisible hand. I blink, adjusting to the reality of where and who I am, and after a minute I lift my head and look at Penny and Rose, who are still talking as if they haven't noticed that I dozed off.

Relieved, I sit up and rub my arms, aware that my skin still bears goose bumps from the dream-cloaked memory. "It's lunchtime," I announce, ready to move on. "We can't spend all weekend reminiscing when there's work to be done."

Penny grumbles and sets the photo album and journal aside, but Rose volunteers to go out and pick up lunch. "Have you ever tried a veggie sandwich?" she asks, looking at me with an arched brow. "There's a sub shop in the village, so I could be back in a flash."

"Okay, bring me a sandwich," I tell her. "But you'd better put some meat on mine."

Rose makes a face, but she heads down the stairs, and two seconds later we hear the front door slam.

Penny stacks the photo album, the journal, and the stationery box on the bureau. "That was more fun than I thought it'd be. I'm glad Grandma put all those pictures together for us. I only wish Daddy had liked her a little better."

I stare at her, amazed. "Why would he send us to St. Simons every summer if he didn't like Grandmother?"

"He *needed* her," Penny answered, "but I don't think he liked her much. Don't you remember how he was always making jokes about the husbands? Sometimes I think he blamed her . . . you know, for how Momma died. *I* know Grandma had nothing to do with it, but he had to blame somebody."

Penny's statement raises the hair on my arms. I know what she means, but I would never have voiced the thought aloud even though I've often wondered if Grandma didn't pave the way for Penny's and Rose's multiple marriages. She really wasn't the best example.

And even though we don't talk about it, we all know the awful truth about our mother—she killed herself in the bathtub, not slitting her wrists in a theatrical gesture, but by efficiently slicing deep into her upper arm with a straight-edged razor, severing the brachial artery. I learned the truth from Grandmother, not from Dad, who refused to talk about Momma or utter the word *suicide* until the day he died.

But as awful as the story was, we needed the truth to make sense of our situation. Why would our mom leave us? Why did God allow her to die? Could death swoop down like a big, black bird and take anyone it wanted, at any time?

Questions haunted our childish imaginations and woke us in the middle of the night, leaving us terrified and in tears. Dad tried his best to comfort us, but our father was an awkward nurturer, and the dreams kept coming back.

Yet Grandmother realized what we needed. A careful dose of the truth, administered at the right time, by the right person, in the right way.

"Sometimes," she told me after a nightmare woke me one night not long after Mother's death, "a woman gets the blues right after a baby's born. No one can understand that dark feeling unless they've experienced it, but it's like a heavy cloud that just won't blow away. Your momma resisted that cloud for months, honey. She fought it until she didn't have the strength to fight anymore." Tears trickled down Grandmother's cheeks as she wrapped her arms around me. "When she thought the sky had plumb run out of blue, that's when she took her life."

At eighteen, I read *exsanguination* on the coroner's report and learned the medical details. Mom had worked as a nurse's aide, so she knew how quickly a person could bleed out. Yet despite all the explanations I collected over the years, I've never fully understood how she could choose to leave three little girls who needed her.

But now, tired and heartsick, without the love of my husband or the comfort of my sons, I am beginning to understand the suffocating darkness of despair.

TWELVE

GINGER

After lunch, Penny suggests that we can move through the house more quickly if we concentrate on one room at a time. Since we've felt Lillian's presence with us ever since we arrived, we decide to tackle her bedroom first.

A restless energy invades my bones as we walk to the back bedroom and begin to clean. Rose moves her suitcase and personal belongings to a corner, and I can't help feeling a bit ruthless as we open dresser drawers and toss items into bins. Worn slacks and shorts, underwear, and bathing suits all go into trash bags. Ditto for outdated shirts. The few pieces that could qualify as vintage fashion—a few dresses, suits, and a coat—are folded and placed into a box marked for the thrift store.

Rose pulls a patterned hatbox from a closet shelf and opens it, then begins to laugh. "What in the world?"

"What?" I glance in her direction. "Did you find a hat?"

"Not exactly."

Rose lifts a beige garment and holds it up with both hands. Elastic tabs dangle from each leg, and the main structure appears to be made of shiny and unyielding fabric.

"That's a girdle," I tell her, grinning. "Probably from the forties or fifties."

Rose flicks one of the elastic tabs with her index finger. "What are these things for?"

"They held up her stockings," Penny says. "That was before the invention of control-top panty hose."

Rose laughs and drops the girdle back into the hatbox. "What do you think? Would a museum like to have one of these?"

"Only if it has a special room for instruments of torture," Penny answers. "I say you should throw them out."

Rose looks at me to see if I have any objection, so I shrug.

"I've gotta hand it to Grandma," Rose says as she drops the hatbox into a garbage bag. "She really cared about her appearance. Did you know she wore Spanx until the day she died?"

I take a wincing breath. "You're kidding."

Rose shakes her head. "I'm not. The week after she died, a nurse from the home called to tell me that the dentist wanted to know why Grandma hadn't shown up at his office. Apparently she had an appointment to have her teeth whitened."

Penny and I look at each other in astonishment, then Penny laughs. "Do you think she wanted to look good for her funeral?"

"Wouldn't surprise me," Rose says.

I stop what I'm doing as Penny's comment about Victoria's Secret comes roaring back on a tide of guilt. Grandma cared about her appearance . . . was that how she kept Walter happy?

From a small drawer in the dresser, Penny pulls out a stack of neatly folded handkerchiefs. "Remember these?" she says, shaking out a yellowed square of fabric. "Remember how Grandma used to recite that story about the lady sitting on the bench?"

"The story where the lady fell over?" Rose picks up another handkerchief, then brings it close to her face. "Um, smell this. Still smells like Gran's perfume."

While Penny leans over for a sniff, I bite my tongue, which is itching to express my impatience. I feel like I'm working at double speed, applying more energy than usual to the task at hand, while my sisters are leisurely strolling down memory lane. But they aren't to blame for the crisis looming over my head, and I probably shouldn't rush them through this ritual of saying good-bye to

Grandmother. In a sense, we are celebrating her life as we clean out her cottage and take stock of all she meant to us.

Maybe I need to do the same thing with my marriage. As Penny and Rose talk about our grandmother, maybe I should be thinking about Michael, making a mental list of the ways he's influenced my life. The man has strengths and weaknesses, virtues and flaws, and the more rational I can be when dealing with him, the better off I'll be.

I yank a blouse from a wire hanger and wince when the neckline rips. Maybe I need to tame the rage boiling beneath my skin, let it cool to at least a steady simmer before I make a list of Michael's faults.

I toss the hanger and the blouse into a trash bag and draw a deep breath. I can do this.

I reach into the closet and pull out another shirt; this one slides easily from the hanger. I fold it and place it in the thrift store box for someone else's grandmother.

Maybe I can contest the divorce and save our marriage. Michael will need to clean up his mess and take responsibility for his actions, of course. Though he may not have intended to, he has established a second family. That woman's child will grow up looking like my sons, and while Michael may be unfaithful, a liar, and a skunk, he has always been a good father. He will want to play a role in this child's life, which means he'll want to have visitation and contact, and he'll want to provide financial support.

Can I say nothing while a chunk of our household income goes to support Michael's other family? Can I come home from work and paint on a smile while his child visits our house?

Yet staying married will be better for our sons. Staying married will allow me to keep my job. Staying married will preserve, to some extent, our family's reputation for stability and integrity. No matter how vicious the rumors, after a while people will see that we're still together and assume that the rumors must have been exaggerated . . . because, after all, if Michael had done something truly reprehensible, I wouldn't have remained with him.

I pull out a white cotton shirt with a red paint stain on the sleeve; I toss it in the trash.

If I can somehow convince Michael to preserve our marriage, we'll have to face potentially serious repercussions at the university. He may lose his job and have to find work elsewhere. He may have to sacrifice a great deal to maintain life as we presently know it.

And I will have to try to forgive . . . something my faith commands me to do, but an act easier to read about than carry out. I'll have to live with Michael, continuing to serve his meals, clean his house, and sleep beside him, all the while wondering if he's with me because he wants to be, or because I shamed him into acquiescence.

Postadultery life with Michael . . . What will it look like? I'm fairly sure I can maintain a cheerful facade in public, but what will I feel when we're together behind closed doors? I can fulfill most of my wifely duties, but will I ever be able to make love to him again? Or will I forever cringe at his touch?

If I can't find a way to accept and be happy in this new reality, the best thing for me to do is clear out. I would rather be lonely and resigned on my own than miserable and bitter in a sham of a marriage.

Can I do it? At this moment, I think I can. I can wipe Michael out of my life as resolutely as I can throw Lillian's underwear away.

I pull a bathing suit off the closet shelf and stretch one of the leg openings, then chuckle when the elastic crumbles and the opening gapes like a mouth. "Let this be a lesson to us," I say, my voice clipped as I pull other items from the shelf. "Elastic doesn't hold up well over the years. Sort of like marriage."

Penny snorts, but Rose only looks at me, her eyes troubled. Yet she should know what I mean. She may be happy with Wort, but she's been in two other marriages that didn't survive. And two out of three isn't exactly a winning average.

"I think," I announce, "that it may be time for me to start a new life. The boys are in college, I'll have my inheritance for a nest egg, and I'm young enough to move to another community. I could do it—start over, I mean."

Penny looks at me with bright eagerness, but Rose's brows tangle in a knot over her eyes. "Don't forget," she says, "that Michael did drive down from Savannah in the middle of the night to talk to you. The man obviously loves you, Ginger."

"You think?"

"I know. You shouldn't make any rash decisions," she cautions. "You're gonna need lots of time to think about this. Make sure you weigh all your options—even the ones that seem far-fetched right now."

For an instant I'm bemused by the realization that Rose is offering *me* advice, then I'm stupefied by the notion that Michael and I might somehow work things out and stay together. With a younger woman and a baby mixed into the equation, that solution is about as likely as the lines on my face vanishing without surgical intervention.

PENNYROYAL

Leaving Ginger and Rose to continue cleaning, I drag a stuffed trash bag out of Grandma's bedroom. Before hauling it outside, though, I find Ginger's purse on the kitchen counter and her cell phone in an inner pocket. She won't mind if I use her phone again, because unless I miss my guess, Miller Conrad is still waiting for me on Jekyll Island.

As Rose's voice rolls down the hallway, I slip the phone into my pocket and drag the bag onto the front porch, gratefully inhaling the fresh air. After heaving the bag into the Dumpster, I settle onto the porch swing and punch Miller's number into the phone. Fortunately, he answers before I lose my nerve.

"Hey, it's Penny," I tell him, relaxing in the warmth of his greeting. "I hope you're enjoying Jekyll Island."

"It's nice," Miller says, "and I'm on the golf course right now. Found a nice room in a resort, so I'm having a good time."

"I'm glad to hear that. Because you don't know how much it pains me to say this, but it doesn't look like I'm gonna be able to get away this weekend. My time with the sisters has been—well, unexpectedly eventful. I don't think I can skip out without causing either Ginger or Rose to blow a gasket."

"Too much shopping, huh?"

"Hardly! Too much work! My older sister is a perfectionist, and she's not gonna let us out of here until Grandma's house is clean enough to eat off the floor."

He chuckles. "I hope y'all are at least having a few laughs."

"Trust me, this weekend has been anything but a funfest. Ginger—she's the oldest—just learned that her husband got a coworker pregnant. She's having a rough time."

"I'm so sorry to hear that." His voice deepens with compassion. "Have they been married long?"

"Twenty-six—no, twenty-seven years, I think. None of us expected to hear that kind of news this weekend."

"I'm sorry, but I know she'll survive. That sort of thing can happen to the best of us, can't it?"

I'm dying to ask if it's happened to him, but I don't want to move too quickly. I have to break things off with Bob before I take serious steps toward Miller. For now, all I can do is let the doctor know that I like him, I trust him, and I'd like to know him better.

"Thanks for understanding," I tell him. "I really enjoy talking to you."

"Same here. I have the feeling I could tell you almost anything and you'd understand."

"I'd at least try." I laugh, but at that moment Rose steps out onto the porch. She lifts a brow when she sees me, then she gestures to the phone and mouths, *Can I talk to Bob?*

I shake my head and turn sideways on the swing, cutting off her view. "Listen, I need to let you go. We still have bathrooms to scrub and an attic to empty."

"Thanks for calling, then."

"Will I see you at lunch on Tuesday?" I hold my breath, afraid he will say no.

"Count on it. I have to eat, right?"

My heart sings with delight as I disconnect the call. When I turn to face forward again, Rose is standing in front of me, her arms folded across her chest and her lips set in a grim line of disapproval. "That wasn't Bob."

The girl is way too observant. With an effort, I hide my chagrin. "I was talking to a friend."

"The guy on Jekyll Island?"

"So what if it was?"

"So you were flirting, that's what. I know you, Penny Jensen, and I know what you're like when you're on the prowl. You were flirting with another man, but you're still married."

I exhale a deep sigh. "I told you, Bob and I are finished. Not only is the romance dead, but we don't want the same things. I don't think we ever will."

"What does he want that's so unreasonable?"

"Kids, for one thing. At my age, what woman wants more kids?" I snort softly. "Bob never wanted kids either, but a few months ago his younger sister and her husband had a baby. Suddenly Bob was dropping by their house every weekend, helping paint the nursery, buying baby toys, and picking out lullabies on his guitar. He would pull up long lists of baby names from the Internet and leave them lying on the kitchen table, probably hoping to stir up some kind of biological reaction from me. I replaced his lists with brochures about Italian cruises and tried to sidetrack him by suggesting that we consider buying a vacation time-share."

"Don't you want more kids?" Rose's voice is soft with disbelief.

"Are you crazy? I already have Reese, though I try not to talk about him around Bob. All Bob knows is that my first husband got custody and Reese and I talk on the phone every couple of weeks. If Mr. Math ever finds out how old Reese is, my goose is cooked."

"I don't get it. Why wouldn't you want them to get together?"

"Because Bob thinks I'm only thirty-nine. If he finds out that Reese is twenty-four . . ." I whistle. "Well, you do the subtraction."

Rose's eyes appear to be in danger of dropping out of her face. "I hate to ask such an obvious question, but why does Bob think you're thirty-nine?"

I shrug. "Meeting me in that 'under forty' chat room might have something to do with it . . . but he should know that you can't believe everything you read in a profile. After we started dating, I didn't tell him the truth because I didn't want to disappoint him. Next thing I knew, we were married."

"But—but—your driver's license. Your birth certificate."

I wave her objections away. "Bob never pries into my past. Or my purse."

A frown settles between Rose's brows. "Didn't you have your tubes tied after Reese was born?"

"Yeah, I did."

"And Bob doesn't know that?"

"You think I go around advertising that I've shut off the chute? I thought I could make him happy enough to forget about babies, but now he's talking about setting up a nursery."

Rose's eyes flick at me, then shift to the space beyond the porch railing. "I can't believe none of your other husbands wanted children."

I snort. "It's not so hard to believe. Grayson wanted to concentrate on his legal career, and he wanted me to focus on being the perfect lawyer's wife. Zack thought a baby would hamper our ability to travel to NASCAR events on the weekends. Langston might have wanted children—his mother certainly wanted grandchildren—but when it came down to it, Momma Thibodeaux didn't want to share her son with anyone, not even a wife and kids. So there you have it. I've already raised my son. I'm done with kids."

"Your ex-husband raised your son," Rose says, a hair of irritation in her voice. "You saw Reese, what—twice a year?"

The words snap, raising a welt on my conscience. "Are you saying I wasn't a good mother?"

Rose sinks onto the swing next to me. "I think I'm saying that you weren't much of a mother at all. And sometimes I think it's completely unfair that you gave birth to a child while I wanted one so desperately . . ." Her voice clots as she lowers her gaze and looks away. "Never mind all that. There's one thing, though, I know for sure—you're not being fair to Bob. You need to tell him the truth about how you feel. Don't treat him the way Michael has treated Ginger. Don't leave him with no options."

I inhale through my teeth and feel a dozen different emotions crash head-on. I want to be furious, but I can't be angry with Rose, not when she's suffered so much. Yet my situation isn't at all like Michael's; I haven't had an affair, and there's no baby in the making.

"I already know how Bob feels," I assure Rose, "and I'm gonna tell him the truth when I get home. If he honestly wants a kid, then he won't want me. So, like I said, our marriage is over."

"You're a fool," Rose says, but her words brim with affection. She looks at me, her eyes large and liquid. "You are married to a man who loves you completely, and yet you're willing to throw that love away. I may be your sister, but I will never, ever understand you."

She gets up and goes into the house, but her words hang in the air, shimmering like my unfulfilled hopes and dashed dreams.

ROSEMARY

Frustrated by Penny's attitude, I step into the house, pick up Justus, and carry him down the front steps. I set him on the grass and stroll to the side of the house, a sheltered spot where Penny can't see me from the porch. I don't want her reading the emotions on my face.

We Lawrence girls have made an art of marriage: we win a man, we marry him, we love him just so far and no further. Even Ginger has her limits and secrets she keeps from Michael. Does he really know her? Does he know what she made me do?

I clench my fists as the thought fans the deep-buried embers of anger that have never gone cold. I cannot bear this smoldering resentment any longer. I'm tired of speaking in code and skirting around topics that might make someone uncomfortable. I've lived with insincerity and false faces for so long I've forgotten what genuineness looks like.

Poor Bob Jensen seems like an honest guy, a man who's truly given his heart to his wife. Does he know Penny is about to drop a bombshell on him?

My own words echo in my ears: *You are married to a man who loves you completely, and yet you're willing to throw that love away.*

If Penny or Ginger knew what I was planning for tomorrow, they'd throw my words back in my face. How can I leave Wort? The man loves me, yes, but he doesn't depend on me, and he's strong enough to survive anything. In fact, my leaving tomorrow might save him from watching me die through a long and painful bout with breast cancer or something even worse. Every cloud has a silver lining, and eventually Wort will find it.

And it's not like I'm leaving him with nothing. He'll have our ranch, of course, and my inheritance from Grandma Lillian's estate. He'll have a place on the board of Racehorse Rescue, if he wants to keep it, so he won't have to move or uproot his business because of me. He doesn't have any pressing dates on his calendar, so the funeral won't even upset his schedule.

I know he'll grieve, but he's no stranger to grief. Wort has already lost both of his parents, as have I. And together we mourned the death of our child when no one else did; together we lived through the day that should have been a joyous birthday, the fulfillment of a heartfelt longing and the promise of our continued future. Wort would have been a great father—as rough as he looks on the outside, he is as soft as butter when he holds a child in his arms.

Once I am gone, he will have another chance at fatherhood. He can remarry. He can have a dozen kids and later bounce grandchildren on his knee.

Yes, Wort loves me, but I cannot fulfill his dreams. He loves me too much to divorce me, but I am empty and barren, forever scarred by my past mistakes. Since Wort won't let me go, I have no choice but to remove myself from his life.

Dying should be easy. If we know anything, we Lawrence girls know how to leave without creating a fuss.

GINGER

I can't help noticing a palpable tension between Penny and Rose when they come back in the house. Penny lets the screen door slam behind her and stops in the living room with her hands on her hips, eyeing the tied garbage bags on the floor. "Looks like you've been busy," she says, her voice crisp and slightly breathless. "So does that do it for Grandma's room? Are we finished with the downstairs?"

"No one's touched the coat closet." I gesture toward the narrow door across from the staircase. "You might find a few leftovers from the Depression in there."

After a glance at Rose, Penny walks to the closet and throws open the door. Something in her posture tells me she's no longer thrilled to be here, and while I'm not overjoyed by the prospect, what good would it do to go home? Michael's at the house, and I'm not ready to face our devastated marriage. I'd much rather be doing something constructive than sitting in my living room with a cheating man, a box of tissues, and a broken heart.

"I think I'll go up and check out the attic," Rose says, her words low and resentful.

As she walks past me, I catch her upper arm. "Are you going to tell me what's going on?"

"What do you mean?"

"I mean the thing between you and Penny. Spill it, please."

Rose pulls her arm from my grip, and after a pointed glance at Penny's back, she sighs. "I caught Penny flirting with that guy on the phone. I told her she was crazy if she really meant to divorce Bob."

Penny steps out of the closet, her face flaming above Grandmother's heavy wool coat. "She's not your mother, Rose. You don't have to tell Ginger everything I tell you."

Ignoring her comment, I walk over to confront her. "You're divorcing Bob? What's he done?"

"Bob didn't do anything." Rose moves into the line of fire. "He wants kids, that's all. So she's gonna divorce him and go after that man she keeps calling."

"Penny Jensen." I know I sound like a scold, but old habits die hard. "You've been chasing another man while you're still married? Why, you're no better than Michael!"

Penny flings the coat onto the floor and glares at us, a scowl knotting her brow. "I am *nothing* like Michael! You know, maybe y'all should focus on your own men and stay out of my business."

"Excuse me for caring, but someone has to talk sense to you." I sink to the edge of the love seat and fold my arms. "What's the problem with Bob?"

Penny opens her mouth to answer, but Rose is quicker—and armed with opinions. "She's built her marriage on a lie, that's what. Bob thinks she's still able to have children. She didn't tell him she's had her tubes tied."

I blink, incredulous. "Is this true?"

Penny scowls at me. "Not telling every little thing about yourself isn't lying. I didn't tell him because the subject never came up."

"If you know he wants kids, the subject has come up," I point out. "But you didn't tell him the truth? What kind of a marriage is based on half-truths?"

"Well, gee, what kind do you think?" Penny impales me with a sharp look. "What kind of a marriage do you have if one partner is having a baby with another woman? How much truth did Michael give you on those nights he came home late? And what made him take up with another woman in the first place?"

Her retort stings me into silence.

Rose leaps to my defense. "You can't blame Michael's actions on Ginger. She's not the one who had the affair."

"Maybe not, but whenever a marriage fails, it's usually because of problems from both sides. At some point two people become strangers. At some point they stop wanting the same things. They fall out of love."

"It's not that simple," I whisper, my voice ragged and torn. "Staying close isn't as easy as you make it sound."

"I never said it was easy." Penny's eyes rake my face. "So maybe you should stop judging me and look after your own relationship. Go home to Michael, if you can, and pretend his affair came out of the blue. Pretend you are still as close as hand and glove. You may fool yourself, you may fool your friends, but you can't fool me."

In that moment of soul-shattering clarity, I'm not sure how anyone manages to survive sisterhood.

PENNYROYAL

Grandma always warned us that we should never start an argument with a woman when she's tired . . . and now I think she should have added, "or unhappy." After our most recent dustup, we all retreat to separate corners and work in chilly silence. I can't speak for my sisters, but I find myself tossing perfectly good items into trash bags and tying them shut with malicious satisfaction. Ginger tosses several stuffed bags down the staircase, probably hoping one of them will knock me over like a bowling pin.

Without consulting anyone, at suppertime I leave the cottage and drive to the nearest grocery store, a Winn-Dixie. I'm not waiting for Ginger to suggest what we should have for dinner, and I don't care if Rose starts moping because a head of lettuce sacrificed itself to feed us.

In the grocery, I toss French bread, lettuce, mustard, mayonnaise, cheese slices, and cold cuts into my cart. I add a couple of bottles of orange juice, a bag of chips, a bag of ice, and a two-liter bottle of diet soda. Because I'm a grown woman and I can eat what I want, I pick up three packages of peanut M&M's. I'll share if Ginger or Rose wants some; otherwise, I'll enjoy them as a little reward for all the physical labor I've been doing. Emptying closets must burn a ton of calories.

When I drive back onto Fish Fever Lane, I'm relieved to see that Ginger's and Rose's cars are still present. We might argue from time

THE FINE ART OF INSINCERITY   217

to time, but I'd hate it if one of them took off before we could clear the air.

I haul out the grocery bags and drop them on the kitchen table. "Supper's here," I call, suddenly missing Grandma's big brass dinner bell. When she rang that thing, we could hear it from almost anywhere in the village.

I hear footsteps on the stairs, then Ginger comes around the corner and gives me a grudging smile. "Thanks. I really didn't feel like going out again."

Rose steps out from the hallway and lifts a brow when she sees what I've bought. "Yum, cheese." She smiles. "Looks good."

I sit down, pleasantly surprised that I've managed to do something right.

My sisters take their usual places, and we begin to make sandwiches.

"I'm so tired I can barely feel my fingers," Ginger says, fumbling with a knife from Grandma's silverware chest. "Can't we just liquefy this stuff and drink it?"

"You can feed me through my veins," Rose deadpans, layering a slice of bread with cheese and mustard. "I haven't been this worn-out in a long time."

I rip open the bag of chips and dump a handful on the paper towel I'm using for a plate. "I think I'm just gonna eat chips—they're easy. And a bag of peanut M&M's, of course. They're protein, right?"

Rose giggles, and even Ginger manages a small smile.

We eat in silence, our weariness speaking for us, and after a minute Rose stands to pull glasses from a thrift store box. "I don't know why we didn't just set some dishes aside until we were done with all this."

I know why—because Ginger isn't happy unless any job is 100 percent completed—but I don't say a word as Rose asks if anyone else wants orange juice.

Both Ginger and I lift our hands, so Rose pours a glass for each of us, then drops back into her chair to finish her sandwich. When our meals have all but disappeared, Ginger wipes her hands with a napkin and purses her lips in a thoughtful expression. "I've been thinking," she says. "I know that's dangerous, but maybe I missed something in the definition of love. What does it really mean? No one seems to interpret the word in the same way—after all, Penny obviously loves peanut M&M's, but that doesn't mean she couldn't live without them—"

"Oh, yes it does," I interrupt.

Ginger lifts her gaze to the ceiling as if appealing to a higher authority, then shakes her head. "In college, I told my friends I loved them, but if one of them were to die tomorrow, I'm not sure I'd feel obligated to fly off to their funerals."

"What brought this on?" Rose turns to look more directly at Ginger. "Are you thinking about Michael?"

Ginger snorts, acknowledging the obvious. "When I told my college friends I loved them, I meant that I held them in high esteem. It didn't mean I'd drive across the state to meet them for lunch."

"I don't think they expected you to go that far," I point out. "A college friend is one thing; a husband is something else."

Rose taps her nails on the table. "Are you thinking that Michael didn't love you enough?"

"I don't know what I'm thinking," Ginger answers. "All I know is that when I told Michael 'I love you,' I meant I'd never betray him. That I'd always stand by him. That I'd be there for him, no matter what. But obviously those three words didn't mean the same thing to him."

"Or he changed," I add, trying to keep my voice gentle. "People do change, you know."

"Do they?" Ginger looks at me with something raw and wounded in her eyes. "Is that why my pantry always holds cereal boxes older than your current marriage?"

I lift my hand, an automatic defensive movement. Ginger's stung me so many times that I can't help pulling back when she launches a barb, but she doesn't seem interested in preaching at me now. She's looking at me with real interest in her eyes, and the idea that she might honestly be seeking an answer from me is . . . astounding.

"I don't know," I finally tell her. "I just keep thinking of Grandma, and how she had to marry seven times before she finally found her soul mate. I know there's a man out there who will meet all my needs, and every time I got married, I thought I'd found him. But as time passes, I learn things, the fuzzy feelings go away, and I realize that I haven't found my perfect soul mate after all. So I have to keep looking."

Ginger turns to Rose. "And you? Wort obviously loves you. You care deeply for him. So how do you make it work?"

Rose stares, her eyes widening, then she shakes her head. "Wort's precious to me," she says simply. "And so are my animals and my friends. If that's love . . . well, that's all it is. If something is precious, you want to care for it and protect it."

Rose's explanation makes no sense at all, but the thought of her shoveling manure and hauling bags of chicken feed reminds me of something Grandma used to say: "Service is nothing but love in work clothes."

Grandma bubbled over with simple sayings . . . but maybe they were also profound.

THIRTEEN

ROSEMARY

The first sound I hear Monday morning is the rataplan of rain on the tin roof. The soothing sound carries me back to rainy afternoons spent in this bedroom, long hours when I would curl up with my head in Grandma's lap, dozing as her fingers twisted and played with my hair.

Fresh air from the window rolls into the bedroom, bringing with it the ozonic smell of rain. I breathe deeply and smile, relishing the scent. If I could have special-ordered the weather for my last day on earth, I would have ordered rain. The sound, the smell . . . they're as soothing as Grandma's hands.

With an effort, I pull myself from the embracing folds of sleep and roll out of the canyon in the center of Gran's bed. Monday—our last day at this house. My last day, period.

I place my feet on the cool floor and whistle to wake Justus. He lifts his head from his pillow bed and blinks in my direction, his nose crinkling as he stops his labored panting to parse the air for my scent.

"I'm here, buddy." I push myself off the bed and kneel by his side, cupping the top of his head with my palm. "You ready to go out this morning? Do you think you can manage the porch stairs?"

Justus yawns and attempts to stand, but the sight of his struggle is too much for me. I scoop him into my arms and carry him to the back door outside the entrance to Grandma's bedroom. I step onto the concrete pad and set Justus in a patch of grass, not caring if an early-rising neighbor happens to glance outside and see me in my pajamas.

As Jussy sniffs for the perfect potty spot, I tip my head back and close my eyes, listening. The fat raindrops falling around me are malingerers dropping from the trees, but thunder rumbles in the distance.

"Know what that is?" Grandma once asked me.

Terrified by the booming crashes, I shook my head.

"Bless your heart, darlin', it's only the angels bowling."

The memory ripples through me, shivering my skin like the caress of a gentle spirit.

Will I be with Gran tonight? She often talked and sang about heaven; the church she attended never held a service in which they didn't sing at least one hymn about being washed in the blood or one day flying to a place beyond the pearly gates. As a kid who took things literally, I couldn't help being horrified by the idea of a bloodbath, but flying to a kingdom with pearly gates . . . *that* idea captivated me. Maybe that's what I'll focus on when I crash through the railing and sail out over the South Brunswick River.

"Rose? Rosemary!"

Even from outside I can hear Ginger's voice, heavy with impatience. I'm tempted to ignore her, but if I do, she'll stick her head out the door and yell for me. It'd be a shame to ruin the neighborhood's peace and quiet.

I push my thoughts aside and thrust my head into the hallway. "Ginger?"

She appears at the end of the hall, her features sharp and her eyes narrow. If anything, she looks worse than she did yesterday, so I'm guessing she didn't sleep last night, either. She's wearing jeans and a dirty T-shirt, and she hasn't put on even a touch of makeup.

The woman in front of me doesn't look a thing like Ginger, but I understand why.

"We're running out of time and we still have to go through the attic," she says, pushing stray tendrils of hair from her cheek. "Will you go up there this morning and see what needs to come out?"

I nod. "Sure."

Ginger's restless hands keep moving; one fusses with a pleat in her mom jeans while the other strokes her neck. "I've got to run to the grocery for some more trash bags and cleaning supplies. Penny's in the front yard, hacking at that leggy azalea bush and the kudzu. I told her to let them go, but she seems determined to behead something this morning."

"No problem."

"I'll get some breakfast too," she calls, walking away. "I won't be gone long."

I wave to the back of her head, then step outside again to fetch Justus. After settling him on his cushion in Gran's bedroom, I grab fresh clothes from my suitcase, then leave them on the bed, deciding to clean in my pajamas. I can shower, change, and put on some makeup after the dusty work is done. That way I'll be fresher for the drive home. I'm *not* saying good-bye in rags and a bare face.

I go upstairs, my feet silent on the wooden treads. I'm about to pull down the attic ladder when my cell phone rings. Worried about Wort, I hurry down the steps and pull the phone from my purse, then glance at the caller ID. I ought to ignore anyone but my husband, but the number rings a distant bell of memory.

"Hello?"

"Rosemary Dodson?"

"Speaking."

"I hope you don't mind me calling your cell, but your husband gave me this number. I'm Greta Miles, and I run a program for autistic children called Equine Facilitated Learning."

I can think of a hundred reasons to hang up, and only one to keep listening: the word *equine*. When it comes to horses, I'm all ears. "Can I help you with something?"

"I hear that y'all take in retired racehorses."

"That's right."

"Good! Because we're always in need of stable, calm animals for the children in our program."

"We don't do trail rides," I explain, moving back toward the stairs. "Our animals are retired. They deserve their rest."

"Oh, we don't do trail rides, either. The EFL program doesn't demand much of the horses—we ask only that the animals not be prone to biting, kicking, or bucking. Our children don't necessarily ride; sometimes an hour of brushing alone is great therapy. The simple act of leading a horse by the halter—I've seen it work wonders."

I lean against the stair railing, interested despite my plans for the day. I usually spend two or three hours every morning grooming our animals, so this task will fall to Wort or Marisa unless we—*they*—find someone else willing to spend a lot of time in the barn. Like these children.

"How does this program work, exactly? I'm not unfamiliar with the concept, but I've never investigated it."

A smile slips into Greta's voice. "Children with emotional disorders experience amazing benefits after only a few sessions with horses. After basic lessons about how to handle a horse, the children learn how to issue elementary commands—real elementary stuff. When the horse responds, the child is affirmed—and we've seen autistic children who don't speak begin to verbalize directions to the animal."

A sprig of hope rises in my breast—maybe my animals will have an even richer life after I'm gone. "That's amazing—and it makes perfect sense, because horses tend to mirror the temperament of the person handling them."

"Exactly." Greta's voice rings with satisfaction. "We've been using EFL in Alachua County for three years, and we have several ranch families involved in the program. But there's a waiting list of children, so when I heard about your work with retired racehorses, I wondered if the program would be a good fit for you. After all—just because we're retired doesn't mean we've been *completely* put out to pasture, does it?"

When the woman laughs, I find myself smiling at the idea of my beloved animals feeling useful and loved. This kind of program wouldn't demand much of Wort or my assistant, so if we can do it . . .

"I think it's a wonderful concept," I tell Greta. "How can we help?"

"Can you and I get together next week? I could come out to your place with a standard equine evaluation form. It wouldn't take me long to assess your animals and choose the ones most likely to be suitable for the program."

I sink onto a lower stair as my thoughts slam into a brick wall. I won't be here next week; the pages in my mental calendar run out after tonight. And next week Wort will probably be too busy handling funeral preparations and visitors to talk to this woman.

"The week after next would be better," I tell her, gentling my voice. "Why don't you give us a call before you come out? If I'm not available, ask for Marisa Coloney, my assistant. I know she'll be as excited about the program as I am."

"Great. I'll do that. And, Mrs. Dodson?"

"Please call me Rose. Everyone does."

"Thank you, Rose. On behalf of all our children, thank you so much."

As I set my phone on the fireplace mantel, an unexpected jealousy stirs inside me. Marisa will get to watch my horses interact with children; she'll be around to watch the animals do something to change lives for the better.

I would have enjoyed watching my noble retirees provide a unique service to special kids. I would have enjoyed that . . . a lot.

GINGER

By the time I return to the cottage with supplies, coffee, and a bag
of breakfast sandwiches, Penny is sitting at the counter, her hands
and arms covered in scratches. Rose is standing at the sink, still
in her pajama bottoms and tank top. Neither of them appears to
be speaking to the other, but the arrival of food thaws the chilly
atmosphere.

Rose regards the bag with a wary eye. "Anything vegetarian?"

"Veggie sausage patty," I tell her, setting the tray of Styrofoam
cups in front of Penny. "And for you, Penn, double sugars in the
coffee. You can have whichever sandwich you want; I'll take whatever's left."

While they pull food onto the counter, I add the new cleaning
products to those already lined up by the sink: powdered cleanser,
window cleaner, mildew remover, toilet bowl cleaner, bleach, paper
towels, heavy-duty scrubbers, rubber gloves, and more trash bags.

"That ought to do it." Penny grins at my arsenal. "Good job."

I know it's silly, but her comment goes a long way toward mending the breach between us. And because there are only two stools at
the breakfast bar, I grab a coffee and a biscuit and take them into
the living room, where there's plenty of space to eat.

Ever the peacemaker, Rose stands and gestures to her seat. "You
want my stool?"

I smile. "No, thanks. I'm fine over here."

And because my hands are itching to hold the morning newspaper I usually read over breakfast, I sit on the sofa and reach for the nearest piece of reading material I can see: my grandmother's journal.

I lift the cover and discover that she inscribed the flyleaf:

Though I speak with the tongues of men and of angels, and have not love,

I am like sounding brass, or a tinkling cymbal.

And though I have the gift of prophecy, and understand all mysteries, and all knowledge;

and though I have all faith, so that I could move mountains, and have not love, I am nothing.

And though I bestow all my goods to feed the poor, and though I give my body to be burned, and have not love, it profits me nothing.

Love suffers long, and is kind; love doesn't envy; love doesn't promote itself, is not puffed up,

Does not behave itself unseemly, seeks not her own, is not easily provoked, thinks no evil;

Rejoices not in evil, but rejoices in the truth;

bears all things, believes all things, hopes all things, endures all things.

Love never fails: but where there are prophecies, they shall fail; where there are tongues, they shall cease; where there is knowledge, it shall vanish away.

For we know in part, and we prophesy in part.

But when that which is perfect is come, then that which is in part shall be done away.

When I was a child, I spoke as a child, I understood as a child, I thought as a child: but when I became grown up, I put away childish things.

For now we see through a glass, darkly; but then face-to-face: now I know in part; but then I shall know even as also I am known.

*And now abides faith, hope, love, these three; but the greatest
of these is love.*

As I flip through the first few pages, I realize this journal is
more like a logbook. The volume covers ten years, and each page
contains only a few lines for each day. Apparently Grandmother
began writing on February 12, 1990, and she finished on December 31, 2000. These are the unknown years, to me at least, because
by 1990 we girls were married and busy with families of our own.
We didn't see much of Lillian during that decade.

"I think I know why Grandmother decided to keep this diary,"
I call to my sisters. "It ends at the beginning of the millennium.
She must have wanted to keep a record of the last decade of the
twentieth century."

"You don't know that," Penny calls.

"Prove me wrong," I answer, unruffled.

I stop on the pages for March 11 and 12 and run my finger over
the row that contains entries for 1991. Sure enough, on the twelfth
Grandmother wrote, *Glory be! Ginger had her baby yesterday, a fine,
healthy boy. She's named him Ryan Albert. Michael called to give me
the news, and I could hear pride in his voice. A happy, happy day.*

My throat tightens as I blink tears away. Those were happy days,
but they are long gone. I'm glad Grandmother didn't live to see the
disaster Michael and I have become.

I skim other pages, reading of Grandmother's garden club
meetings, church suppers, and Sunday dinners on the ground. And
then, later in March, her handwriting becomes irregular: *Walter
is convinced he's going to die. He asked again if I'd go with him to
Europe; again I said no. So he left without me. He went with that
man, and I don't know if I'll ever see him again.*

I flip backward through the pages, looking for some other refer-
ence to "that man." Nothing. Grandmother doesn't mention him,
doesn't say anything else about Walter and a trip to Europe. But
why would she write that she might never see him again?

An ominous feeling settles over me as I lower the book into my lap. "Penny, Rose," I call, my voice sounding hollow in my ears, "did y'all ever hear anything about Walter going to Europe? This would have been in '91. Grandmother didn't go with him."

"Walter went to Europe?" Penny swivels on her stool, coffee cup in hand. "Why didn't Grandma go?"

"I don't know."

"I never heard anything about it," Rose echoes, "but if Walter had asked me, I'd have gone with him in a heartbeat."

I return to the journal and search for answers. Why didn't Lillian go with her husband? Her health was good and she loved to travel. She went everywhere with Walter, so I can't think of a single reason why she wouldn't have accompanied him to Europe.

I skim through other entries, impatiently skipping references to neighbors and church meetings and concerts by the lighthouse. Finally, on April 13, *No word from Walter . . . not even a birthday card. I spent most of the day at the church, where I prayed for understanding. Some there are telling me to file for divorce; Henry Wagman even asked me out for coffee. But I am a married woman, and I want to keep my vows. But how do I face those questioning faces when folks ask where my husband is?*

I read the entry twice, feeling each word like a cut to the heart. I may soon be writing something like this in *my* journal, wondering how to answer my friends when they ask about Michael. I knew Grandmother had a checkered matrimonial past, but I never knew she and Walter went through a rough patch . . . if that's what this is.

I flip forward a few more pages. The word *Europe* jumps out at me from an entry dated June 23: *Spoke to my left-hand neighbor today; he asked about Walter. I told him the truth—no sense in trying to hide it from someone so close—and he asked why I didn't divorce "the lousy pervert." I told him I've decided it's time someone showed Walter a little mercy . . . and though I said it with a smile, I think I meant it. How can I sing about the love and forgiveness of God if I don't show it to anyone else?*

I count on my fingers—March, April, May, June. Four months with a runaway husband would surely be considered abandonment. Maybe not legally, but socially.

"Walter left Lillian," I call, a note of indignation in my voice. "He left in March '91 and I'm already up to June. He hasn't come back yet."

"But he *did* come back." Penny stands and walks toward me, bringing her coffee with her. "We know he came back. He didn't miss a Thanksgiving until the year he died."

Thanksgiving—November. I flip to the end of the book and search through the autumnal entries. Sure enough, November 28 is Thanksgiving. Grandmother wrote, *Walter drove me up to Savannah for T'giving dinner at Ginger and Michael's. Her boys are adorable, and Penny's Reese is so big! Rose brought a new beau—Jonah somebody. She says she's not serious about him, but I wonder . . .*

I turn the pages backward, searching for Walter's name in the text. Finally, on November 14: *Walter is home! M deserted him in Florence, and Walter spent a month alone, no friends, no support. So he's come home to die. The doctors say he may live ten more years if he tries the new drugs, and he says he wants to spend those years with me—if I'll have him. I want to be angry with him. I want to turn him out, and there are some who say I should. But I took a vow to love, and the Lord who loves me loves Walter too. So I will do my best to be Jesus to my husband and show Walter what genuine love looks like . . . and how it forgives.*

As Penny one-fingers the piano keys, I lower the journal, my mind racing with speculation and unexpected answers. Walter, the old man we cherished as our grandpa—my goodness, we didn't know him at all. But Lillian did. She knew him, she loved him, she welcomed him back home, forgiving a betrayal so socially unacceptable she couldn't even name it in her diary.

Forgiveness . . . seems to me the hardest effort of all. How did she do it?

"Girls," I call, my voice in tatters, "when did Walter pass away? Do you remember?"

Penny turns to look at Rose. "It was '98, wasn't it?"

"June '98," Rose says. "I remember because it was right after Jonah left me."

I return to the book, bending over it as I turn the ink-stained pages to June. I find the row for 1998 and skim the entries, reading of trips Lillian and Walter took, of people they had over for dinner.

Finally—June 15, 1998: *My precious Walter went home today. He was upstairs, changing a lightbulb in the closet, and I heard a thump, like he'd dropped something. I called out, but when he didn't answer, I went up and found him in the blue bedroom. The doctor later told me that Walter's heart simply gave out, but I think Jesus sent the angels to take him home. I'm sure they were jostling each other in line, trying to see who'd be selected for the job of escorting my sweet man, but I still hated to see him go. Love divine, all loves excelling . . . Lord Jesus, welcome him home.*

I hug the book to my chest, feeling the stiff leatherette crack beneath my hands. I can't speak, couldn't force a word if I wanted to.

I can see my grandmother sitting on this sofa, alone in the house. Her age-spotted hand trembles as she records her thoughts at the end of every day, especially when the recollections are hard to relive. By recording these memories, she is leaving a testimony, bearing witness to the fact that she lived, struggled, and loved. A record she intended for us.

Besides Walter and this journal, who else did she have to share her memories with? Her children were gone. And we three girls, I'm ashamed to say, were busy with our own families, too distracted by school, work, and children to give our grandmother much consideration.

How many years have I thought of Grandmother Lillian as a terrible example for us? I loved her as one would love a ditzy, demented old woman, but I spent far more time focusing on her failures than her successes. Yet her successes were monumental. She took in three motherless girls and loved them dearly. She provided a stable place for us to call home. She gave us space to escape from grief, and in her private life, she found the courage to do something I'm not sure I'd be able to do . . . something I'm not sure I can do even now.

She cared enough to love the man who abandoned and betrayed her, and then she dared to forgive him. To keep him at her side. To shelter him among her family, to let him be adored by her grand-daughters and great-grandchildren. To call him *precious* after thirty years of imperfect marriage.

I find it hard to imagine the depths of that love.

PENNYROYAL

After finishing my sausage biscuit, I go back to the kitchen counter and look in the bottom of the fast-food bag, hoping to find a left-over turnover or something. No luck, but yesterday's doughnut box is still on the counter, so I lift the lid—not a single pastry left. Did Ginger eat every last one? I wouldn't be surprised.

All this physical labor has made me hungrier than usual, so I think wistfully of the apples in the trunk of my car and step toward the front door. "I'm going out for a minute."

Rose's granite eyes lock on me. "Fixin' to call *him* again?"

The years fall away and I answer in a singsong voice, brim-ming with a fifteen-year-old's sarcasm. "No, I'm not calling him again."

Rose's mouth curves in what looks like bitter amusement. "At least you're being truthful. Family members shouldn't keep secrets from each other."

I can't tell if she's being serious or ironic, but I can't let her com-ment slide. I turn from the door and march back to the kitchen, then face Rose from the opposite side of the breakfast bar. "Oh, yeah?" I spread my arms and grip the edge of the countertop. "How honest have you been with *your* husband? Have you told Wort everything about your past?"

Rose holds my gaze without flinching, but something moves behind her eyes. I took a random shot and scored a direct hit.

"Wort knows everything he needs to know," she says, yet her voice sounds uneasy. "I've never lied to him."

While I can't imagine what deep, dark secret Rose might be shielding, it's exhilarating to learn she has one. Knowing her, she's probably guilt-stricken because she broke down one day and ate a piece of pepperoni.

"But you haven't told Wort everything"—I drive my point home—"so by your own standards, that's deception. And that's why I can't stay with Bob. Our relationship is built on a lie, and I can't play along anymore."

Rose tilts her head as the beginning of a wavering smile touches the corners of her mouth. "And in the future, things will be different for you . . . how?"

It's a reasonable question, but I wasn't expecting it. I shift my gaze as Rose's words hammer at me. "I'll . . . I'll be totally truthful with my next husband, whoever he is. The man I've recently met"—I feel myself blushing, but it'd be useless to try to hide the truth about Miller now—"is older. He's probably in his midfifties, he's single, and he's settled. He won't be bugging me about starting a family."

"You're gonna tell him everything?"

"Of course."

"Starting with how many times you've been married?"

I stare at her across a sudden silence, then glance into the living room, where Ginger is still reading Grandma's journal. Rose hasn't played the dating game in years; she's probably forgotten about the delicate give-and-take, the cautious sharing of secrets, the slow dance of learning to trust. But she's not gonna leave me alone until I convince her that I'm telling the truth. Worst of all, she'll keep talking until Ginger knows all about my love life, and then I'll have Miss Nosy asking dozens of questions about Miller and Bob and anyone else I'm interested in.

I meet my younger sister's gaze head-on. "How about if I call him right now?"

Rose's eyes light with mischief. "Seriously?"

"If that's what it takes to prove I'm determined to do things right next time."

Wearing the smug smile of a well-fed house cat, Rose walks to the fireplace, pulls her cell phone from the mantel, and brings it to me. I accept it, a little amazed she'd take me up on my offer. I've never seen this side of Rose before.

"Call your new Mr. Wonderful." She folds her arms. "Call him and tell him how many times you've been married—oh, and that you're still living with your husband, who has no idea he's about to be sent packing. Tell him you want to base your relationship on complete honesty."

"And if I do this"—I balance her phone on my fingertips—"what's in it for me?"

Rose shrugs. "Who knows? Maybe true love. Maybe, finally, a lasting relationship. But you'll never know until you give honesty a try."

Another voice chimes in: "Yes, do that." I turn toward the living room, where Ginger has set her book aside and is watching with keen interest. She stands and walks toward the kitchen, her eyes snapping with challenge. "I'd love to see how this experiment turns out."

I consider Rose's dare, then punch in Miller's number. One ring.

"He's probably golfing." I cross an arm over my chest. "He may not pick up."

Two rings.

"I think he's on the course, so I should probably try later—"

"Let it ring," Rose commands. "Be patient."

Three rings.

I glance at my watch. "It's still early, so he may be in the shower. After all, this is a holiday—"

"Hello?" Miller's voice.

In the hollow of my back, a drop of sweat trickles over the track of my spine.

"Hey, it's Penny." I close my eyes as words gush out in a breath-less rush. "Sorry about the unfamiliar number, but I'm using my younger sister's phone. I told her about you."

Miller's voice holds the hint of a smile. "I hope it was a good report."

"How could it be anything else?"

Rose reaches for the phone. "Let me talk to him."

I jerk back, moving away from her grasping hand. "She wants to talk to you. I don't know what she has in mind."

"I'd like to meet her," Miller says. "And this is as good a time as any, right?"

"If you say so. Just a minute." Reluctantly, I hand the phone over.

Rose gives Ginger a delighted smile as she puts the phone to her ear. "Hi," she says, eyeing me as she steps away. "This is Rose, Penny's younger sister. I'm fine, thanks. I just wanted to be sure she actually dialed your number and wasn't bluffing. Yes, nice to meet you too. I think Penny wants to talk to you now."

She gives the phone back. "He's all yours."

If only that were true.

I take the phone and steel myself for whatever's coming, know-ing that this man must think I come from a family of lunatics. "Miller, this may sound crazy, but Rose says a good relationship requires total honesty. So I want to be completely truthful with you before our friendship develops any further."

"Sounds promising," he says, his voice warm in my ear.

"Yes, well, I hope it is. I want to tell you that I'm forty-five years old and I've been married five times." When he doesn't scream or hang up, I grasp the remaining shreds of my courage and continue. "I told you I'm still married, but I didn't tell you that my husband and I haven't separated yet. But we're fixin' to, and I'll be filing for divorce very soon. That's the absolute truth, so help me. My sisters are my witnesses."

For a long moment I hear nothing but a faint buzz on the line, then Miller laughs. "That's—that's a lot to absorb all at once."

I smile, relieved that he hasn't called me a name that would send Grandma running for a bar of soap. "You must think I'm from a family of fruitcakes."

"No, I have an unconventional brother myself. Actually, I have two sisters and three brothers. The Conrads have a thing for large families."

"Nothing wrong with that." I perch on a counter stool and cast a triumphant glance at Rose. If she thought this little exercise would ruin my budding relationship, she's about to be sorely disappointed.

"The more, the merrier," I add. "So unless there's anything you want to confide to me—"

"Maybe there is." His voice slows to a relaxed drawl. "You know, I'm really glad we're having this conversation. I've been trying to find a way to broach a sensitive subject."

A tiny note of alarm chimes in my head. What could my new-found Prince Charming have to confess? A passion for golf? A weakness for football? My throat tightens. "Go on."

"I'm fifty-four," he says, "and I've been married three times. I'm currently separated from my third wife, and the divorce is already in the works. I own my own home, my own car, and a share in our medical research firm."

"Nothing wrong with any of the above." I relax and cross my legs. "I'll soon be coming into an inheritance from my grandmother. It's not a fortune, but it's nothing to sneeze at, either."

"I think we could survive an inheritance," he says, laughter in his voice. "But I also have a dog."

"I like dogs. I have a son, but he's grown. His name is Reese, he's twenty-four, and he lives in Indiana. He tells me he's about ready to get married and settle down."

"Glad to hear you have a son," Miller says. "Because I have *five* sons, ages six, ten, twelve, eighteen, and twenty. The two older ones are in college, but the younger three live with me and visit their mother on weekends. They're with their mother now, but I'll be picking them up when I go back tonight."

A shiver contracts my spine, and my smile freezes. Miller's still talking, rattling off the names of his children, but his words are bouncing off my brain like bullets repelled from Superman's chest.

"What's wrong?" Rose waves her hand before my eyes. She hasn't heard Miller's side of the conversation, and she'll laugh when she finds out what I've just learned.

"Five kids?" Somehow I find my voice and croak into the phone. "Five *boys*?"

Rose's face goes blank with shock.

"Listen, Miller"—I turn so I won't have to see Rose's expression turn to gloating—"I need to give the girls a hand with the cleaning. Take care and I'll see you later."

I disconnect the call and hand the phone back to Rose, my confidence shriveling. I should have known I'd discover a major flaw in the perfect Dr. Miller Conrad.

Ginger drops her hand onto my shoulder and gives me a surprisingly sympathetic smile. "You don't have to search for a husband who'll love you if you have one waiting at home."

"Miller has five children." I acknowledge the fact aloud, then shake my head. "The man must be bonkers."

"He must love kids," Rose says, but the delight in her voice has faded. She turns toward the sink, and after a silent interval I lean forward to check on her. Tears glisten in the depths of her eyes, but I can't figure out why *she's* crying when I've just given up the perfect man.

ROSEMARY

Anguish rises inside me like an overinflated balloon, and the tender touch of Penny's inquisitive gaze is enough to prick the bubble. I burst into tears, the repressed longings and agonies of past years flooding onto my cheeks as I run for the shelter of Gran's bedroom.

I slam the door behind me, but I've no sooner flung myself onto the mattress than Penny appears in the doorway, her eyes wide. "What is wrong with you?"

I can't speak, don't want to speak, but Penny won't be ignored. "Why on earth are you crying? I'm the one who just found out that my perfect man is raising a basketball team."

"What man is perfect?" Ginger asks, following in Penny's wake. She steps into the room and stares at me, her face a mask of curiosity. I turn toward the wall and try to stanch my tears, but I can't—they're oozing from old wounds, flowing from a buried spring running fast and deep.

"Rosemary, what's wrong?" Ginger drops to the bed and curls a stiff arm around my shoulder. But hers is the *last* comfort I want right now, the last touch I'll ever want. I jerk away, rolling out of her embrace, and end up standing on the other side of the room. I wrap my arms around myself and shudder as my sisters stare at me in openmouthed bewilderment.

This is not the way I wanted to spend my last day. I had decided not to let them see my pain; I didn't want them to know my secrets. I have to find a way to handle this, to bring up some small upset so their suspicions won't be aroused later.

"Rose," Ginger finally whispers, "you can talk to us. What has Wort done?"

The stupid question draws a reflexive guffaw from me. Ginger will always think of him as a deranged Hells Angel. I can defend him until my throat is raw, but Ginger will always distrust him.

Maybe it's time to hold a mirror up to *her* face.

"My babies." I choke out the words, knowing this is far from a small upset. "I can't forget about my babies."

Penny glances at Ginger, then walks around the end of the bed and takes a step toward me. A deep line appears between her brows as she feels her way into the conversation. "Honey . . . what babies?"

Of course, she doesn't even accept that I *had* babies! Blindsided by her ignorance, I try to clamp my throat over the sob rising from my chest, but I can't. I begin to wail in earnest, sobbing, coughing, shrieking like an adolescent on a hormonal crying jag. The floodgates have opened and I can't stop the tide of tears.

I collapse on the bare mattress and bury my face in my hands, dimly aware of my sisters whispering nearby. I cry until I'm exhausted, then I close my eyes and roll onto my back, resting in the posture of a dead woman.

The room fills with a thick quiet, broken only by my occasional sobbing hiccup. I open my eyes enough to see Penny elbow Ginger, silently urging her to take charge. Ginger takes a stiff step in my direction, but she has no right to speak to me about this.

Unable to bear Ginger's pseudo-sympathy or Penny's questions, I pull myself off the bed and stride out of the room, down the hallway, and out the front door. The gravel road beckons, the wind whistles in the tree canopy, and I obey their summons, walking down Fish Fever Lane at a brisk pace.

I'll go back to the house once my heart calms and my tears dry. But for now, I want to leave my sisters alone with one of my secrets. Maybe Ginger will lift the lid and expose the truth I've left behind.

I doubt it, though. I've known both of those women all my life, but I don't think they've ever really wanted to know me.

Sprawled across Ginger and Michael's bed, I pressed my hands to my sandy, swollen eyelids. From a gap under the door, Bill Cosby's voice seeped into the silent bedroom, followed by a burst of canned laughter.

I placed my hands over my ears and tried to drown out the sound. None of the Cosby kids would find themselves in this kind of mess; Dr. and Mrs. Huxtable were too loving, too firm, and too involved to ever allow one of their teenage daughters to turn up pregnant.

I certainly hadn't meant to find myself knocked up at twenty. Harper and I were tiptoeing toward commitment, and though I was pretty sure he loved me, he hadn't actually said those words. He liked me, I was sure of that, and I never felt as loved as I did when he held me in his arms.

Still, Harper hadn't been around when I read the result from the home pregnancy test. For more than an hour I sat in a stunned huddle on the bathroom floor, trying to figure out how to tell my dad that his baby was fixin' to have a baby. In the end, I couldn't do it.

So I left the house and drove to Ginger and Michael's apartment. Ginger had just come from visiting Penny in the hospital and was so jazzed about Reese's arrival that at first she didn't notice the expression on my face.

"The baby is adorable," she said, shedding her shoes and untying her scarf as she led the way back to her bedroom. "I want one just like him, but not yet. Michael has to finish grad school first, and I want to be sure we're financially stable and settled wherever he lands a professorship—"

The dam broke in that instant, turning me into a watery, slobbery mess.

"Why, Rose!" Honest surprise filled Ginger's face. "What on earth?"

I stepped into her bedroom and closed the door behind me, then slid down the wall and sobbed out the oldest story in the book. Pregnant. Poor. Not married.

I thought Ginger would yell, or at least lecture me about how stupid I'd been. She didn't like Harper; she never had.

Instead she let me finish; she listened silently while I spilled every tear and every regret. Then she handed me a box of tissues and waited until I blew my nose.

"Sit," she commanded, pulling me off the floor and gesturing to the edge of the bed. While I sat, still sniffling, she folded her arms and looked at me with her steeliest gaze. "Where is Harper Jones now?"

"This minute?"

"Exactly."

I told her Harper was working at Harvey's grocery store on Bemiss Road. He didn't get off until four.

"Did you call him? Have you told him anything about this?"

I mouthed my answer, a silent no.

"Good. You stay here, fix your face, pull yourself together. I'm going to see this boy, and I'm taking care of this for you."

I melted in relief. Ginger would fix it. Ginger could talk anybody into anything. I didn't know what she was going to say to Harper or how she intended to tell Daddy we had another baby on the way, but I was happy to let her take charge.

She grabbed her purse, applied a fresh coat of lipstick, and slid her feet back into her shoes. Without even saying good-bye, she went out the door, her scarf fluttering from her neck.

Feeling suddenly weary, I stretched out on her bed, both hands protectively shielding my stomach and the life within. I woke to the sounds of Michael's laughter and the Huxtables. The window had gone dark, and the room had filled with the dense hush of twilight. How long had I slept?

I sat up, pushed my hair from my eyes, and stared at my reflection in the shadowed mirror on the closet door. A crease marked my cheek, an impression from the pillowcase. I must have slept like a stone.

I stood and opened the bedroom door, then stepped into the living room. Michael and Ginger sat on the couch, and, after nodding at me, Michael rose, stretched his legs, and mumbled something about going to study at the library. He slung his book bag over his shoulder and left without looking at me again.

"Did you have a nice rest?" Ginger asked, as casually as if I'd dropped by for a nap.

She patted a spot on the sofa. I sat next to her, pulling my long sleeves down over my cold hands. "Did you find Harper?"

She clicked the remote, muting the television, and shifted to face me. "I found him"—she looked directly into my eyes—"and he doesn't want you to worry because he's going to do the right thing. He gave me this." She pulled a bulky white envelope from behind a sofa pillow.

I eyed the envelope with suspicion. "What is that?"

"It's two hundred fifty dollars. It's enough for an abortion."

I jerked away as alarm raced up my backbone. I hadn't asked for an abortion, hadn't even thought about getting rid of the baby. The life inside me was a child, a boy or a girl. It hadn't done anything wrong. I might be foolish, but the baby was innocent.

I shook my head. "I don't want an abortion."

Ginger exhaled a sigh, her face filling with regret. "I know you don't, Rose. Harper doesn't want one either, but he knows you two aren't ready to be parents. So he wants you to get the procedure done so y'all can start over and do things right. You've got the money and I've already made the appointment. You can stay here tonight, and first thing tomorrow we'll go down to the clinic—"

"No!" Tomorrow was too soon, too quick. I hadn't even had time to get used to the idea of being pregnant.

"The longer you wait, the more complicated the procedure is," Ginger explained. "You want to do it quick, so all the doctor has to do is vacuum it out. It will only take a few minutes unless . . ." She tilted her head. "How far along do you think you are?"

I swallowed hard. "I don't know."

"How many periods have you missed?"

My cheeks burned as if they'd been seared by a flame. "Two."

Ginger drew in a quick breath, her eyes widening. "Good grief, Rose, why didn't you realize something was wrong?"

Fresh tears sprang to my eyes. "How was I supposed to know? I've never been regular, and Harper said he was being careful—"

"You trusted a guy to be *careful*?" Ginger groaned and knocked her fist against her forehead. "Why didn't I teach you better? I trusted the school, that's why. I figured your friends would tell you everything you needed to know."

"I—I—didn't mean—" I stammered, mortified by my ignorance.

"It's okay." Ginger lowered her hand and took a deep breath. "You're going to be fine. I'll call Dad and tell him you're spending the night with me. He doesn't need to know anything else, and we won't tell Penny, either. The fewer people who know, the better."

"What about Michael?"

"I haven't told him a thing. I told him you came over and took a nap because you were having cramps." She leaned forward, planted her elbows on her knees, and clasped her hands. "When it's all done tomorrow, I'll take you home and get on over to the church. I have a choir rehearsal at eleven o'clock."

Like a child caught in a rip current, I surrendered to Ginger's insistence. She wanted me to get rid of the baby. Harper wanted me to get rid of the baby. Daddy didn't know about the baby, but he would probably want me to get rid of it too . . . if he bothered to voice an opinion at all.

So the next morning, when Ginger drove into a parking lot, pressed the envelope into my hand, and pointed toward the clinic door, I got out of the car and walked forward.

FOURTEEN

PENNYROYAL

Under the sofa, I find a dust-covered piece of embroidery, a rectangle hand-stitched with one of Grandma's pithy sayings: *Most men believe in dreams . . . until they marry one.*

I sweep behind the sofa and love seat. I hate to think of Bob agreeing with the sentiment of that sampler, but I know he'll be hurt when I tell him I want a divorce. I've also been hurt, though. After all, I believed Bob was a romantic until we'd been married awhile. Then he began paying more attention to his Mensa pals than to me. His lack of attention hurt, but when I withdrew to lick my wounds, he only became more involved in his activities than our marriage.

I didn't sign on for a marriage of companionship. I want a man who loves me more than anything else. Is that so much to ask?

I am carrying a loaded dustpan toward the front porch railing when I hear the steady roar of an approaching car. Since we're not expecting anyone but the thrift store guys, I give the SUV only the quickest of glances, then I halt in midstep: the car is a silver Xterra and looks exactly like Bob's.

I dump the collection of dirt and dead insects into the hedge, then peer through the drizzle as the car comes to a halt next to the others parked in front of Grandma's cottage. Then I realize the SUV is not a car *like* Bob's, it *is* Bob's, and my husband is behind the wheel.

For a moment I feel like a fly caught in a spider's web, unable to move. What is Bob doing here? He's supposed to be at home, working on his computers or building a Mars mobile rover or something. . . .

But he's here, and he's seen me. He kills the engine.

I don't know why he's come to St. Simons, and I can't think of a single good reason. This leaves me with two choices: I can walk back into the house, where Bob is probably heading next, or run through the backyard, leap the fence, and hide somewhere in the neighborhood.

No . . . as much as the last idea appeals to me, I'm too old for hide-and-seek. And I need to catch him before my sisters do.

I manage a shaky smile and walk toward the Xterra, my mind racing as I struggle to maintain a nonchalant attitude.

The car door opens and Bob's head appears above the roofline. I'd recognize that receding hairline anywhere.

"Bob?" I inject a bright note into my voice. "What on earth brings you here?"

He turns and watches me approach, but he doesn't answer and he doesn't smile. The observing oaks bend their branches and gossip about us in whispers, but I keep walking, finally facing my husband in the narrow space between our two parked vehicles. For some insane reason, I feel like I'm in an old Western, about to enact the shoot-out at Fish Fever Lane.

"Bob?" My smile quavers. "Is something wrong?"

He reaches into his pocket and for an instant I'm actually afraid he's going for a gun. But instead he produces my cell phone, the one I left charging on the kitchen counter.

"I found this," he says, his voice flat, "and Saturday afternoon it kept ringing, so I answered it. Talked to a guy named Miller Conrad, who wanted directions to your grandmother's house on St. Simons Island. Seems he wanted to show up here and surprise you . . . until I told him I really didn't approve of another man visiting my wife."

The empty air between us vibrates, the silence filling with dread. Somehow I remain on my feet, though I'm certain the ground has

shifted beneath me. I've been found out. "Bob, you have to understand—"

"Understand what, Penn?" His face remains locked in neutral,
though he has to be ticked off about what he's learned. "All weekend I've been trying to understand how a woman who says she
loves me—who said as much a couple of days ago, right before she
left to visit her sisters—could invite some other man to meet her in
Georgia. Could tell him that her marriage is over. I've been turning
that question around in my head, but I can't seem to come up with
an acceptable answer—and I'm not a dummy, by any means. So
maybe you can explain it to me, because I'm certainly not having
any success coming up with an answer on my own."

"Bob, I . . ." I glance at the houses around us, wondering if the
sound of my husband's now-impassioned voice has drawn any of
the neighbors to their windows. What a drama for the residents
of Fish Fever Lane. Not even Grandma dared to stage one of her
breakups in the middle of the road.

"All right." I lift my hands in surrender and resign myself to
the inevitable. Fine. I deserve everything that's coming to me. I'll
never see Miller again, but that's okay. The important thing now is
to calm Bob's feelings, avoid a public confrontation, and hope for
an amicable divorce.

"Come out of the rain." I step forward and take his arm, pulling
him toward Grandma's house. I lower my voice as we walk. "I'm
sorry about what you found out, and the way you found out about
it. I was getting ready to explain that things aren't working out
between us, and I know I should have told you sooner."

"What things aren't working out?" he asks, his voice choked.

"Well . . ." I point to the porch swing, where our conversation
would be more private than if we went inside. "Shall we sit?"

I take his elbow again, but he pulls away as if my touch is
unbearable. The unspoken reproach hurts, but I lead the way up
the stairs and across the porch, then sit on the right side of the
swing. After a minute Bob sits, too, leaving a wide gap between us.

I'm grateful the swing forces us to face in the same direction, giving me a reason not to look into his eyes. "Bob"—I smooth my voice and launch into my standard speech—"I'm sorry. You deserve to be happy, and you deserve all the good things you want out of life, but I can't give you those things. I've begun to realize that I probably shouldn't have married you. I'm not gonna fight you and I won't be greedy, so it won't be a difficult divorce—"

"What makes you think I want a divorce?"

Surprise siphons the blood from my head, making it even harder to think. "Well, it's obvious—I mean, we've grown apart—"

"How can you say that?" He reaches across the space between us and takes my chin, pulls it around until my unwilling eyes lock with his. "My feelings for you haven't changed at all."

"But they will." Though my intentions remain firm, my voice quavers. "When I tell you the truth."

His face twists into a question mark. "Please do. I love hearing the truth."

I close my eyes. "I hoped we wouldn't have to do this. I didn't want to tell you, and I didn't mean for this to drag on for so long—"

"Spit it out, will you?"

My eyes fly open. "Okay! I'm not as young as you think I am. I'm not thirty-nine, I'm forty-five."

His expression remains serious, but one corner of his mouth curls upward. "Forty-five's not such a vast age."

"It is if you want babies. I can't give you those; I had my tubes tied not long after my son was born."

There. My secrets are out, all the biggies, exposed and naked and writhing in the harsh light of day. Bob has heard them, he will despise me, and he will grant me a divorce as soon as he can. Goodbye number five; make way for number six. Maybe next time I'll find the kind of love Grandma Lillian finally found in Walter.

Bob releases my chin and stares straight ahead, his gaze wide and fixed on nothing. Giving him a minute to absorb the full significance of my deception, I brace myself for his anger and derision. I've had emotional reactions heaped on me before, from husbands who were far meaner and more physically powerful. Bob's rebuke will probably contain more syllables and send me running for a dictionary, but the end result will be the same.

After an interval woven of eternity, Bob turns his face to mine, his eyes as soft and tender as a caress. "If you don't want children," he says, his voice calm and even, "then I don't want them, either. And while I never believed you were thirty-nine, I really don't care how old you are. I fell in love with *you*, Penny, with your spunk, your spirit, and your heart. I love you. I want you. And I'm not gonna give you up simply because you think it's time to move on."

Stunned by the ardent expression that fills my husband's face, I sit very still, my deck shoes angled on the plank porch like frog flippers. He *loves* me? After what I've put him through, he still wants me?

"Penn." Bob drops a warm hand to my shoulder. "Don't look at me like you've never seen me before."

"I don't think I have." My voice is a ragged whisper, and my eyes keep flicking away, afraid to rest too long on his earnest face. "Who *are* you? And why did I think you were smart?"

A trace of a smile touches his lips with ruefulness. "Most people think I am, yet I've never met anyone who confuses me like you do." He touches my face. "I felt you pulling away, so I tried to give you space. You resisted my attempts to draw you closer, so I settled back to wait—"

"I thought you were bored with me. I thought all the romance between us had died."

"Sweetie, if you want romance, all you have to do is smile at me and I'll melt into a puddle of goo. But no matter what happens, I want you to know this: I love you, Penny Lawrence Thacker Mitchell Barthol Thibodeaux Jensen, and I believe I can make you happy. But you've got to be willing to stay. I can't love you like I want to if you won't let me."

I shake my head, disbelieving. "But . . . I went behind your back and I hurt you. I didn't exactly have an affair with that man, but I was—well, I was ready to move on."

"I spent a great deal of time considering that on the drive up." Bob's distracting and talented fingertips trace a warm path from my shoulder to my neck. "But I'd had a good talk with Dr. Conrad— once we got over our initial embarrassment, that is. He's a decent guy, and he didn't want to cause trouble. He assured me that things weren't serious between you two."

"They could have been," I insist. "Given a little more time, I could have fallen hard for him."

Bob chuckles. "Penny, I don't think you know what it means to really fall for someone, but I'd like to show you what love's really about."

I slide closer to him, still amazed, but drawn by the tenderness in his touch. "How are you gonna do that?"

"I'm going to promise you something. You can be honest with me about anything, and I promise to love you through it. Tell me when you're glad, when you're mad, and when you're sad. Say you're annoyed at me; say you're miserable because of something I did. Let me know when I do something wonderful, so I can learn what makes you happy. Tell me anything, but be honest. As long as you are, I'll love you forever."

I lean into the curve of his arm and breathe in his clean, masculine scent, unable to believe that my number five turned out to be more understanding than I imagined. I could still let him go . . . but why should I? I barely know this marvel of a man.

If he really wants to keep me, I might learn to enjoy being kept.

"I can do that." I reach up to stroke his stubbled cheek, then kiss the tip of my index finger and press it to his lips. "If you will forgive me for being an idiot, from now on I will always tell you the truth."

"I forgive you," Bob says, lowering his mouth to mine. "And I always will."

GINGER

I'm hunched over, tears of loss rolling down my cheeks as I scrub the sink in the upstairs bathroom, when I hear footsteps on the steps. I lift my head, expecting to see Penny, but Rose comes into the room, a caddy filled with cleaners in her gloved hands and a dishtowel over her shoulder.

"I'm here to do the glass." She nods at the window without looking directly at me. "If you'll let me get in that corner for a minute . . ."

I step to the side and wipe my tears away, then grab a length of tissue to blow my nose. Once I'm sure I look reasonably present-able, I lean against the wall to watch her spray the windowpane. "Are you feeling better?"

She nods, and from where I stand I can see that her eyes are also red.

I wait for her to say something, but apparently she doesn't want to talk about her bedroom breakdown. "Listen, Rose," I begin, "I know you've struggled with infertility. The miscarriage was terrible and I felt really bad for you, but you've got to learn how to put the past behind you and move forward. You're still a young woman, you have a great life, and I'm sure the future holds all kinds of wonderful things for you."

"I'm glad you're so sure of that." Rose speaks in a dispassion-ate voice, and I can't tell if she's sincere or only humoring me. She wipes the glass clean with a vigorous circular motion, then turns to spray the mirror on the medicine cabinet. When she's finished, she gives the glass a final swipe, then arches a brow. "Anything else in here need cleaning?"

I point to the grimy bathtub. "There's that."

"Okay."

She sprays the faucet with glass cleaner, then sprinkles powdered cleanser around the edges of the tub. As she gets on her knees to begin scrubbing, I move back to the sink and open the vanity cabinet. The small space has been emptied out, but something remains . . . something ominous.

I pull my head out of the vanity as a sense of approaching disaster engulfs me. "This is *not* good."

Rosemary stops scrubbing and turns in my direction. "What's the problem?"

"I think I've found mold under the sink here. Black mold. Isn't that stuff nearly impossible to get rid of?"

"There you go, jumping to the worst possible conclusion. Let me take a look." Rose drops her scrub brush into the tub and crawls forward, then lowers her head to peer at the dark spot beneath the U-shaped pipe. Frowning, she extends a gloved hand and scrapes at the spot on the vanity's base. Part of the black grime comes away, but most of it remains.

"I can't tell." Rose stares at the goop on her gloved fingertip. "It might be mildew. If it is, a good dose of bleach will kill it."

"But what if it's mold?" I groan and drop to a more comfortable position on the floor. "Mold is like death to a real estate contract, and we have to disclose it to the buyer. Sometimes mold hides, and if you find a little bit, you can almost bet it's living in the walls, growing up the pipes, and sending spores into the air. No one will want to live here if the place is filled with mold. No one at all."

"Calm down," Rose says. "The house passed a professional inspection, didn't it? We're off the hook." Rose straightens and reaches for the plastic caddy. She pulls out a bottle and sprays the offending black blob. Together we sit back and watch as the foamy liquid bubbles on top of the suspect spot.

Maybe I am overreacting. Maybe the situation with Michael has caused me to look for the worst in everything, to expect disaster in the most insignificant developments. . . .

"Some things," Rose says, her voice abstracted, "ruin everything they touch."

I peer at her. "Isn't the mold remover working?"

Rose shifts her gaze, sees that I'm staring at her, and draws her mouth into a tight smile. "It's working. So never mind."

That's when I realize she wasn't talking about mold at all. But who does she think she's talking to? I'm her sister; I practically raised her. "Don't change the subject, Rose, I know that look. Something's on your mind, so out with it."

Rose pastes on an unconcerned expression, but when I refuse to glance away, she squares her shoulders and straightens her smile. "I was just thinking that some people are a lot like mold. Me, for instance. I move in with Harper, he leaves me after a year. I marry Todd, who carries on with my best friend. I marry Jonah, who leaves me when I can't get pregnant. I marry Wort, we get pregnant, and then we lose our baby. If it weren't for me, even our mother—"

Her voice breaks and her chin quivers with the thought she can't bring herself to say.

But I know what she's thinking because I've thought it myself. And believed it.

"I'll give you room to finish cleaning the tub." I push up to a standing position and cough the scent of mold remover from my lungs. "I think these fumes are giving me a headache, so I'm going out for some fresh air."

PENNYROYAL

Grandma once told me that you can always tell if a woman is truly in love by the way she looks at her husband. If she smiles at him like a woman pulled over by a traffic cop, that's genuine love.

"Are you sure you don't want to stay?" I lock my hands behind Bob's back, pulling him close. I smile up at my husband, noticing once again how nice and tall he is and how warm his blue eyes are.

"I'm going back to get things ready for your homecoming." He kisses the top of my forehead. "Your sisters are nice, but I'm gonna suffer an estrogen overdose if I get drafted into cleaning detail. Go ahead, have a good time, relive a few old memories. I'm glad y'all are having this chance to be together."

He kisses me, and for a dizzying moment I cling to him, blown away by the realization that I was ready to leave this man. How could I have been so blind? I am amazed at his inner strength—none of my other husbands ever stood up to me in the way Bob did today. None of the others was willing to work at keeping me.

"Be careful on the drive home." I wipe invisible dust from his shoulders and squeeze his bicep. "The roads are wet, and I don't want to lose you."

"I'm not going anywhere without you. See you soon."

Bob releases me and jogs down the porch steps, a new jauntiness in his stride. I linger on the porch and sit on the railing, leaning against a column as I wave and watch the Xterra pull away. He honks—two quick taps—as he nears the end of Fish Fever Lane.

Just like Daddy used to do.

That's when it hits me—how many times in my childhood did I sit in this exact spot and watch Daddy drive away? Every time he left, I felt a frightening hollowness open up inside me, a yearning I've been trying to fill for as long as I can remember. I tried easing the ache with food; that only put on more pounds than I could comfortably carry. I tried looking for male attention, and for a while that worked—I felt pretty, clever, and desirable when boys wanted to spend time with me.

Throughout junior high and high school, falling in love was as easy as turning a page, though my relationships lasted about as long as a first kiss. After high school graduation, I set out to find Mr. Perfect, but not until today did I realize that he simply can't exist.

Nobody's perfect—not me, not Bob. But because no one is fault-less, we all stand on even ground. Now that I've exposed the lies I told my husband, I feel as if I could tell him anything and not have to worry that he will be disgusted, offended, or so turned off by the truth that he'll abandon me. I can barely believe it, but the man *really* loves me.

I have never felt so free.

R O S E M A R Y

It's time.

Standing at the living room window, I rub my arms and watch Penny say good-bye to her husband. Her carefully laid plans have flown right out the door because her intelligent husband put a few clues together and drove up here to confront her.

I've left a trail of clues too—especially in this cottage, where several times I've said more than I intended to say—but no one has noticed them. Ginger is too focused on her own personal tragedy, and Penny is off in her romantic la-la land.

No one is likely to stop me from driving off the Sydney Lanier Bridge . . . and that's a good thing. Because Justus and I are ready to go. The cleaning is done, I've spent time with my sisters, and though we haven't exactly made peace, we haven't declared war, either.

Maybe peace will come after I'm gone.

I glance upward, where the wet wind moves in the trees. The rain has stopped, so driving will be easier . . . and yet I will still have a wet roadway to blame for the accident. The insurance company will pay out without complaint; no one will be bothered by guilt. I am making this choice, and I will follow through.

Now . . . I need only to convince Penny and Ginger that I'd like to pull out early.

Ginger is upstairs, and Penny is still on the porch, humming to herself.

She's wearing that smitten look, and I wouldn't be surprised if she decides to take off not long after I leave. She'll be home tonight, snuggled in her husband's arms, while Justus and I will be . . . at rest, I hope.

I walk back to Gran's bedroom, glance around, and lift my suitcase to the stripped bed. I drop my toiletries bag and hairbrush into a side pocket, then double-check the closet and the bathroom. When I'm sure I haven't left anything behind, I zip the bag and roll it down the hallway and out the front door.

Penny lifts a brow when I walk past. "Loading your car early?"

I nod.

"That's a good idea. Wouldn't want those thrift store guys to take your suitcase when they come to empty the house."

Penny doesn't wait for my answer but leaps out of the swing and hurries into the house, probably to pack her own bag. I roll mine over the cracked sidewalk, then drag it through the gate and the gravel. Into the back of the car it goes, then I turn and take a last look at the cottage.

All I need is Justus, his bed, and Gran's bird blanket. I should probably say good-bye to my sisters, but I'll need a cheerful facade for that.

I lean against the car and close my eyes, wrapping my heart in resolve. I can do this. I can think of how much good Wort can do with my inheritance, how he can grow his business. I can focus on how Racehorse Rescue will thrive with a million-dollar bequest from my life insurance, about how many more animals can be saved from slaughterhouses. And I can breathe a silent prayer for Wort's happiness . . . that he will find a woman who can give him the sons he wants, and that he won't be lonely when I'm gone.

I open my eyes and straighten myself with as much dignity as I can muster. Moving forward in a strange numbed comfort, I go back into the house to fetch my dog and say my farewells.

GINGER

I shouldn't be surprised that my sisters want to leave before the work is finished; walking out on me seems to be a popular choice these days. Apparently neither of them cares enough for my company to want to stay for the nice dinner I proposed, but at this point I'm not sure I'd want to stay myself. I'm exhausted, physically, and mentally. I can't seem to stop crying, and I need to get back to real life and find out what's left of my world.

I thought Penny would be the first to abandon ship, but when I come down the stairs, sweaty and smelling of disinfectant, Rose is standing near the door, her dog in one arm and Grandmother's bird blanket in the other.

"It's stopped raining"—she glances out the window as if she's afraid to meet my gaze—"so I thought I should hit the road before the next deluge. I don't want Wort to worry."

I look at Penny, expecting her to share my surprise, but she's peering out the window too.

I gesture to the furniture, still in place. "But the thrift store truck hasn't even come yet. Once all this stuff is out, we have to sweep the floors—"

"Don't worry, we'll take care of it." Penny smiles at Rose. "Give the Wortster a hug from me, okay? Maybe Bob and I will drive over to see you one of these weekends. You let me know when it's a good time."

"Sure." Rose gives Penny a smile that seems a bit too small, while Penny gingerly reaches around the dog and pats Rose's back.

"All right, then." I step forward, not surprised that Rose wants to leave. This was probably the worst possible time to arrange a get-together, but how was I supposed to know that my life would come crumbling down this weekend? Life happens on its own schedule.

"Drive safely, kiddo." I give Rose a quick shoulder pat and open the door for her. "Tell Wort hello for me."

A muscle quivers at Rose's chin, but she steps through the doorway, striding across the porch and down the stairs. I watch until she reaches the picket gate, then I close the door and glance at the clock. "Lunchtime," I announce, "and the thrift store truck should be here any minute."

"Want me to go grab some food?" Penny reaches for her purse. "I could be back in a flash."

I nod, realizing that Penny is anxious to finish and go home. Maybe the truck will be here by the time we've eaten lunch. If so, all we'll have to do is give the house a final sweep and then find the nearest U-Haul agent. Penny and I will both need a trailer to transport the furniture we've chosen, but if we pick up the trailers *now*, we might be able to persuade the thrift store men to give us a hand with the loading. . . .

I turn, about to ask Penny if we should go rent our trailers, but she's already out the door. I could call her, now that she has her phone.

I find my purse on an end table and fish my cell from the inner pocket. Before I can dial Penny's number, however, the phone rings. The caller displayed is B Jones, and it takes me a minute to recognize my Realtor's name and number.

"Hello?"

"Ginger! So glad I caught you. Listen, I neglected to get Social Security numbers from you and your sisters—the accountant will need them before she can cut your checks. Can you help me out?"

"Sure." I give her my Social Security number, then glance around. Penny took her purse, of course, so I have no way of getting the information for either of my sisters. "Listen, Penny ran out to get lunch, so I'll have her call you the minute she gets back. As for Rose, she's already driving home to Jacksonville, so let me give her a call. I'll get back to you as soon as I can."

"Thanks, I'd appreciate it. Talk to you soon."

I move to the window and scan the road, but I can see no sign of an approaching truck. The movers promised to arrive around lunchtime, but maybe I should wait until one, then call and make sure they're still coming.

I press the quick-dial button for Rose's cell phone. After several rings, the service provider switches me to Rose's voice mail.

Good grief, why won't Rose answer her phone? I click my teeth against my tongue, thinking, then dial her home number. Her husband should be around. Maybe he'll know Rose's Social Security number.

The phone rings four times, then Wort answers, breathless. "'Lo?"

"Wort, this is Ginger." I smile into the phone, determined to be polite. "Listen, Rose must have turned her ringer off and I need her Social Security number. Would you happen to know it?"

"Um . . . no. Rosie handles all our paperwork and financial stuff."

I suppress a groan. "Are there any papers nearby that might show it? Last year's tax return, for instance?"

"Wait a minute, let me look around."

I hear a clunk, then the distant sound of file drawers being opened and slammed shut. When Wort finally comes back on the line, his voice is rough with frustration. "Listen, Ginger, I can't find anything. Let me look around some more and I'll call you back."

"Thanks, Wort. Appreciate your help."

I hold the phone for another minute, wondering if there's any other way to get the information I need, but apparently I'm not going to be able to check this item off my to-do list any time soon.

I toss my phone back into my purse, pick up the broom, and head back upstairs.

PENNYROYAL

By the time I arrive back at the cottage with lunch, I see that I've been preceded—barely—by a huge truck operated by the Heavenly Treasures Thrift Store. Ginger must have heard the vehicle rattling down the road because she's on the front porch, arms waving as she tries to tell the driver how and where to park to make loading easier. Unfortunately, our darling Dumpster is in the way.

I leave my car by the side of the road, well out of the crash zone, and grab the pizza box I picked up in the village. Ginger may complain about having pizza again, but I suspect she'll be so busy bossing the thrift store guys around that she'll scarcely notice what she's eating.

One of the movers, a thin man with a thick mustache, hops out of the cab and winks at me as I walk around the truck and beeline for the gate. "Is that lunch for me?" he calls.

"Not if you've already eaten," I holler back. "My sister and I are starving."

When Ginger sees me on the sidewalk, she props one hand on her hip. "Before I forget, Penny, you need to call the Realtor. Barbara needs your Social Security number before she can cut your check."

"Fine." I climb the porch steps and gesture toward the front door. "You want to eat inside, or out here?"

"I was thinking about my piano . . . and the rental trailers." Ginger swivels to face me as a frown creases her forehead. "If we had our trailers now, we could ask these guys to help us with the load-ing. I wouldn't mind paying them a few bucks."

"But we don't have the trailers yet." I point to the road, which is solidly blocked by the truck. "And we don't have any way of get-ting them before these guys leave. I could get out, but there's no way you could get your car out with that truck blocking the way."

Ginger bites her lip. "I guess we could ask the guys to move the piano and kitchen table onto the front lawn, at least. Then maybe you and I could manage to get the piano and the table into the trailers."

My stomach clenches at the thought of pushing a piano, even a small one, across a tangle of grass and oak roots. "I don't know, Gingerbread. The table won't be so bad, but pianos are a major hassle. You might have to call a piano mover . . . if you can find one who'll work on a holiday."

"I should have thought of this earlier, made plans ahead of time." Ginger is chewing on her lower lip now, in danger of draw-ing blood. "If I hadn't been so upset about Michael, I wouldn't have messed this up."

"Calm down." I step toward her and grip her elbow. "You'll think of something. You always do."

My assurance erases the tense lines on Ginger's face, but only for an instant. They spring back into prominence when her cell phone begins to ring.

GINGER

What can possibly go wrong now?

Irritated by the shrill chirp of my cell, I hold the screen door open as Penny carries the pizza into the house. I ought to ignore the phone—with all that's going on here, whoever's on the line would certainly understand and call back. Neither Ryan nor Ross would call today because they're bound to be out partying with friends. Michael is probably with his girlfriend, so he's not likely to be inquiring about my welfare. But . . . that's okay; I'll think about him later. I am here to settle Grandmother's affairs, so my personal problems can wait until I get home.

Penny sets the pizza box on the kitchen table, then gestures to the noisy cell phone on the kitchen counter. "Aren't you gonna answer that?"

"Nope."

"What if it's important?"

"It's probably Michael, and I'm not ready to talk to him." I grab a glass of water and toss it back, preparing to go out and oversee the thrift store pickup crew.

"You gotta admit he's persistent." Penny shakes her head and throws back the lid of the pizza box. After picking up a slice of the pie, she looks more closely at the phone. "Ginger, this isn't Michael. The caller ID says Rose Dodson."

I turn and blow hair out of my eyes. "Who?"

"Why would Rose be calling so soon?" Penny crinkles her nose. "Wait—that's Rose's house. Must be Wort on the line."

"Took him long enough to find that Social Security number." I snatch up the phone. "Hello, Wort? Did you find Rose's Social?"

"No—and I've been trying to call Rose. She won't answer her phone."

"I told you, Wort, she must have turned the ringer off."

"But that's just it, Rosie never turns her ringer off. I think she's up to something, something that's not good—"

"Hang on, Wort, slow down. Why don't you start at the beginning and tell me what's up."

I'm tempted to hand my babbling brother-in-law over to Penny because the restless thrift store guys are milling around in the front yard, obviously waiting for direction. I'd send Penny out to deal with them, but she'll turn on the charm and turn a one-hour job into at least a two-hour affair. . . .

"I was looking for Rosie's number in the desk drawer," Wort says, his words coming out at double speed, "but right on top, set out like she meant for me to find them, were these envelopes. So I opened them—and found her will and a life insurance policy."

There's no help for it; I have to send Penny outside. I catch her eye as she bites into her pizza, then gesture to the porch. Sighing, she wipes cheese off her chin, then drops the rest of her slice onto the box lid and saunters toward the front door.

I return my attention to Wort. "You found what?"

"Rosie's will and a life insurance policy. I never knew about this policy; she never said a word."

I blink as my mind spins. "Well . . . maybe she wanted to surprise you. And maybe she set them out because she was worried about the drive up here. Grandmother Lillian used to set out her will and her funeral dress every time she took a long car trip. Some people are cautious like that."

"Rosie's not that cautious. And she's not usually organized. Plus, there's something else: the date."

"What date?"

"The date on the insurance policy; Rosie's circled it. The policy's dated September second. Today's the fifth. This policy is almost exactly two years old."

I turn to look out the door. Penny stands at the porch railing like a queen holding court, smiling as she talks to the moving men. Even from this distance, I can tell that the three guys are enchanted.

I shake my head and try to focus on what my brother-in-law is saying, but so far he's not making any sense. "Wort, I don't understand. Rosie'll be home in a little while, so why don't you ask her about the policy? I don't think she meant to keep it from you—"

"For a smart woman, you can be awfully dense!" Wort roars, barely bridled fury in his voice. I pull the phone away from my ear, mystified by his sudden anger, until he adds, "Don't you get it? There's a suicide clause that prevents payment unless a period of *two years* has passed."

Without warning, the events of the weekend collide in my head like the bits of glass in a mosaic, jumbles of words and expressions and signs that fit together in a perfect picture: Rose not wanting anything from Grandma's house. Rose weeping over her babies. Rose believing she ruins everything she touches.

Rose insisting that she bring along an arthritic dog that is living—barely—on borrowed time.

"Wort"—my heart begins to thump almost painfully in my chest—"surely you don't think she could—that she would—take her own life."

On the porch, Penny turns toward me, her eyes wide and her face contorted with alarm.

"I do," Wort says, his voice ragged. "But I don't know what she was thinking, so I don't know how to stop her. But y'all know her. *You* know her, Ginger, so what would she do?"

The question snaps like a whip, making me flinch. I close my eyes as images of my baby sister jostle in my head, competing with each other for space. Would Rose take pills? Find a gun or a noose?

Maybe she'd follow our mother's example and make a quick end of things with a knife. There are no freestanding bathtubs between here and Savannah, but there are dozens of cheap hotels. . . .

Truthfully, I don't know what my sister would do to kill herself, but I do know I can't let her do it. I have to go after her.

"We're going to find her," I tell Wort as I catch Penny's attention and reach for my purse. "We'll find her on the road, even if we have to follow her all the way home. Don't worry, we won't let her down."

I disconnect the call, drop my phone into my purse, and shove my way past the screen door. Penny is still staring at me, her face as pale as paper. "Did you say what I think you said?" she whispers, her hand going to her throat.

I jerk my thumb toward the house. "Get your keys; we have to take your car." While she darts inside, I lean over the porch railing to address the three moving men. "Gentlemen, please take anything you find inside this house—except the suitcases and any personal items near them. Everything else goes."

Penny runs out, her purse on her arm and her keys in her hand. As the moving men begin to trudge toward the stairs, I take her hand and pull her down the steps.

"You're giving them everything?" Penny says with a gasp, running alongside me. "Even your piano?"

I point toward her Altima, parked several yards away. "Just give me your keys and get in the car. I'm driving, and we're going to find Rose."

FIFTEEN

GINGER

Though I have been perspiring all weekend, I feel suddenly slick with the rancid sweat of fear. Penny sits next to me, one hand braced on the dashboard, the other on the back of my seat as I tear through the village and drive toward the highway that leads to the mainland.

"What makes you think Rose wants to kill herself?" Penny asks, her voice choked. "She seemed fine to me."

"Did she? How much time did you actually spend talking to her?"

"I've been with her for the past three days. I'd have noticed if something was wrong."

"You did ask me if she seemed weird."

"Rose has always seemed a little weird."

"Did you notice that she didn't want anything from Grand-mother's house? That she kept that dying dog with her all the time?"

"She loves that dog."

"She should have put him down days ago. She didn't . . . and I think she wanted to take him with her."

An RV with Michigan plates is oozing through a red light, so I steer around it, horn blaring, and gun the engine when we hit a stretch of open road. "How long has Rose been gone?" I ask, not daring to take my eyes off the road.

"I don't know." Penny's breath comes in gasps and snatches. "An hour? An hour and fifteen minutes? She should be nearly home by now."

"But she's not home. And she's not answering her phone."

"She could be taking her time. She could have been held up by traffic."

"And she could be gathering the nerve to make this her final trip. Wort seemed convinced, and the more I think about it, I am too."

Penny's face pales except for two red patches, one glowing in each cheek. "If you're right about what she's up to, she might not be in a hurry. Knowing her, she might have driven up by Christ Church before leaving the island. She always loved that area."

"We don't have time to look for her at every tourist spot. We need to drive out and look for her car, maybe check out a few motels off the highway." My voice is flat with the thin sound of fear.

I lay on the horn as I approach an intersection where a single car waits; fortunately, the vehicle hesitates before pulling out. I grip the wheel and urge the Altima forward, for the first time bemoaning the fact that the roads on St. Simons are mostly quiet two-lanes. We near the roundabout, a traffic nightmare, and as I turn right to enter I see two rumbling semis traveling front to back, as close as train cars on a track. I slam on the brakes to let them pass.

"Why are you stopping?" Penny shrieks at me. "You have to go!"

"I *can't* go." I knock the back of my hand against the windshield, indicating the trucks. "You want me to kill us too?"

After maneuvering through the roundabout, we finally hit a stretch of four-lane highway. Driving like a madwoman, I slant from lane to lane, dodging cars and blowing past the doddering tourists out for a bit of holiday sightseeing. We fly toward a horizon that has gone greenish gray, and Penny groans when thunder booms overhead and rain begins to fall in sheets.

"We're all fixin' to die," she wails, peering out at the bruised and swollen sky. "We're gonna skid on the bridge and end up in the river!"

That's when I feel the answer like an electric tingle in my stomach. If she hasn't already done it, Rose is planning to drive off the bridge. In this weather, under these treacherous conditions, no one will suspect that her death was anything but the result of a tragic accident.

I press the car onward, my heart beating in time to the quick thump of the windshield wipers. How can I know if we're too late? We haven't had a TV or radio on all day, so we wouldn't hear a news report. We'll only know if we find that section of highway closed, see red flashes and police cars, find the road lined with blinking yellow caution lights and detour signs.

"Penny"—my voice rings with authority—"call Rose. Dial the number again and again. Don't quit until she answers."

Penny sniffs, then grabs my cell phone and punches in Rose's number. From the corner of my eye I see tears zigzagging down her cheeks as she holds the phone to her ear, her lips soundlessly begging our sister to pick up.

ROSEMARY

"Are you done, Jussy?" I run my fingers through the grass to avoid startling my precious pup with an abrupt touch. "Should we get back in the car?"

Rather than drive straight out of town, I took Justus to one of my favorite spots on the island, the beautiful grounds of Christ Church, near Fort Frederica. I don't know if dogs are actually allowed in the cemetery on the historic property, but the threat of rain has kept the tourists at bay, and Justus certainly hasn't the moxie to bother anyone. Surrounded by the dead—the island's earliest settlers and some of the most recent—we walked among the scabrous tombstones and ancient granite markers, then I spread Grandma's bird blanket on a grassy patch. For a long time, my dog and I rested on the handmade quilt and looked up at the moss-draped live oaks and the bruised sky beyond.

But now thunder threatens from the east, and the first fat drops of rain have begun to fall. So I scoop Justus up in my arms, gather Gran's blanket, and run over the cracked sidewalk to the shelter of the car. Once inside, Justus nests in the worn folds of the quilt on the passenger seat while I let the engine warm.

My purse, sitting on the console between the seats, seems to be buzzing, and for a minute I can't figure out why. Then I remember that I muted the ringer as I got in the car. I didn't want anything to disturb us on our last drive.

I pick up my phone and turn off the power. I won't be needing it anymore.

Lightning flashes, its stark yellow bones showing through the gray skin of the sky. A thunderclap follows, a rumble so loud it seems to shiver the oaks while its baritone plays over the cemetery.

When the sound has faded, I put the car in reverse. "Time to go," I whisper, reaching out to pat Justus's head. I bite back tears and pull away from the sanctuary of the aged church, then turn onto the highway and follow the signs that will lead us to the marina and the Sydney Lanier Bridge.

GINGER

Rain is falling in earnest by the time we drive by the marina. I clutch the steering wheel and sit as straight as a soldier, alarmed at the pellets of rain bouncing off the hood of Penny's car. We pass through the intersection where the road forks toward Brunswick, but the Sydney Lanier Bridge lies to the south. Rose would come this way to go home.

After we veer toward the southern fork, however, I spot blinking yellow lights on the blurred horizon. A spasmodic trembling begins somewhere inside me, and I can't stop it, can't speak, and can barely draw breath.

Penny has gone as stiff as a stone in the next seat. She stares forward, her eyes slitted as she peers through the pouring rain, and after a minute she cracks a tentative smile. "No cop car," she says. "Just traffic signs. The side of the road over here has washed out—they don't want you to drive into a gully."

"Are you sure?"

"Think about it. This road would be closed if—if something had happened."

We haven't driven more than two miles when Penny points straight ahead. "There she is. That's Rose's car."

I stamp on the gas and steer left until we are side by side with our sister's blue SUV. Fortunately, Rose wasn't speeding, but the astonished and guilty look she gives Penny assures me that Wort's hunch was correct.

"Motion for her to pull over when she can," I say, struggling to maintain my position by the side of Rose's vehicle.

Penny is mouthing and pointing to the caution signs at the side of the road, but Rose simply stares at us, her eyes wide and blank. When she finally slows, I slide into the right lane ahead of her and put on my blinker, intending to meet her at the first solid shoulder on the highway. But my tires have no sooner hit the gravel than Rose's car roars around us, taking off like the proverbial bat out of hell.

Penny gasps. "She's getting away!"

I have no choice but to follow. I put on my blinker and look through my left window, trying to ease back into traffic, but it's nearly impossible to see through the curtains of rain.

Finally I face forward and stamp on the gas pedal again, hoping that God and his angels will get us to our sister before she does something desperate.

ROSEMARY

I used to think that Ginger had some weird kind of big sister ESP because she always knew what I was up to when I felt inclined toward trouble. Now I know she hasn't lost her gift.

I don't know how Penny and Ginger managed to figure out what I had planned. I don't know where they came from or how they came to be behind me, but one thing is clear: they intend to follow me until I pull over.

I pound my palm against the steering wheel as the towering bridge looms in the distance. Why can't I disconnect from these women? Life would be so much simpler if we weren't bound to one another, so why can't they see that? If Penny and Ginger stop me from following through with my plan, they'll be sorry after a while. Life will go back to the way it's always been; nothing will change.

At the foot of the bridge, I glance in the rearview mirror and see the Altima, a blur of light blue, still behind me. Ginger is riding my bumper like a race-car driver drafting off of his opponent, handling Penny's sedan as if it needs to be taught a lesson.

She won't give up. She'd follow me to hell and yank me back from the abyss if I went there, all because she's *responsible* for me.

The realization makes me want to laugh and cry. My stubborn older sister, as inflexible as an oak, will stay with me no matter what. She'll cling to me on the curve of the bridge. She will zero in on my vehicle if I change lanes; she will allow no one to come between us. And if at the crest of the curve I veer toward the sea, Ginger might stubbornly follow me into the wide-open space.

I cannot die today . . . without risking my sisters' lives.

My car climbs toward the summit, fear blowing down the back of my neck when gravity pins me against the seat. My head falls against the headrest as I pass a slower-moving Honda and overtake a pickup truck with a rifle in the rear window. Yet no matter how much I increase my speed, Ginger and the Altima remain in my rearview mirror, looming over my back bumper like some kind of warrior guardian angel.

Above my hood ornament I see nothing but sudsy gray sky. My heart leaps uncomfortably into the back of my throat as we near the center of the span; if I'm gonna turn, I should do it *now*, should jerk the steering wheel toward the empty lane at my right, hold it until the car rams into the concrete guardrail and breaks through with the force of sheer velocity.

A scream rises at the back of my throat, but I choke it off by holding my breath. The hood tips downward and I see the bridge's falling curve, the gentle arc that will lead us back to land . . . and safety.

For the next several moments my hands handle the car automatically and my heart returns to a normal rhythm. When I am clear of the bridge and on a straight stretch of U.S. Route 17, I shift into the right lane, put on my blinker, and pull onto the grassy shoulder. My palms are slick with sweat, but my mind has gone numb and my body responds with reflexive movements. I turn off the engine and tremble in the driver's seat, my hands clutching the steering wheel like claws. Outside the car, whooshing traffic splashes my windshield and wind whips at the tall grasses.

I don't look in the rearview mirror because I'm sure Ginger and Penny followed me over the bridge and onto the shoulder. Someone pounds on my window, and without looking I know who it is. Instinctively I turn to face her.

Ginger stands outside, her eyes wild with distress as the wind plasters her hair against the side of her face.

"Open up, Rose!" She shouts to be heard above the wind and rain and traffic. "Open the door and step out here!"

And just as I've obeyed her for the past forty-two years, I obey and fall into my oldest sister's embrace.

"I know." She grips my upper arms as if she's afraid to let me go. "I know what you meant to do. And I'm so glad you didn't, Rose. I'm so glad."

Penny runs up, and her eyes widen as she looks from me to Ginger. "Are you two okay?"

Ginger tightens her hold on my shoulders. "Come on. We'll pick up your car later."

Maintaining her iron grip, she guides me to Penny's Altima. I protest and gesture toward my SUV, but after clumping my purse, keys, and phone in the empty seat, Penny reads my mind and goes back for Justus. I watch as she ducks into my car, then she emerges with Gran's bird blanket tucked around my dog. With her hair straggling in wet hanks around her head, she climbs into the car and struggles to close the door in the pouring rain.

Finally we are together again, safe and sound . . . even if we didn't want to be.

GINGER

Somehow, through some power or strength I don't understand, I drive back over the bridge and onto St. Simons with the same detachment I once employed when Ross cut his head open during a game of football. In that hour, like this one, my hands remained loose on the steering wheel, my palms remained dry. While Michael rode with Ross in the backseat, I drove quickly and efficiently, careful not to endanger my passengers or myself.

But on that day, like this one, cold panic sprouted somewhere between my shoulder blades and spread its twining tendrils down every nerve. My stomach twisted in a knot, and an iron hand closed around my throat, threatening my airway and my voice. I couldn't speak if I wanted to. Silence fills the car like a cloud, keeping us sisters apart and preserving my veneer of calm.

Penny and Rose can't know I'm about to lose control. They depend on me; they always have. But if Wort hadn't called, if I hadn't believed him, Rose could be floating in the river now.

I press my lips together and turn my head toward the window, not wanting Penny to see the emotions that must be playing on my face. The trembling rises from beneath my ribs again, threatening to spread to my arms, my hands . . .

I grip the steering wheel more tightly. What is wrong with me? No matter how I try to hang on to order, my life keeps slipping out of my control. My husband is planning to leave me, my sons are going their own way, and my baby sister was actually planning to commit suicide. Why didn't she tell me something was wrong? Why didn't she call me for help? I can't help her if she won't talk to me; I can't give advice if no one ever asks me for it.

All the people who love me are walking away from me, but why? Have I grown hideous and repulsive? I glance at my reflection in the rearview mirror, almost expecting to see horns sprouting out of my forehead. No, I haven't changed; other people have. Any amateur shrink could diagnose Michael's situation as a case of midlife crisis, but what about Rose? She's too young for a midlife flare-up, and we can't blame her feelings on postpartum depression. Wort seemed to think she's been planning this for at least two years. That's a long time to be depressed, no matter what the reason.

When we were growing up, Penny's and Rose's problems were easier to handle. I told them when to do their homework; I made sure they didn't watch too much TV. I didn't let them go to school dances with boys who had a reputation, and I waited up until their curfew, making sure they were home before I locked up the house. Even when we stayed at the cottage, I would sit with Grandmother in the porch swing, counting fireflies until we heard Penny and Rose riding their bikes up Fish Fever Lane.

Penny and Rose weren't above trying to sneak past me, but generally they didn't give me too much trouble. They respected me, and I relied on that respect.

But what do I do with Rose now? On the mad drive over the bridge, all I could think about was catching her and stopping her. But now that she's in my car, what do I say? Forbidding her to try such a silly thing again is not going to work.

We are no longer children, and Rose and Penny are dealing with issues I know nothing about. They don't come to me for help, and even if they did, how could I solve their problems when I can't even handle my own?

Twenty minutes ago, I operated under the sincere but misguided belief that I could find my baby sister, grip her by the arms, and tell her not to kill herself, not now, not ever. But after seeing the desperate expression on her face when I peered through her window, I know that approach won't work. Yet I have no idea what I should do . . . or if the problem is simply too big for a big sister to handle.

SIXTEEN

ROSEMARY

Five minutes after getting out of my car, I am sitting behind Ginger and crossing the bridge again as we head back to St. Simons. I'm soaked through and shivering like a woman with fever. In the front passenger seat, Penny's teeth chatter as she holds Justus close, keeping him warm.

No one speaks on the way to the cottage. When we pull up outside the house, Ginger gets out and waits as if I've become an emotional invalid and she's my nurse.

"Come on in the house." She takes my elbow. "I have to call Wort, who's worried sick. After that, the three of us can talk. I think I have the things we need to make tea in my suitcase."

I glance at Penny, who remains uncharacteristically silent as she carries Justus up the porch steps. She opens the door—apparently no one locked it—and walks through a room emptied of everything but a few dust bunnies and dead flies. Penny kneels in front of the fireplace, where she gently lowers her bundle.

Maybe she meant to fool me; maybe she thought I would believe Justus was only sleeping. But when his head lolls in an unnatural direction, I know my dog has made the journey I planned to take with him.

Ginger goes upstairs as I sit cross-legged on the wooden floor and look at Jussy, my heart squeezed so tight I can barely breathe. Penny goes into the bathroom and comes back with a towel, which she tosses to me. While I attempt to dry my hair and arms, she stands with one eye open in a wary slit, as if I'm a bomb she expects to blow at any moment. "I'm sorry," she finally whispers. "So sorry about the dog. I'll help you bury him, if you want."

"Was he . . . was he alive when you picked him up?"

"I don't think so, honey. He didn't seem to be breathing."

My head feels like it's packed with water-soaked sponges. Tears leak from beneath my eyelids, so I dab at the tears with the towel, then give up and let them fall where they may. "It's okay," I manage to say, my voice emerging as a hoarse croak. "He was sick and ready to go. But I wanted to go with him."

Penny sinks to the floor next to me, her hair like wet ribbons around her face. "Why, Rose? Why would you want to die?"

"Because." My voice, like my nerves, is in tatters. But in nearly dying, I've come to a place of liberation. Penny and Ginger know what I wanted to do; they know I would have done it if they hadn't been behind me. And since they know the worst, maybe there's no reason I shouldn't tell them everything.

I came here hoping to find Grandma's survival secrets. Maybe the biggest of them has been staring me in the face all along: honesty. Grandma never worried about maintaining her dignity; she felt free to play, even to let us see her hidden fears, her emotions, and her dreams.

Now it's my turn.

Ginger comes down the stairs, and the relieved look on her face tells me she's talked to Wort. She carries cups and teabags to the microwave while I reach out and stroke Jussy's wet fur. No one speaks until the old microwave dings, then Ginger drops teabags into the steaming cups and comes over, a drink in each hand. She hands one to me and the other to Penny, then she sits on the raised brick hearth. I look from her to Penny. Tears are rolling down Penny's face, but though Ginger's eyes have welled with what looks like hurt, her cheeks are dry.

I swipe at my wet nose with the back of my sleeve, then wrap both hands around the warmth of the Styrofoam. "I wanted to die because everything I touch eventually gets ruined. Wort would be better off without me. So would the ranch."

"Rosie," Penny says, "that's crazy talk."

Ginger puts out a restraining hand. "Let's hear her out."

I lower my gaze and try to sort out the feelings jumbled inside my heart.

"My babies," I begin, clearing my throat. "I've lost two babies. Two years ago, Wort and I had a little girl, did y'all know that? We made it all the way to the nineteenth week. I had such high hopes, but then we lost her. We buried her on the ranch, under a tree. When I knew I was losing the baby, I stayed at the house because I didn't think the hospital would let me have her . . . afterward. We placed her in an old trunk Wort found out in the barn. I lined it with satin and dressed her in lace. And we buried her ourselves."

From the corner of my eye I see Penny cover her mouth, but I'm watching Ginger. For an instant the concerned expression she managed to shoehorn into her features twists into revulsion; then her features rearrange themselves in lines of compassionate interest.

"Rose, we know that was an awful time. We worried about you back then."

"Did you? Funny, you never mentioned it."

"I sent a card!"

"Yes, you did. And eventually you managed to visit. But you never mentioned my child. Neither you nor Penny ever talked about the baby . . . and that made me feel like she wasn't worth talking about."

"That's simply not true." A gleam of resentment enters Ginger's eyes. "But sometimes people avoid painful topics because they don't want to make things worse."

"I don't think you could have made the situation any worse." I lift my chin. "There's a lot y'all don't know about what happened. Like the reason I miscarried."

Penny snorts softly. "Honey, at your age—"

"My age had nothing to do with it." I swivel my gaze from Penny to Ginger. "Apparently I have scar tissue on my uterus. The doctor said I'll probably never carry a child to term."

"Why would you have scar tissue?" Penny frowns and straightens her shoulders. "You need a second opinion, that's all. You probably have endometriosis, and I know women who've had treatment for that—"

Ginger touches Penny's arm, cutting her off. "Why don't you wait—?"

"I'm allowed to talk to my baby sister." Penny pushes Ginger's hand away. "Even if there *is* scar tissue, Rose and Wort could always adopt—"

"The scar tissue is Ginger's fault . . . and mine. Mostly I'm to blame." My words fall like stones in water, casting ripples in all directions. Penny gapes at me, then shoots a questioning glance at our big sister.

Fresh misery darkens Ginger's face. She swallows hard, then grimaces in a way that makes me wonder whether she's trying to remember or striving to forget.

"What?" Penny looks from me to Ginger. "What's going on between you two?"

Ginger ignores the question. "That's not fair, Rose. I only did what I thought was best for you at the time."

"Did you?" Rancor sharpens my voice. "How could you know what was best for me? You hurried me to the clinic before I had a chance to think things through. You told the doctor we wanted the simplest abortion procedure—"

"What are y'all talking about?" Penny's voice rises. "What clinic? What abortion?"

"The summer I dated Harper Jones." I stare at my eldest sister and drive the words like a wedge into the space between us. "I got pregnant. I didn't know what to do, so I went to Ginger for advice. She said she'd take care of everything."

Ginger straightens her spine. "Harper wouldn't have made a good husband for anybody. He was reckless and irresponsible—"

"You told him I wanted money for an abortion." My fear of Ginger has vanished, replaced by a liberating rage. "I went with you to the clinic and I lied to the doctor about how far along I was. When the vacuum procedure didn't work, he had to do a D and C, and in the process he not only sliced up my baby, he cut up my uterus. He made it so I could never have babies, not ever."

Ginger's gaze is boring into me, but her lower lip quivers. "You were in no shape to make that kind of decision, Rose; you needed someone to take charge. I didn't know the doctor was going to hurt you, but all medical procedures carry some risk—"

"But I wanted my baby. I wanted *lots* of babies, and now I'll never have any. Wort will never be a father, not as long as he's married to me." I shift my gaze to Penny. She's not the most material woman I've ever met, but she knows how it feels to want something desperately. "Ginger was supposed to look out for us. She was always the mature one, the responsible one, the one we could trust to tell us the right thing to do. So I didn't question her, you see? I was twenty years old, unemployed, and dating a jerk. And by listening to her, I ruined my life."

When I look at Ginger again, she's staring at me like a woman who's just been knocked over by a charging lamb.

PENNYROYAL

I can't believe what I'm hearing. Part of me wants to pinch myself, because none of this seems possible—not the storm outside, not our mad ride across the island, not the venom Rosie has just spewed all over Ginger. I keep expecting Rod Serling to step inside the house and announce that we've stumbled into the Twilight Zone.

But clearly, Rose is serious . . . and Ginger isn't denying a word Rose has said. I never knew about the abortion, and I can't imagine our churchgoing Ginger ever suggesting such a thing. And I thought I knew my sister.

I may not even know Rose. I never knew she had problems with fertility; I'd always assumed she was like me and didn't particularly want kids.

I sit in the living room, the third point in a perfect triangle, and feel the space between us grow wider. For years I've made incorrect assumptions about my sisters, and now I can't believe the depths of my ignorance. I saw all the clues, but I never put them together. Ginger has always hovered over us, she's always taken responsibility for us, on occasion she's even sacrificed for us. And yet something's always been missing, particularly where Rose was concerned. Rosie's sensed it too. She's heard the edge in Ginger's never-ending advice and felt the sharpness in her tone. What did she tell me earlier? *Sometimes I think Ginger hates me.*

I press my fingers to my lips as a realization takes root and blooms in my brain. Why . . . Ginger may not hate Rose, but she sure doesn't love her. She may not love me, but sometimes I have felt a bit of affection coming from her. But between Ginger and Rose . . . there's been nothing. No affection, no love at all.

Maybe Rosie's intuition was dead-on.

"Gingerbread"—I wrap my arms around myself and try not to shiver—"I just realized something."

Ginger lifts a brow. "And how did I ruin *your* life?"

"You didn't ruin it, and maybe that's my point. You don't think you ruined Rose's, but you're looking at the situation with logic and not with heart."

"I don't know what you mean."

I take a deep breath. "You are always looking out after us because you think it's your duty. You see us as your responsibilities. But we don't need you to be our guardian; we never did. What would be nice is if the three of us looked after each other . . . because we love each other."

Ginger catches her breath. "You can't think I don't love you. After all I've done—"

"But I *do* think that . . . because it's true." I shift my gaze to Rose, then catch her hand and hold it. "I love you, Rosie, and I'm so sorry about the loss of your babies. I wish I'd been there for you, both times, and I'm sorry I wasn't."

Rose chokes on a sob, then claps her free hand over her mouth and looks away. I feel a pang that strikes like a blow to the heart, but I'm not finished. "Grandma used to recite this one saying, and every time I heard it, I thought she seemed . . . I don't know, unsophisticated. But now I think she was wiser than I realized."

Ginger doesn't answer, but Rosie turns her head and lowers her hand. "What'd she say?"

"She said, 'You can give without loving, but you can't love without giving.' Grandma didn't have a lot, but she shared everything she owned with us because she loved us. Most of all, she shared her heart."

I look at Ginger next. "You've always given us a lot of guidance, but I don't think you've ever given us much of yourself. But like Rosie says, both of you are precious to me. If you're honest . . . I don't think you can say the same thing about us."

Ginger stiffens. "I don't know what you want me to say."

"All I want"—I speak slowly, as if she were a child—"is for you to open up and tell us what you're really thinking and feeling. Don't worry about the hurt; don't worry that you'll upset us. Just be honest . . . no matter how painful it is."

I look at her, waiting, but all I hear is the whisper of the wind beyond the windows.

GINGER

Not love my sisters? The thought is so ridiculous that after a moment I actually begin to laugh, though I feel a long way from genuine humor. After all I've done for them, how can Penny say that I don't love them? And how can Rose look at me as if I'm the devil incarnate?

My laughter becomes brittle, then stops as suddenly as if someone flipped a switch.

"It's okay." Penny lifts her shoulder in a casual shrug. "If there's one thing Bob taught me, it's that people aren't really free to love us until they know us, warts and all—and then the warts don't matter because it's so freeing to be loved completely. This afternoon I told Bob the truth about everything, and he forgave me for the hurt I've caused him. So I can see the truth about you and forgive you, Ginger. For not loving us and all that."

Rose says nothing, but lowers her gaze and rubs her wet hair with a towel. So . . . Penny is forgiving me for only God knows what, and Rose won't speak to me. Great. Just great.

I'm tempted to explode like a volcano, but Rose might not survive an onslaught of scalding lava. So I draw a long, quivering breath and stand. Seething with resentment and humiliation, I stalk up the stairs, heading to the bedroom where I retreated on so many other afternoons when I'd had a fight with my sisters. Neither Rose nor Penny calls after me, so apparently they are more than willing to let me go.

I step into my old bedroom and slam the door, creating a sudden vortex that spins a clump of dust on the wooden floor. The beds have been removed; nothing remains but my suitcase, my empty cooler, and the few books I'd set aside for my library. Grandma's recorder and the bag of cassette tapes lie on the floor, overlooked and ignored.

I walk to the window and clench my fists, resisting the surge of rage heating my chest and face. I can taste bitterness in my mouth—caustic, foul, and sharp. First my mother leaves me, then my dad dumps me at Grandmother's for three months out of every year. My husband betrays me, and now my sisters announce that I'm a hypocrite.

How can my sisters hold such a distorted view of me? I have done nothing but work for them, worry about them, and fret over them. I have given my life for them. I surrendered my childhood for them. Yet anyone listening to them talk would think I'd committed outright genocide.

I close my eyes and study the memory of the photograph in Grandmother's book, the family portrait taken when Rose was born. Our expressions say it all—Penny felt curious, Daddy popped with pride, exhaustion had bested Momma, and I wrestled with confusion. Or did I? Maybe my lowered brow and curled upper lip meant something else entirely. Maybe what I struggled with on that afternoon was resentment.

But how can anyone resent a baby? My thoughts flit to Ross and Ryan, my much-loved sons. When I saw the double lines in that first home pregnancy test indicator, I never once thought about terminating my pregnancy. From that moment of awareness, I considered that unborn life my child. Everything that followed—the ultrasounds, the first kick, the quick sound of the heartbeat—only reinforced a precious truth: I was carrying a baby, a human life, a gift from God. During the sixth month of my first pregnancy I began to bleed. I nearly went to pieces thinking I might be losing our son or daughter. I clung to Michael. I begged God to intervene. When the doctor finally said the risk had passed, I wanted to dance in relief.

Why should my pregnancy be any more real, any more precious than Rose's?

Both Rose and I have twice conceived life within us. But while I've adored my children, kissed their pudgy toes, changed their diapers, and taught them how to talk and do long division, Rose has never been able to hold a living baby of her own in her arms. And I'm the reason why.

I shiver as a cold knot of regret forms beneath my breastbone.

I shouldn't have manipulated Rose into having the abortion. If Penny and Rose are dead set on hearing an apology from me, I can give them one that's heartfelt. Abortion was a quick fix, and it was all I could think of in the situation, but now I see that I should have been more thoughtful. I should have explored other options, including allowing Rose to keep the baby. Maybe things would be different for her now if I'd taken more time.

So why didn't I take more time for Rose? The question is like a hallway with a dozen shadowed doors, and I'm not eager to open any of them. But Penny's right about one thing: I've always assumed that I love Rose, but I can't honestly say I like her very much. Why is that?

Be honest . . . no matter how painful it is.

I pace in front of the window and chew on my thumbnail. Rose is my baby sister, so she required more care than Penny did. Rose has always been dreamy and absentminded, so she tended to drift more than Penny did. Rose marches to her own drummer, a characteristic that consistently annoys me, and she's melancholy, another trait that drives me batty. She's impulsive and disorganized, and her refusal to eat meat makes planning any menu more difficult than it has to be.

And she's the reason Momma left us.

The thought slips in with all the others, and at first it barely registers. Then I remember my expression at Momma's hospital bedside, and cold reality sweeps over me in a crushing wave, one so powerful that it steals my breath and leaves me teetering on my feet.

My resentment began in that hospital room and crested when Momma died. All these years, I've blamed Rose for Momma's death. If Rose hadn't been born, our mother wouldn't have suffered from postpartum depression. If not for the depression, she wouldn't have taken her life . . . and I would never have wandered into that blood-soaked bathroom on the longest afternoon of my life.

I sink to the floor beside my suitcase and struggle to catch my breath. This honesty is painful, and it's going to cost me a measure of pride . . . while a heaping dose of vulnerability is shoveled in to take its place. Over the years I championed my sisters publicly and criticized them privately. I wanted to shine while they remained lesser lights. I pretended to be the guardian, but in reality I wanted Rose . . . gone.

Penny was right, Rose was right, but how could it be true? I resented Rose's presence, I resented her *life*. I resented sharing Penny and Daddy with her; I resented having to watch over her. As she grew I resented her ethereal loveliness, her creativity, and the way dogs and cats climbed all over her while they purposely avoided me. When she hit that bit of trouble in her junior year, I resented having to share my new home with her, and I especially hated her turning up pregnant before Michael and I could even *think* about having a child.

No wonder I found it so easy to schedule an abortion. If I could go back in time, if I'd been able to have my way, I would have arranged an abortion for Momma before Rose was born.

But I was a kid, and kids aren't able to control the adults in their lives. I had to let Momma go. I had to watch Daddy flounder in grief. I had to put up with Grandmother's childlike silliness.

But Grandmother wasn't always silly. That must have been a facade she wore because she thought it pleased us girls. The woman who journaled her thoughts about love and forgiveness was no emotional lightweight. She was a woman who stayed with her husband because she wanted to love and forgive, not because she wanted to fulfill her duty. She was more mature, and more loving, than I have ever been.

If I'm to be honest, I have to admit that I took care of Rose and Penny because people expected me to, because it was my duty. But Penny is right; I didn't love them. If I had, I might have found some joy in the job.

Displaying a little joy might have helped them love me . . . and it might help Michael too. I should take a lesson from Penny and learn how to be vulnerable, how to need my husband.

I close my eyes as my thoughts wander back to the last time I saw Michael at home. In that last hour, I yelled at him for disappearing when I had things to do, I quizzed him about my to-do list, and I fussed at him for not wanting my grandmother's piano. I was all about duty . . . and not a bit about love.

"Oh, Grandma." I push my hair back from my forehead and prop my elbow on my suitcase. "Why didn't you tell me I was going about it all wrong? Surely you saw what I was doing."

Maybe she did . . . but after seven marriages, Lillian must have learned that scolding rarely accomplishes anything. When Walter came back from Europe after abandoning her, she didn't scold or reject him. She forgave him and welcomed him home.

I draw a deep, shuddering breath, afraid that I won't be capable of doing the same . . . or if Michael will even want to come back.

Maybe my marriage doesn't deserve to be saved. Maybe the miracle is that my relationship with Michael survived twenty-seven years of wheedling, to-do lists, and matter-of-fact reminders. No wonder Michael strayed, and no wonder he sees divorce as the best answer for everyone caught up in this situation.

But we are still married . . . and for the first time I have seen myself through my sisters' eyes. I cannot be that ordered, joyless woman anymore. I want to serve my family like Grandmother did—from a reservoir of love. Maybe Michael and I can be honest with each other and make our marriage into something new. Maybe we can't. But if we can change, things can be different for us.

Grandma always said that the magnitude of our fears revealed the measure of our faith. If we are too afraid, our faith shrivels. But if our faith is strong, our fears fade away.

Overcome with a need to hear our grandmother's voice, I pull the tape recorder closer. A cassette sits in the machine, so I plug the cord into the wall, then hold my breath and press *play*. I hear a hiss of static, a quiet chuckle, and then my grandmother's crackling voice: "Dear Lord, how I pray for my girls. Be with young Rosie, Father, and keep her safe. Be with Penny, and let her feel your tender love. And Lord, bless my sweet Gingerbread. Teach her how to lean on you instead of trying to carry the world on her own shoulders. Show her how to love. And help her be the guiding light that draws her family close."

I realize I am crying again only when I taste salty tears running into my smile.

ROSEMARY

Penny has managed to light the charred remains of a log in the fireplace by the time Ginger comes down the stairs. Both Penny and I look up, not certain what mood we'll find Ginger in, but something in my chest relaxes when I see that the glint of anger has vanished from her eyes.

Penny backs away from the fireplace. "Sorry about the fire," Penny says, launching into an apologetic explanation. "But it's just so damp and chilly with the rain—"

"I don't mind." Ginger sits cross-legged on the floor near us, then a slow smile creeps onto her face. "You were right."

I watch, my heart aching, as my proud sister's eyes fill and her chin wobbles.

"I didn't believe it at first, but both of you were absolutely right. All these years . . . I haven't loved either of you like I should. I saw you as responsibilities and not much else. I focused on doing my duty, not out of joy, but out of pride. I knew people were watching, so I did what I had to do in order to keep the family in line. But I didn't love you. And I'm sorry for that . . . because you are amazing women and you deserve to be loved."

Tears, glittering like jewels in the firelight, drop from Ginger's cheeks. "And you, Rose—I didn't even do my duty as far as you were concerned. I was a kid when Mom died, and when they told me she killed herself because of postpartum depression, I placed all the blame on you. Somehow I never outgrew that way of thinking. But it was so wrong of me."

Her eyes are more focused now, as if a film of indifference has been peeled away. "I was wrong about the abortion; I should never have suggested it or manipulated you the way I did. I'm so sorry for the hurt you've carried all these years, and for the babies you haven't been able to have. But Rose—Rosie—if you think you ruin everything you touch, you're as confused in your thinking as I was. Look at Wort—you have taken a rough-edged motorcycle man and turned him into a giant teddy bear who rides to raise money for sick kids. You took a dilapidated old house and turned it into a sanctuary that not only helps animals, but it also blesses all the people who visit because they don't have the space or the money to take care of animals. You're the most giving person I know, Rose, and one of the most tenderhearted. And though I haven't loved you the way I should in the past, I'd like a chance to love you better."

I can't stand to listen a minute more. As tears blur my vision, I rise to my knees and reach across the space between us, and for the first time ever I feel my eldest sister relax in my arms. "It's okay, Gingerbread. I forgive you."

She releases me, then swipes at her wet cheeks with the back of her hand. "While I was taking a good, hard look at myself, I realized you're not the only ones I've treated like a responsibility. I've acted out of duty to Michael too. I thought loving him meant keeping his house picked up, making sure his sons stayed in line, and bringing in some extra money to help out with the budget. But did I make him happy? Or did I help him because helping made *me* happy?" She shakes her head. "I haven't been loving Michael, either. So I think I can understand why he went looking for a woman who's willing to treat him the way a husband ought to be treated."

Penny drapes an arm around Ginger, then rubs her hand. "I don't want to excuse what Michael did, but I understand what you're saying. So . . . what are you gonna do?"

Ginger draws a deep and unsteady breath. "I'm going to call him before heading home tonight. I'm telling him that I don't want a divorce; I want a second chance. And if he doesn't want to give me one, I'll be brave and show him that I'm not the same woman. I'm not perfect, either . . . but I can change."

And in listening to Ginger, I realize that I have some apologizing of my own to do. Penny told me Wort called earlier, frantic about finding my life insurance policy. I need to tell him I'm sorry . . . and then I need to find someone who'll help me come to terms with my past.

If my sisters can open up about their hidden wounds, maybe it's time for me to learn how to open my heart and be painfully honest with others.

Maybe that openness was Gran's secret.

GINGER

The weekend has come and gone, and nothing happened as I thought it would. We Lawrence girls are leaving Grandmother's cottage for the last time, and none of us is taking anything we hoped to get . . . yet we're leaving far richer for the experience of having been together.

By now Grandmother's square piano is probably at the thrift store, where it'll be a conversation piece until some music lover with more time than sense decides to take it home and refurbish it. The solid pine table and its six chairs are keeping company with the sofa, love seat, corner cupboard, beds, dressers, and boxes of household miscellany. Bits and pieces of Grandma's life will spread throughout coastal Georgia, and my prayer is that they will enrich other lives as much as they enriched ours.

Each of us girls will soon be receiving a check for two hundred thousand dollars, but though the inheritance is greatly appreciated, I've come to realize that Grandma's legacy has nothing to do with material goods and everything to do with her example. We are the women we are—flaws and all—because we're Grandma's girls.

When the last trash bag has been removed, the last rag picked up, and the last speck of dirt swept from the floor, my sisters and I gather in the kitchen as I ceremonially drop the key on the counter.

I have to smile as I look at the things we've taken from the house. After we buried Justus in the side yard, Rose folded the bird blanket and wrapped it around the Romper Room cookie jar in the trunk of her car.

Penny is leaving with Grandmother's photo album and the stationery box of mismatched pictures.

And I'm going home with the tape recorder and cassettes, a few of Grandmother's books, and her journal.

"Well"—I shift my gaze from one precious face to the other— "I guess this is good-bye."

"For the house," Rose says, propping her elbows on the counter. "Not for us."

"No, not for us," Penny echoes. She opens her arms and draws Rose and me into a group hug. For a long moment the three of us stand in a compact knot, relishing one another's warmth and this unexpected closeness. I close my eyes, startled by the sting of fresh tears behind my eyelids.

When we pull apart, I see that I am not the only emotional Lawrence girl. Penny is weepy, too, and Rose peers woefully at both of us through tear-clotted lashes.

"Are you sure you're gonna be okay?" Penny asks. I nod, struck by the reversal in our roles.

Penny and I both look at Rose, who senses the question on our lips.

"I'm gonna be fine," she says, a tinge of wonder in her voice. "Wort's meeting me at this little inn we recently discovered outside Jacksonville. We'll spend the night there, and we'll talk. I plan on telling him about everything I've been feeling."

"We need you." Penny squeezes Rose's hand. "Don't ever leave us, Rosie."

Rose answers with a tentative smile, and together we walk out the front door and across the front porch. As Penny and Rose head down the stairs, Penny glances over her shoulder. "Coming, Gingerbread?"

"In a minute," I tell her. "I want to make a quick call first."

Surrounded by the sheltering silence of my grandmother's

house, I sit on the swing and dial home . . . holding my breath until my husband answers. "Michael"—I turn to wave good-bye to my sisters—"I'm coming home . . . and I hope you'll be there when I arrive."

He greets this news with an instant of shocked silence. "Does this mean—?"

"I don't know what it means, but I'd like you to be home. Because though I've tried, I can't imagine a future without you in it. I've changed, Michael, and I want to make our marriage work. But I need to know one thing—forgetting about the college, your job, and the threat of a lawsuit, do you want to stay married to me? I won't stop you if you want to leave."

"I don't want to go," he says, his voice low and intense. "And I'd give anything to undo what I did."

The despair that has hovered over me all weekend lifts, replaced by a sense of strength and purpose. "We can't undo the past, but we can face the future together. We need to talk, Michael. I want to hear everything you have to say, and I want to share what I've learned about myself. We can go to counseling, therapy, whatever it takes. I believe we can weather any crisis if we stand united."

I tell him I'll see him soon, then I stop on the threshold to lock the front door. My sisters are getting into Penny's Altima—she'll drive Rose to the spot where we left her car.

As I walk to my SUV, I can't resist taking a last look at the house that sheltered us through so many storms. Grandmother Lillian, I have to believe, is peering down through clouds of glory and watching her girls.

"Out of all the grandmas in the world," I whisper, looking up at the luminous sky, "you're my favorite."

ACKNOWLEDGMENTS

No novelist writes alone, for she is involved in an invisible partnership between herself and her reader. For helping to improve my contribution to this partnership, I am indebted to the group of women better known as the Traditions Book Club, who for seven years have read, laughed, and wept with me as we explored books we love. Many of them read this manuscript in its early stages, and I'm grateful for their insights.

I also owe thanks to my editors, Becky Nesbitt and Traci DePree, and to my agent, Danielle Egan-Miller, and her staff, Joanna MacKenzie and Lauren Olsen, for their inspired suggestions.

I am especially grateful to my cousin Ginger Wiggins who read this novel in its roughest incarnation and reminded me of stories I'd forgotten about our precious grandmother . . . who would certainly have worn Spanx, if she'd known about them.

READING GROUP GUIDE

Discussion Questions

1. Of the three sisters, whom do you most closely relate to? Why?

2. The title, *The Fine Art of Insincerity,* implies that one or more of the characters is being insincere. Which character do you think is the most insincere? The most sincere? How does this character (or any of the others) hide her true feelings? Do these women really know one another?

3. The novel unfolds from three first-person viewpoints: Ginger's, Penny's, and Rose's. Though each scene is identified with the point-of-view character's name, do you think you could have identified the viewpoint character without the label? How do these three voices differ?

4. While she's cleaning out her grandmother's bedroom, Ginger debates whether she should divorce Michael. She says she'll be able to carry on with most of her wifely duties, but one—she won't be able to make love to him. Why do you think that is? How does Ginger define love at this point?

5. Why do you think Grandma Lillian assembled the photo album at the retirement home? How did it affect each of her grand-daughters?

6. At dinner on Sunday night, the granddaughters discuss what love is. How would you define it? Which of them comes closest to a good definition for love? Do you think any of their definitions have changed by the end of the novel? Whose?

7. Why do you think Penny is constantly looking for romance? Has it anything to do with the reason she doesn't want more children?

8. Penny says, "I know there's a man out there who will meet all my needs, and every time I got married, I thought I'd found him. But as time passes, I learn things, the fuzzy feelings go away, and I realize that I haven't found my perfect soul mate after all." Is there a "perfect soul mate" for every woman? Can any man satisfy a woman's every need?

9. An old and familiar saying reminds us that love isn't a matter of finding the right person, but of *being* the right person. Which sister needs to learn this lesson most?

10. How has each woman changed at the end of the novel? If you could keep writing and plot out the likely future of Ginger, Rose, and Penny, what would those future scenes look like? Will all three relationships succeed?

11. At one point Grandma Lillian had a crisis of faith that changed her outlook on life and marriage. Can you identify that crisis? How did she change her actions at that point?

12. Do we ever really know what goes on in another family's home? How is the theme of reality versus appearance echoed in the story?

Author Q&A

1. The "grandma gene" is such a great conceit for the novel. Is this the single idea that *The Fine Art of Insincerity* sprang from?

Yes. Since my grandmother married five times and one of my relatives duplicated her record, I once jokingly referred to a "grandma gene" that likely skipped a generation . . . and thus the idea was born.

2. What sort of research was involved in writing this book? Was it geared more toward looking outward and observing, or looking inward and meditating?

Probably equal parts of each. Actual research required a trip to St. Simons Island to spend a week in a rented beach house. My mother, my aunt, and one of my cousins went with me, and we shared "grandma stories" while we were there. Of course, not everything in this novel is drawn from real life. Eventually I had to create characters and spin their unique story problems.

3. *The Fine Art of Insincerity* is a fantastic title for this book. While I'm sure each reader will draw his or her own conclusion, who do you think is the most insincere character? Is being true to oneself as important as being true to others?

Choosing a single character as the most insincere is difficult, because they all have a claim on the title. But I think Ginger scores points for not being honest with herself—her personal ideas and convictions were terribly inconsistent, but she wasn't able to see those inconsistencies until her sisters pointed them out. Only then could she see that her shifting stands had actually inflicted pain on her loved ones. We all have those blind spots—and we depend on those who love us to help us see them.

4. You write a great blog titled *A Life in Pages* with all sorts of fun video links and random thoughts on popular culture and peculiarities of life. How has blogging changed your relationship with your fans? Do you have any favorite blog entries from the past couple of years?

Well, bless you for reading my blog! I do try to put something up every day, but warn people not to expect writerly profundity with every sunrise. I think blogging helps my readers see me as a real person and not merely as a writer, and when we connect person-to-person, we connect as friends. The blog has led to some lovely unexpected friendships with people across the United States.

5. The epigraph to this book is a wonderful passage from 1 Corinthians and sets the tone well for the rest of the story. How did you pick this particular passage? Was it a muse, or did you come to it after you had finished writing the story?

The idea to use 1 Corinthians 13 came to me during the second or third draft. That passage seemed to sum up all I wanted Ginger to realize—that no matter how much she talked about caring for and worrying about her sisters, if she didn't really love them, all her efforts were worthless. A lot of us spend a lot of time talking about people we could love . . . if we didn't spend so much time talking.

6. You are a star of the Christian writing community, and firmly ensconced in it as a speaker, teacher, writer, and role model to many. Do you think that with this comes a certain responsibility with what you are writing? Do you ever hold back or edit yourself because of this role?

Yowsers, I've never thought of myself as a star. A veteran, certainly, and I have the gray roots to prove it. When I write, I feel a dual responsibility: I don't want to disappoint my Lord or my reader. Since I write for people beyond the church as well as those in it, I try to incorporate genuine characters involved in honest, sometimes gut-wrenching situations. I feel responsible for providing a story that will surprise, challenge, and entertain. A story that will transport the reader to another world, invite them to slip into another character's skin, and experience some aspect of God's truth.

7. How much of the plot of this novel did you borrow from real life? Is Grandma Lillian similar to your own grandmother? Did you have many "girls only" weekends akin to the one Penny, Ginger, and Rose shared in the novel?

Lillian is modeled after my own five-times-married grandmother, a woman with an eighth-grade education and four daughters to feed and clothe. My grandmother never married a man wealthy enough to leave her a beach house—I doubt she even knew *anyone that wealthy—but she did the best she could. She did wear a girdle until the day she died, and she did call each of us grandkids into her room and assure us that she loved us best. She made the most delicious fried apple pies and sang the silliest songs . . . and we all adored her.*

And while I do have two sisters, I was thinking more of my mother's relationship with her sisters when I envisioned the "girls only" weekend. My mom and the aunts often get together and have proven to be the glue that holds our extended family together.

8. Why did you decide to set the book on St. Simons Island? Was there something in particular about the place that leaped out at you while you were in the process of creating these characters?

I chose St. Simons because my mom and her sisters love the place and have spent several weekends there. If a writer has to spend a week researching a locale, why not set the book in a charming, historic spot?

9. You have written a great number of novels, nonfiction books, and even children's books, but what in particular will you remember about the process of writing this book? Was this a story particularly special to you? It is very intimately written even though it is fictional.

This book will always be special to me because it sprang from my family's shared history. And because I am Ginger in many ways (being the firstborn, the bossiest, the one with a to-do list perpetually at hand), writing this book served as a cautionary tale for me. If I'm not careful, if I don't stop and listen, I, like Ginger, can be at risk of hurting the people I love most.

10. Being the consummate writer, you are always working on something. Can you give us a glimpse into the future and tell us a little about what you are working on next? Do you think you will ever revisit the characters of Penny, Rose, and Ginger?

[Laughing] I think I'll be content to let Penny, Rose, and Ginger rest . . . but you never know what the future holds. At present I'm working on a story about three people who meet on a train trip through several Southern coastal cities. To research the book, I traveled the same route with my cousin Ginger (who bears no resemblance to the Ginger in Insincerity*) and took hundreds of photos. So for the next several months, I'll be thinking about trains . . . and three characters with interesting challenges. Sounds a bit familiar, doesn't it?*